MARCHING THROUGH GEORGIA

MARCHING THROUGH GEORGIA

AN ALPHONSO CLAY MYSTERY OF THE CIVIL WAR

BOOK THREE

Jack Martin

OPEN ROAD

INTEGRATED MEDIA
NEW YORK

ISBN: 978-1-5040-7817-7

This edition published in 2022 by Open Road Integrated Media, Inc.
180 Maiden Lane
New York, NY 10038
www.openroadmedia.com

MARCHING THROUGH GEORGIA

PROLOGUE

JUNE 27, 1864—KENNESAW MOUNTAIN, GEORGIA

"WILLIE!"

The scream seemed to contain all of the grief, anguish and despair in the world. Major General William Tecumseh Sherman shot bolt upright in his cot, drenched in sweat that was only partly due to the humid Georgia night, and glared wildly about the interior of the tent, dimly lit by a flickering oil lamp. Tears ran down his cheeks; a sob escaped him. Moments later the flap of his command tent was thrown back, and a sentry peered nervously at his commanding general.

"Uh, General Sherman sir, you all right?"

Sherman wiped away the tears with his shirtsleeve, and was surprised to find that he had again only taken off his tunic before collapsing onto his cot. "Fine, son, fine. Just a bad night. We all get them at times." He grimaced a smile at the sentry, while in his mind's eye he still saw his nine-year-old son William at the moment of his death six months ago; his body ravaged by the yellow fever that the South had inflicted on the child. Not on him, on his son, the son he had brought down to the South for company. '*Damn the South to Hell!*' he thought savagely.

"Yes sir, I guess we all do," replied the sentry uneasily. "Sir, it's near four in the morning. Generals Thomas, McPherson, Davis, Logan and Hooker just got here for their final orders; that scout fellow Bierce too. Want I get your aides up?"

"No, let them sleep a bit longer. They're going to have a damn long day. Tell the generals and Bierce to come in." With nervous energy Sherman jackknifed out of bed and shrugged into his tunic, not bothering to button it up. The sentry held back the flap of the large tent to admit the visitors.

The first to enter was Major General George Thomas, commander of Sherman's Army of the Cumberland. In contrast to Sherman's disheveled appearance, the massive hero of Chickamauga was carefully groomed and neatly dressed. His dignified, bearded face bore an expression somewhere between resignation and anger. Following him, Major General James McPherson, the cheerful, youthful commander of Sherman's Army of the Tennessee. Sherman smiled at the sight of McPherson. However, the smile immediately became a frown as he caught sight of Major General Joseph Hooker, the brave, self-promoting commander of the 20th Corps who had been sent west to retrieve a reputation he had lost to Stonewall Jackson during a brief, disastrous command of the Army of the Potomac. Hooker was immediately followed by Brigadier General Jefferson C. Davis, acting commander of the 14th Corps; the unfortunately-named Davis had the flat, cold eyes of a killer, which was what he was in spades. Behind Davis came Major General John Logan, a darkly-handsome, well-connected former congressman who Sherman grudgingly conceded had the makings of a fine officer. The last to enter was the slender, hand-some Captain Ambrose Bierce, who was obviously completely unintimidated by the high rank of his companions. Sherman's mind suddenly flashed back for a moment to a dusty field outside Vicksburg, reminding him what he owed the young scout.

"Very well, gentlemen," said Sherman abruptly in his quick, high-pitched voice. "We went over the details after dinner. Any last-minute questions before you go to your posts?"

The ponderous Thomas spoke without preamble in a soft Virginia drawl, "Sir, I must once again urgently request that you postpone this attack. Flanking maneuvers have served us well enough these last two months. Progress is slow, true, but we eventually succeeded in forcing Joe Johnston out of every position he has held, with a minimum of casualties. Most of the boys in the frontal assault will be mine. I fear their lives will be lost with nothing to show for it."

Sherman realized his eyes must be showing his anger, but knew he was incapable of concealing any strong emotion. "Thomas, we went over this all not six hours ago. Johnston has come to expect our flanking maneuvers, and will have weakened his center to reinforce the flanks. He will not be expecting us to punch straight up the center. When we do, he will crumble, just like Bragg did at Chattanooga last fall."

Thomas paused for a long moment before replying, as if he were silently counting to ten. "Bragg was always a careless officer. Johnston is not careless. I assure you, I know him from the prewar army, where he was the finest chess-player around. He will leave enough men and cannon in the pass to turn it into an abattoir."

"Goddamn it, Thomas! We can't keep going so slowly. It's no longer a matter of battles in the field, but of politics. The election is barely four months away. Grant is bogged down in Virginia, and the papers are full of the so-called fiasco of the Wilderness Campaign. Here, we inch along day after day, and have no victories to show for it, much less Atlanta. And the Democrats have just nominated that Goddamn traitor McClellan to run against Lincoln on a peace platform! If the armies don't show some victories, the Rebs will gain at the ballot box what they can't get in the field."

The floridly handsome Hooker chose this moment to speak for the record. "Sir, do you really want the events of the summer written in letters of blood?" It did not escape Sherman that Hooker had not actually said he favored or opposed the attack.

"Hell yes, so long as it's the last Goddamn chapter!" exploded Sherman. "I told you all last night, this attack will take place, and we will smash Joe Johnston! Now, anyone have anything to say that will be of use to the attack?"

Surprisingly, it was Bierce, by far the lowest-ranking officer in the tent, who spoke. "Sir, I personally scouted the route up through the pass tonight as far as I dared. A couple of Rebels heard me, and sounded the alarm, so I never made it to the top; had some luck in getting back at all. It is true that the approach to the Rebel position is much less difficult than at Chattanooga, but I still cannot say to what extent Johnston's army has dug in, or what kind of artillery support they have. Our attack might be as great a victory as Chattanooga, or it might be as bloody a fiasco as Grant's assault at Cold Harbor."

Sherman seemed to ignore Bierce. "Gentlemen, this battle will happen, and we will be victorious. To your posts, and wait for the sound of three cannon-shots at first light. Dismissed."

The officers grimly saluted and began filing out of the tent, Bierce at the end of the line. Sherman suddenly said "Bierce, stay for a moment." Bierce turned to face Sherman while the last general in line, the emaciated, deadly-looking Davis cast a sour look over his shoulder and let the flap of the tent drop, leaving the scout alone with the commanding general.

"Captain, it sets a bad example for a commanding general to explain himself to his subordinates," said Sherman without preamble. "Gives them the idea he's not sure of himself. Still, I'll make an exception for you, with what I owe you from Vicksburg, and what with the personal risks you took in scouting tonight. Information has come to me, information from a damn sensitive quarter. Johnston's center is going to be weak, as weak as Bragg's was at Chattanooga. Thomas will smash through and set Johnston's boys running. Once that starts, McPherson will take his army, hook around the right, and if he doesn't trap them altogether he will hit Johnston's boys in the flank so hard we will waltz into Atlanta. That will put McClellan and his damned defeatism in its place!"

Bierce looked troubled. "Sir, if you say you have other sources showing the Rebs to be weak in the middle, then who am I to question it? I just would have been more comfortable if I could have verified it with my own eyes."

Sherman looked at the tall, slender Bierce, and remembered how little Willie had been tall and slender for his age when the South's yellow fever had taken him. For some reason, it struck him that Willie might have grown up to look very much like Bierce.

"Bierce, I know whatever course I choose, good men are going to die. Don't care what the generals think; but I want you to know that they didn't die because I was a pig-headed fool like Rosecrans or Burnside. And I want you to know that no matter how today turns out, I had a good, solid reason for going at the middle."

"May I ask what that reason is?"

Sherman hesitated. "Don't take this wrong, Bierce. I have absolute trust in you; more than anyone else in this army, except Grant and maybe McPherson. But I gave my word that what I was told would stay with me, and stay with me it will."

Bierce looked appraisingly at the red-headed, slightly wild-eyed general. "Well, I can respect that sir." He saluted, and started for the flap of the tent.

"Captain Bierce, just what part will you be playing this morning?"

Bierce paused. "General Thomas wants me to be behind the skirmishers in the first wave of Hooker's boys. He has tasked me with providing quick warning of any . . . unexpected barriers to the movements of large masses of men, and to report it back to him instantly."

A feeling of dread, brother to premonition and first cousin to panic, suddenly hit Sherman. *Willie!* "Captain Bierce, I want you to take as much care of your person as your duties allow. Remember that you have nothing to prove; there is no question of your personal courage."

Bierce laughed, a barking, unlovely sound. "Why Sir, General Thomas said much the same thing to me. Generals are not usually concerned with the fates of captains. It is flattering that you both have made an exception for me." With a jaunty salute, Bierce lifted the flap of the tent and was gone.

A whisper of doubt began to creep into Sherman's mind; he physically shook his head back and forth, as if to shake it out through his ears. No, he thought. The information was good, and by noon this war would be well on its way to being won.

Bierce looked behind him, and could just make out in the dim pre-dawn light the gaggle of horsemen on a small hill less than a mile away. He knew that would be the cautious, majestic Thomas; his two corps commanders, Hooker and the morose Davis; and a crowd of aides, messengers, and assorted hangers-on. A quarter-mile closer he could just make out the batteries of three-inch guns, assembled courtesy of Colonel J. Howard Kitching, Hooker's chief of artillery. Lying on the ground in his front and to his sides were huddled masses of blue-clad infantry, grimly clutching Springfield muzzle-loaders; over them stood their officers, who seemed to the cynical Bierce to be already assuming heroic poses appropriate to the illustrated magazines.

The silence was broken by three cannon-shots, separated by four or five seconds each. Officers screamed "Charge!" The men leapt to their feet and began jogging at the double-quick up the slope while Kitching's guns loosed salvo after salvo at the top of the pass, shells whistling over the heads of the advancing men. However, the cannon stopped belching fire before the men were halfway to the Confederate lines, to avoid hitting the men in blue. Bierce jogged along with the men, not far from the front; a manic smile spread over his face as he began to believe there really would only be token resistance.

Then the banshee howl of the Rebel yell burst forth from thousands of throats, and all Hell broke loose. Rebel cannon by the score sent clouds of grapeshot into the front ranks, leaving masses of torn flesh where living men had been a moment before. The ripping fire of thousands of Enfield muskets created a continuous, crackling sound interrupted only by the roar of the cannon and the screams of the Rebels, most of who concentrated their fire on the bravest officers, causing whole regiments to be suddenly leaderless. Incredibly, these regiments kept grimly advancing with few or no officers to lead them, the men unconsciously hunching their shoulders and leaning forward as if advancing in a driving rainstorm.

Ambrose Bierce had a strange love/hate relationship with death, and would have kept running up the slope with the men if there had been the slightest chance of success, regardless of risk. However, he could see that there was not the slightest chance of the attack succeeding, and threw himself prone on the ground, while the men kept flowing around him. When talking with others Bierce was inclined to mock foolish bravery and laugh at those who gave their lives for generals' mistakes. That was a pose, required for some obscure need of his injured soul. Here, watching the men move up the slope to probable death or mutilation and certain failure, he screamed in rage while tears flowed freely down his cheeks. Then he found words.

"Stop, you fools! Go back! Go back! Stop!" But the cacophony of the battle kept all but the very nearest to him from distinguishing his words; and those nearest disregarded the unfamiliar captain lying prone on the ground. Raising his head as much as he dared, he was amazed to see the ever-dwindling first wave approach within yards of the pass's crest. For a moment he dared to hope that the sacrifice would not be in vain, that a miracle would occur. Nevertheless, it was not to be. Just short of their goal the columns seemed to melt away, leaving a residue of bodies on the ground, writhing in agony or ominously still. The survivors began to run back to their starting points; a goodly number were shot in the back by gleefully screaming Rebels. Glancing upward, Bierce saw a lone drummer-boy at the summit, a lad of not more than fourteen years, standing defiantly, refusing to retreat. Apparently none could bring themselves to shoot the boy, and Bierce saw arms come into sight, seize the drummer, and pull him over the summit and out of harm's way.

Bierce stood to join the retreating survivors. However, for some moments he stared at the top of the pass, proximity and the strengthening sunshine allowing him a glimpse of much of the Confederate lines for the first time. To his horror he saw hundreds of rifle pits, located to be mutually supporting; scores of cannon carefully dug in to command the approaches; uncounted barriers and ditches thrown up to disrupt an attack. From where he now stood, it was painfully obvious that General Joseph Johnston had been expecting the attack, and had very carefully prepared for it. Bierce turned and ran for the rear. '*Damn Sherman!*' he thought. Whatever Sherman had been told was lies; no chance that this had been a mistake or misinterpretation by whoever was the commanding general's informant. '*Well, I'll tell Sherman what I saw, and find out who is the traitor that led us into the trap; Sherman's promises be damned!*'

Bierce had by now reached the first of the Union batteries. Out of breath from his run in a hot, muggy Georgia morning, he paused briefly to rest. He turned back to look at the pass of death, where the bodies of some of Sherman's best soldiers lay like autumn leaves. Suddenly, there was a smashing impact on the back of his head. Bierce fleetingly wondered if someone had hit him with a hammer as he fell forward. He hit the ground hard; trying to move, he found that he had lost all control of his limbs. Darkness rushed at him, and he now realized he must have caught a stray bullet in the head, and was dying.

Life had always frightened Ambrose Bierce more than death, after what he had experienced in this war, and before that in Indiana. He welcomed the approaching darkness with no fear at all. Then he caught a glimpse of what lay beyond the darkness, and vainly tried to scream.

Sherman galloped up to the hill where Thomas and his party were stationed, trailing aides behind him like a kite's tail. He had been with McPherson on the flank, waiting for a message that the breakthrough had happened, so he could unleash his young protégé to complete Johnston's destruction. However, the aide from Thomas brought news of disaster, not success. Telling the astonished McPherson to await further orders, he had driven his horse as hard as he dared to find the commander of the Army of the Cumberland. He found the ponderous Virginian at the crest of a low hill, accompanied by Hooker and their respective aides. Savagely jerking the reins to halt his mount, Sherman ignored Thomas' salute and shouted "What the hell has happened? Why is there no breakthrough?"

"A breakthrough does not appear possible, sir. Johnston seems to have heavily entrenched and provided a number of batteries of supporting artillery. Given the defensive nature of the approach, he could hold off ten times his numbers for as long as he has ammunition."

Sherman's wild eyes focused on the nearest streams of survivors staggering back to safety; their regimental flags indicated that they were from Hooker's 20th Corps. "Hooker, why are your men retiring? Why are they not at least digging in close to the Reb lines?"

Joe Hooker glared at Sherman with undisguised contempt. He was a man who never lost an opportunity to show up a superior; but right now his indignation was transparently sincere. "I have ordered a general retreat . . . sir. Finding that I have lost as many men as my orders required, I saw no reason to leave them in danger to no purpose."

"General Hooker, you are insubordinate in word and manner," said Thomas angrily. "I realize that you are under some stress, but it is still inexcusable. Please be so good as to tend to your corps, and only come into my sight or the sight of the general commanding when you are prepared to behave as an officer should." With a curt nod Thomas dismissed his chief subordinate. Hooker looked as if he were about to say something more; but seeming to change his mind, he saluted and galloped off, followed by his own aides.

Thomas turned his attention to Sherman. "I apologize for his conduct, sir. Even though he was not my choice for the 20th Corps, I am fully responsible for his disrespect."

"Never mind that!" Sherman remembered Joe Hooker from prewar San Francisco as anything but a gentlemen, constantly making the rounds of brothels and borrowing money that was never repaid; he concurred in Thomas' low opinion of the commander of the 20th. "Where is Davis? Has he had any luck?"

Sadly, Thomas shook his head. "He heard one of his divisions could not get back, their retreat being cut off; the moment he heard that, he galloped off to direct their rescue without even asking permission."

"Sounds like Davis; one hell of a fool, but afraid of nothing." Sherman hesitated for some moments, then looked at Thomas and said "I want you to know that this is all my fault. You were right, I was wrong."

Thomas looked back, saying nothing. It took nearly a minute for Sherman to realize that Thomas was going to say nothing; in an obscure way, that rebuked him more than a half hour of screaming and cursing would have done. Finally, Sherman issued an order. "Do what you can to call a truce and recover our wounded and . . . the others." Jerkily Sherman saluted and put the spurs to his horse, his aides scrambling to keep pace.

Teresa Duval was enjoying herself as she bustled about the complex of hospital tents. She always found the aftermath of a battle pleasurable, the sight of blood being so . . . stimulating to her. However, she was always careful not to show her pleasure outwardly, staying in her character of a pious nurse from New England, provided courtesy of the Sanitary Commission. The surgeons and staff of the Medical Corp regarded her as an angel of mercy, a nurse more skilled than most doctors in saving the wounded from dying of their wounds. They praised her medical skills to the skies, and in truth she had saved dozens of Federal soldiers from death and preserved dozens more from a lifetime of handicap. If the surgeons and staff noticed that on those rare occasions when she attended Confederate wounded her skills deserted her and the wounded almost always died, they seemed unwilling to draw any conclusions.

In truth, the role of nurse was only one of several which Teresa Duval performed; she was naturally a brilliant actress, and in another life would have dominated the stages of the nation. Far from being a pious Christian from a middle-class New England family, she was a survivor of the Irish Famine, living a bestial life in the slums of New York until the financier Jay Gould plucked her up from the gutter, gave her a veneer of sophistication and manners, and made her one of his most valuable agents. He had arranged for her to be assigned to Sherman's army, and directed her to send him coded telegraphs, innocently addressed to her mother, giving advance knowledge of Sherman's movements and prospects; using that advance knowledge, he was able to anticipate movements in share and commodity prices in the financial markets, and make hundreds of thousands of dollars at a stroke. Gould had also arranged for her to secretly be appointed to Allen Pinkerton's Secret Service, with the understanding that whatever she learned of financial interest while serving the Secret Service would be immediately shared with him. A lesser woman would not have been able to perform all of these apparently contradictory roles without giving herself away immediately. However, Teresa Duval was no ordinary woman.

Duval bustled into a large, shambling barn that stood in the center of the scattered hospital tents, absently wiping her blood-stained forearms with a scrap of cloth, oblivious to the moans and occasional screams of the wounded soldiers around her. She regretted having just amputated a young soldier's leg. She much would have preferred to restore him to combat, killing English-loving rebel bastards, but the bone had been completely shattered by an Enfield round, and amputation was the only way of saving him from death by gangrene. Now she needed to find a doctor to give her another assignment; she had not yet had her fill of cutting on human flesh. She spotted a small, frail-looking captain at a table to her right, and recognized him as Saul Fetterman, the former surgeon of the 27th Ohio whom she had met under peculiar circumstances on the road to Knoxville the previous year. She changed directions and approached Fetterman, who stood staring at a silent form on the table.

"Dr. Fetterman, I finished that poor soul's amputation," she said, feigning sorrow that had no place in her cold heart. "Where else may I be of service in the Lord's cause?"

Fetterman turned his gaze on Duval, who noted his sad, exhausted eyes. She respected his medical skills, and was as fond of him as her nature allowed. Still, she thought of him as something of a fool. She remembered how last year he had volunteered to stay with wounded Confederate raiders, even though it would have meant his capture and imprisonment in the hellish Andersonville. Duval still wondered why she had bothered to take certain actions that saved him from that fate; then decided that she was becoming sentimental as the years passed.

"Miss Duval, you have been doing wonders all day, but there is only so much that a lady should be asked to endure, even one of your great abilities. You should take some rest. It seems like the wounded will never cease coming. In God's name, how many people did Sherman lose today? And for so many of them, there is nothing that can be done. Take this captain; why did anyone bother to bring him in? He has been shot through the head, and cannot live."

Duval glanced at the officer, and did a double-take. "I know this man," she blurted. "Ambrose Bierce; a scout with the Army of the Ohio."

"A pity that a good Christian cannot put such a poor soul out of his misery," said Fetterman morosely. "There is no chance he can recover. See there?" Fetterman pointed to a bloody, clotted wound behind Bierce's left ear. The scout's blue eyes were open, staring fixedly with horror, but there was no spark of animation in them; the only sign of life was the weak, wheezy sound of his lungs, feebly gasping for air. Gently Fetterman turned Bierce's head, and pointed to a bump behind the right ear. "See, the bullet transited the rear of the cranium; I wager that bump conceals the bullet itself. Must have been nearly spent, or it would have cleanly exited the skull. Amazing that he is alive at all."

"Bierce!" came a high-pitched shout from about ten paces away. Duval and Fetterman spun around to see General Sherman, his wild eyes fixed on the table. With jerky movements the commanding general approached the table and looked down into the captain's unseeing blue eyes.

"Sir, I am surprised to see you here," said Fetterman.

"Where else should I be?" snarled Sherman. "These boys are all here because of me. Because of me! And they don't even have the consolation of a victory. I need to see them; they deserve the chance to look at me with hate." He stared down at the wounded scout, and spoke again with a voice beginning to crack. "Damn you, Bierce! I told you to be careful. Told you!"

There was an embarrassed silence for a few moments, and then the general asked the doctor "What are his chances?"

Fetterman hesitated before speaking, "Sir, they simply do not exist. The brain has been penetrated. We need to move him aside to make way for a soldier that can be helped by medical science."

Sherman grabbed the small doctor's shoulder roughly. "God damn you! You will not throw this man aside like trash! You will operate on him, and do all you can to heal him!"

Fear in his eyes, Fetterman replied "Sir, even if I do as you say, all that could be done is close the wound. Infection of the brain is almost inevitable, resulting in a horrible death in a matter of days. Even if by some miracle there is no infection, he would probably remain in this state for the remainder of his existence."

Sherman's face acquired a lunatic cast; his free hand began to undo the flap of his holster. "You whoreson! By God if you don't do as I say . . ."

"General, sir, Captain Fetterman," interrupted Duval smoothly. "I once successfully closed such a wound. Although the man was never the same afterwards, he could live a life . . . of sorts."

Sherman looked with surprise at Duval. "You did?"

"With the blessing of God, I did sir," replied Duval in a pious New England voice. "I need two small pieces of metal, cleaned and heated in flame, some surgical pins, the smaller the better; and a solution of carbolic acid."

Sherman released Fetterman, but then pointed a forefinger like a knife. "You! You get this woman anything she needs, and help her. You save this man's life, or God have mercy on you, for I will have none!"

An hour later, Sherman, Fetterman and Duval staggered out of the barn, circling to the side of the building that still gave shade from the brutal Georgia sun. For the moment they ignored the stream of wounded that was still arriving; there were other doctors and nurses to tend to them for the time being. Tension and lack of sleep having put Fetterman on edge, he suddenly addressed Sherman angrily.

"General, sir, I don't care what you think, how you threaten me, but we have done that man no favor! I have nothing but praise for how Miss Duval conducted the procedure; no one could have shown more skill, least of all myself. Nonetheless, despite all precautions taken, infection will almost certainly take hold in a few days. And if by some miracle it does not, he will spend his life as a vegetable, sir. A vegetable!" Frightened by his own outburst, Fetterman turned away from the astonished Sherman and stared at the horizon, seeing nothing.

Duval felt pleasure at the compliment to her abilities that Fetterman had bestowed in the midst of his tirade. In spite of such a trivial emotion, she felt there was no time to bask in praise; she had an immediate, serious decision to make. She knew Bierce to be a friend of sorts to Major Alphonso Clay, Ulysses Grant's sinister trouble-shooter. Six months before, she had realized that the wealthy, cultivated, dangerous Clay was a man who just might possibly understand the desires that drove her. She had sent him a gift of a pair of objects that she knew would please him greatly, and waited for his response. All patience in vain; none had come, either positive or negative. Teresa Duval was not a woman to give up on anything she desired, and had given much thought as to how to draw Clay into her orbit. Now in her blood-streaked hand she held a small metal object that chance had sent her; and she had always believed in seizing unexpected chances.

"General Sherman, sir, the wounding of Captain Bierce is troubling in more ways than one."

With a bird-like movement of his head, Sherman switched his attention to Duval.

"What do you mean, Miss?"

"It is not surprising that the Captain was shot in the back of the head. It does not even necessarily imply he was running from the battle; bullets come from all directions in a battle. However, the bullet itself disturbs me." She opened her hand to show a flattened piece of lead. "I recovered this just under the skin at the exit wound. Sir, this is not a rifle bullet. It a .44 caliber pistol bullet."

Sherman frowned. "So? He was shot by some Goddamn Reb officer."

Duval shook her head, a vaguely sinister smile on her face. "Rebel officers do use an odd assortment of pistols; but for the most part they use .36 caliber Colts or .42 caliber LeMats. I fear that Captain Bierce was shot by one of our own men, a Southern spy."

"That's damn nonsense! At worse, a wild shot, flying a great distance. . ." Sherman suddenly turned thoughtful.

Duval nodded. "Yes, you see. The Colt .44 is notorious for its short range, not being able to send a bullet much further than about fifty paces. The man who fired it would have seen Bierce clearly."

"Still, there could be other explanations than a murderous attack on a fine young officer under the cover of battle." Sherman sounded dubious.

"Without doubt, General," replied Duval agreeably. "Still, may I suggest that you telegraph to General Grant and ask for the services of Major Alphonso Clay? I believe you saw something of his abilities at Vicksburg, as did I at Knoxville. Besides, I believe Clay to consider Captain Bierce a personal friend. You know the Major's reputation; he would insist on confirming that there is nothing more involved here than the fortunes of war."

Sherman nodded. "I can see that. A hard customer if ever I saw one. Well, I will send a telegram tonight. First I need to see Bierce again." He hesitated, and then gruffly went on. "I want to thank you and Dr. Fetterman for what you did, no matter how it turns out. I am under some pressure, and sometimes say more than I mean." The doctor turned to look at Sherman, realizing that this was as close to an apology as he would ever get. The commanding general re-entered the barn without a backward glance.

"Come doctor," said Duval crisply. "Let us check the tents and see where we can do the most good." Fetterman drew a breath, shuddered, and silently nodded. As the two walked toward the nearest tent, from which came a continuous, high-pitched wail, Duval thought smugly of how she had set things in motion. She cared little for whether Bierce lived or died; what *was* important was that the fascinating Clay would soon be here.

Inside the barn, Sherman stood motionless for nearly a quarter of an hour over the table on which Ambrose Bierce rested. His head was now wrapped in bandages, but otherwise he appeared unchanged; open blue eyes staring rigidly at nothing, the chest wheezily rising and falling at intervals. Sherman knew it was wrong to care so much more about this one man then all the others killed or mutilated in today's butchery. Deep inside, somehow this young captain, to whom he owed his very life, had become mixed up in his mind with Willie, the son who might have grown up to look so much like Bierce. William Tecumseh Sherman cared little for most people, but for those he did care for, he cared with all the fervor of his burning, tormented soul.

His eyes began to fill with tears. The figure on the table seemed to shift back between Bierce and Willie and Bierce again. The South had taken them from him. Irrationally he felt that the South was a coward who would not face him, but would instead take from him whatever he valued. The South, the damned, traitorous South.

Suddenly Sherman murmured. "I will make Georgia howl." There was a pause, and then he screamed the phrase again at the top of his lungs.

"I WILL MAKE GEORGIA HOWL!"

Everyone in the barn who was able to do so looked uneasily at Sherman, and then at each other.

CHAPTER 1

"... AND THERE WERE UNION MEN WHO WEPT WITH JOYFUL TEARS ..."

Major Alphonso Clay and Lieutenant Jeremiah Lot were precariously perched on crates containing the infamous army crackers, trying to anticipate the jolts and swaying that the rickety old freight car inflicted on them. To sleep, even to briefly doze, was to risk being thrown to the floor, or perhaps even out the open side door, left dangerously ajar in the hope of relieving the stifling, humid air in the car. Still, a fall from the train was unlikely to be fatal; at no point was the wheezing locomotive exceeding twenty miles per hour.

Clay studied his black companion with concern, as he had done a number of times during the week-long journey from northern Virginia; the illegitimate son of Clay's uncle and one of the man's slaves was dearer to him than any living person. When General Rawlins, Grant's chief of staff, had delivered to them Sherman's telegram stating that Ambrose Bierce was at death's door, perhaps the victim of a traitorous plot, Lot had literally staggered with the shock. Clay could not recall his friend looking that devastated since a certain evening in Louisiana, two years ago.

Clay had asked Ulysses Grant for permission to investigate Sherman's suspicions, even though it had been a bad time to make the request; cannon were booming in the distance and aides were darting about with worried expressions. It did not surprise Clay to watch the grim, stooping man devote a moment to the telegram as if it were the only thing of importance in the world, bark an instruction for an aide to prepare orders for Clay and Lot, and immediately turn his attention back to the titanic struggle at his front. Clay had long known Grant possessed the twin gifts of total concentration and lack of the capacity for panic. Clay and Lot had commenced their journey within the hour, by horse to Washington, by rail to Cincinnati, where they switched trains to one headed for Chattanooga. Now they were on the last leg of the trip, on a stretch of railroad where no passengers were allowed without priority orders. Sherman's army of one hundred thousand was completely dependent on this one stretch of rail for all of its supplies, a fact well known to Nathan Bedford Forrest and his cavalry. Forrest and his men were devoted to burning bridges and tearing up rails, but were frustrated by the fiendish efficiency of Sherman's engineers under Orlando Poe, who often had the line repaired before Forest's raiders had returned to base. Nevertheless, Sherman's supplies were disturbingly tight, which was why he had ordered all passengers off the trains. Alas, there were exceptions, and among them were Clay and Lot.

Fearing that his friend was immersed too deeply in private misery, Clay attempted to start up a conversation. "Look," said Clay, pointing through the open door to a long string of shattered railway cars. "I had read that Sherman ordered wrecks just shoved off the rails and left to rust, finding it more efficient to seize rolling stock from Northern lines to replace what he loses. Still, seeing it in person reinforces the impression that General Sherman can be a single-minded man."

Lot turned his head and smiled sadly. "You needn't try to lift my spirits, Alphonso, although I do appreciate the effort."

Clay frowned. "Then let us speak on it. I will admit that I had come to value Captain Bierce's merits and discount his faults, and have grown rather fond of him. Still, Bierce is a soldier, and these are the fortunes of war. Why has this hit you so hard?"

Lot glanced sorrowfully at Clay before turning his gaze again to the passing scenery. "He is one of the very few white men who have treated me as an equal. Many pay lip service to abolition, but want nothing to do personally with the black man. Bierce is different. Yes, he referred to me from time to time by . . . an unpleasant epithet; but he says worse about white men. And there was the time he saved my life outside Vicksburg."

"As I recall, he was mainly saving the life of General Sherman."

"He could have done that on his own; he was on horseback, and by then I was not. Instead, he placed himself and General Sherman at greater risk rather than leave me behind. That should not be forgotten. I will not forget it. More importantly, Bierce is a free-thinker, and has not yet found his way into the bosom of the Lord. I fear for his soul should he expire while not in a state of grace."

Clay started to speak, but decided to remain silent. It was not that Clay did not believe in a life after death—far from it. Pessimistically, he doubted that Bierce's place in that life would be determined by a deathbed conversion. Nonetheless, he admired his cousin's uncomplicated faith, and would not challenge it for the world.

"You must prepare for the possibility that Bierce will be dead by the time we arrive," said Clay gently. "Miss Duval has indicated the bullet penetrated the brain."

"She might be mistaken as to the seriousness of the wound."

Clay smiled unpleasantly. "On matters of this nature, I am inclined to trust Miss Duval's judgment."

Suddenly there was a squeal of brakes accompanied by a sharp lurch; the two officers barely kept their seats on the cracker boxes.

"It would seem we have reached the end of the line, quite literally," observed Clay, watching the confused bustle of a large army camp slide into view through the door as the train slowly shuddered to a stop, emitting a final burst of steam that sounded like the dying gasp of a wounded beast. The two officers grabbed the carpetbags containing their effects and leaped the short distance to the ground, flinching as the summer Georgia sun struck them with full force. Blinking, they looked around for a welcoming party; but all they could see was teams of sweating enlisted men swarming over the train, unloading the cars of their precious cargo as fast as possible.

"It looks like we must find our own way," commented Clay. "Well, schedules are irregular, and we could hardly expect General Sherman to personally keep a lookout for our arrival."

As if to immediately contradict Clay, a mounted General Sherman came galloping around the locomotive, accompanied by a single mounted aide. Spotting Clay and Lot, he urged his mount forwarded, viciously reining it to a skidding stop in front of the two surprised officers. Sherman vaulted off the animal, handed its reins to the aide without a backward glance. With a total lack of decorum or respect for the differences in their ranks, Sherman vigorous shook the hand first of Clay, then of Lot.

"Damn glad Sam could spare you," said Sherman without preamble. "Damn glad for more than one reason."

"Sir, is Captain Bierce . . . holding his own?" asked Lot tentatively.

Sherman looked thoughtfully at Lot, the first black officer he had seen with his own eyes. "You were close to Bierce; you and

Clay. It's good you're here; he is unlikely to survive until tomorrow. Man shouldn't die with just strangers around him, even if he isn't awake. Thomas and I think highly of Bierce; but there is little time that either of us can spare to be at his side. Tried to find if he had any special friends willing to be with him when . . . willing to be with him; seems he doesn't. Sad thing to say, very . . . sad," said Sherman, who with the exception of Ulysses Grant had few outside his family for whom he cared or who cared for him.

"I realize you cannot spare much time from the concerns of the army," replied Clay quietly. "If you will direct us to where he is, you need not take more time from your duties."

"Hell, I can spare that much time. Besides, on the way there I can tell you what the Duval woman suspects. More than likely nonsense! Regardless, I would appreciate your take on it."

Leaving his aide holding his mount, Sherman began marching off with long-legged, birdlike steps, leaving Clay and Lot to hurry to catch up.

"Did Miss Duval give any more details on why she thought Bierce was the victim of a murderous assault?" asked Lot.

Sherman shook his head vigorously. "None beyond the fact that a Colt .44 is so short-ranged that the bullet had to have been aimed at him deliberately. I'm still not entirely convinced; bullets do the damndest things in battle, and it's possible some Reb was using a Colt he took off a dead Federal. But by God, she's a damned smart woman with a level head, and I'd feel better if you could put her concerns to rest."

Clay smiled slightly. "Sir, I believe that Miss Duval has an . . . instinct for such matters. I would not dismiss her concerns lightly."

"Well, you will judge for yourself, I expect. Here we are." They had arrived at a large wall tent, one of scores set forth in neat rows. They entered to find a dozen cots filled with wounded men, who were thankfully silent; the surgeons had already done their worst on this tent's occupants, who now stoically waited to see if they lived or died. At the back of the tent Teresa Duval leaned over one still figure, intently inspecting its eyes. She noticed the new arrivals, straightened, and wiped her blood-soaked hands on a rag hung on the side of the cot.

"General, I see you have brought our visitors yourself. Praise the Lord."

"How is Bierce today?" asked Sherman, leading Clay and Lot up to the cot beside which Duval stood.

"Not as good as yesterday, sir." She turned her attention to the Clay. "Major, I am pleased that General Grant could spare you and Lieutenant Lot. You look quite well."

Clay nodded a greeting. "I am as well as ever, Miss Duval. You look as . . . capable as ever."

"I believe you benefited from a long Christmas leave after the affair at Knoxville," she replied. "I hope your holiday was satisfactory, and that you received memorable gifts to mark the birth of our Savior."

Clay looked at her steadily for a long moment, and then said "I did indeed. Two of the gifts were especially intriguing."

"I trust they met with your approval."

There was another long pause. "As surprising as they were, I finally decided that they did."

Lot, whose eyes had been riveted on Bierce, interrupted the enigmatic exchange. "Miss Duval, I must ask for details on Captain Bierce's condition. Please, I must know it all."

"He has shown little signs of consciousness since the operation," she replied. "He opens his eyes in the morning, and closes them in the evening. That is all. I fear he is developing a fever, undoubtedly due to an inflammation of the brain." She forced herself to shed a tear before continuing. "I fear that he will not recover after all, and that the end is near."

Lot struggled to maintain his composure; only Clay could tell how devastated he was by the news. "How long?" asked the lieutenant in a voice barely above a whisper.

Duval simulated a look of tragic concern. "In all likelihood, before tomorrow morning."

Lot nodded solemnly. "Captain Bierce is completely estranged from his family, and has few friends. If I will not be in the way, I would like to stay with him until . . . tomorrow morning."

"Of course you may," Duval replied. "I really do not see what purpose it will serve. I do not expect him to be conscious of your presence."

"Perhaps not. I would nevertheless prefer to be here." Lot turned his attention to Clay. "That is, of course, if you can spare me, sir."

Clay nodded his head immediately. "Of course. I can handle the initial stages of the investigation myself." The slightly built major turned his attention to Sherman. "General, with your permission I would like you to show me where Captain Bierce was found."

"The men who brought him in are scattered on various duties, but I've already had them show me. I'll take you myself." Sherman cast a long, sad glance at Bierce's inert form before saying "Let's saddle up, Clay."

"Until later then, Major," said Duval. Clay glanced at the nurse who had uttered the innocuous words, and saw the slightest trace of a cunning smile adorning the face of the pious angel of mercy. He frowned as he followed Sherman out of the tent; he already had much on his mind, and this complication was unwelcome.

Sherman and Clay trotted up the approaches to the pass over Kennesaw. Suddenly Sherman reined his horse to stop, Clay smoothly following suit. The red-haired general glanced at the surroundings. Aside from a few figures in blue scurrying about in

27

the distance, occupied with collecting and burying the last of the Union dead, they had the field to themselves. A slight, sickly odor of decay permeated the air. Swiftly the lanky general dismounted and wrapped his mount's reins around the branch of a nearby tree; Clay again followed suit.

Restlessly, Sherman surveyed the area in silence. Clay interrupted the general's melancholic thoughts. "Sir, can it be safe for you to be so close to the enemy position? A sniper could leave the army leaderless."

Sherman seemed to snap back to the present. "What? Oh, that's right, I haven't told you. Johnston's boys pulled out last night. We're getting ready to pull up stakes and follow. Johnston must've realized I was about to send McPherson on a flanking move, and wasn't waiting for me to spring the trap. Scouts tell me he didn't leave so much as a cracker behind. Hardest military action is an organized withdrawal in the face of superior force, but Joe Johnston handled it smoothly and without loss . . . damn the bastard!" He looked over the scattered litter that lay in front of the crest of the ridge. "All for nothing. I sent my boys up against the middle, against the advice of nearly every general I had, even that idiot Hooker. All those men dead and crippled, and in the end Johnston leaves on his own. Goddamn it! I had been told . . . Never mind; the fault is mine. Anyway Clay, right here is where some gunners from Hooker's artillery found Bierce." He pointed to a scuffed area of the ground, which aside from a darkish patch of earth showed no sign of violence.

Clay looked at the ground and frowned. "The soil looks as if it had been trampled by a herd of bison. Little can be learned at that spot. I am surprised that you are even sure that was where Bierce was shot."

"Had the spot pointed out to me right after Bierce was brought in by the boys who found him. I remember where the spot was in relation to the tree we used to tie up our horses. Besides, I also remember where it was in relation to the three-inch guns. They're gone now, but the heavy bastards left deep wheel marks which even everything since couldn't erase." Sherman pointed to his left, and Clay saw for himself numerous ruts in the ground. He nodded. "Did they tell you how Bierce's body lay?"

Sherman thought for a moment. "They said he lay on his stomach, facing toward the Rebs."

"Could they tell if he had been shot during the assault itself, or during the subsequent retreat?"

Sherman again consulted his memory. "They were pretty sure it was during the retreat. Didn't see him fall themselves, but they had been going back and forth all during the assault, bringing shells to the caissons, and they were sure his body wasn't there until the retreat was well under way."

"So," mused Clay aloud, "Bierce was facing the enemy lines, even after the retreat was long under way. It indicates he was almost certainly shot from our side. What is even more interesting is that it indicates something about those lines was deeply interesting to him, so interesting as to slow his progress to a place of safety. General, I would like to see the Rebel position more closely."

Sherman shrugged. "Suit yourself." The two officers remounted, and in a minute were among the remains of what had been the Confederate front line. Not bothering to dismount, Clay surveyed the trenches, rifle pits placed to support each other, and numerous artillery positions. The placid blue eyes darted back and forth behind the spectacles, taking in every detail. Finally he turned to Sherman.

"General, I am not a strategist or tactician, but even I can see this is impregnable, if manned by sufficient troops. Why on earth did you order a frontal assault? There was not the slightest chance that one would succeed."

Sherman looked enraged, but as much with himself as with Clay's criticism. "Goddamn it, I know now it was murder to send men against this! I didn't know it would be like this. In fact, I had specific information that the pass would be lightly held."

Clay took another long look at the remains of the Confederate defense. "It would appear that you were misinformed. Just who gave you such information?"

"Doesn't matter now. It was my job to evaluate the quality of intelligence. It was my judgment that failed, and no one else's."

Clay decided to let the matter drop for the moment; he suspected he would be returning soon enough to the issue of who provided Sherman with bad information. Instead, he commented "This might explain Bierce's attention to the Confederate position he was fleeing. He must have made it far enough up the pass to glimpse the true extent of the Rebel preparations. However, it still does not explain why someone from our side would shoot him in the back of the head. I wonder if he had seen something that might explain the, ah, extent to which Johnston was prepared to receive you."

"I guess Bierce himself is the only one who could answer that, and it looks like you won't ever be able to get an answer," responded Sherman moodily. The general shook his head as if to clear it. "Well, if you've seen enough we better be heading back; Army's going to be going after Johnston at first light. Looks like you came on a fool's errand. I'll cut you and Lot orders that will put you on a train back to Chattanooga."

Clay scanned the field, expressionless blue eyes giving no sign of what was going on behind them. "With your permission, I would like to accompany your army on the move. There are still a few matters I need to consider, and I can do that as easily in motion as stationary."

Sherman shrugged his narrow shoulders. "Suit yourself. We'll be living rough, but from what I saw of you at Vicksburg, I expect you can handle that."

Clay did not respond. He continued to gaze over the field, and kept his thoughts to himself.

The sun was just setting when Clay entered the hospital tent in which laid the comatose Ambrose Bierce. He glanced over the rows of cots supporting moaning sufferers, and spotted a seated Lot beside the standing Duval and Dr. Fetterman beside Bierce's inert form. Clay strode over, bowed slightly and clicked his heels, European-style. "Miss Duval, Dr. Fetterman. Doctor, I wish we could have met again under happier circumstances. How is the captain?"

Dr. Fetterman shook his head sadly. "There is no hope at all. The fever is mounting. I expect death within a few hours."

Clay gazed down at Bierce for a moment; the captain's eyes were now closed, but his bandaged head made small restless movements, while a film of sweat coated his face. Clay then shifted his attention to the black lieutenant. Lot was firmly holding one of Bierce's hands with his left, while with his right he held his Bible open, reading from one of the more comforting chapters of the New Testament.

In a low voice, Clay said "Jeremiah, this is doing no good."

Lot turned to look at Clay, who noticed his friend's eyes were brimming with unshed tears. "Alphonso, how do you know that? How? He has not found God, and I think we both know why, both know what must have happened in his childhood. For him to be damned due to monstrous, unnatural sins committed against him . . . well, despite all I believe I hope that enough prayer will save his soul, or at least give him enough life to save his own." Lot turned back to Clay, but instead of resuming his reading, he began to mutter. "Sinful as it is, I would wish the ancients were right about blood sacrifice. I would do almost anything to keep

Ambrose alive." There was a deep sigh. "But of course it never worked; even when the Carthaginians sacrificed their own children, much less animals, they could not save themselves from destruction by Rome." Lot paused for a moment, then began quietly reading aloud from the book that anchored his soul.

In the softest of voices Clay replied "The ancients made a fundamental mistake. The forces to which they sacrificed did not want innocence, be it an animal or a child. They wanted something that could look upon Hell and understand the meaning of what it saw." The preoccupied Lot did not hear Clay. Shocked, both Duval and Fetterman glanced at him strangely.

After a moment, Clay glanced at Fetterman and Duval. The doctor had returned to watching Lot with uncomfortable concern, obviously wishing to give succor but unsure how; Duval looked on with a pitying expression in which lurked a hint of a contemptuous smirk which few aside from Clay would have noticed. Clay addressed Fetterman in a low voice.

"Doctor, I know you have obligations to the other wounded. Still, I would take it as a personal favor if you would keep an eye on the lieutenant as he holds vigil. I would do so myself, but duty requires that I be elsewhere."

While Fetterman nodded solemnly, Duval said "It must be an important task that would take you away at such a time."

"That is so, Miss Duval." Clay bowed slightly, clicked his heels, and exited the tent into the night without further ado.

Although the moon had not yet risen, the occasional campfire and lantern allowed Clay to easily find the holding pen for the Confederate prisoners who had not yet been transferred north. He paused before the abandoned corral inside of which scores of ragged men milled about, and observed that the rickety boards were no barrier to escape. Nonetheless, there were a number of alert sentries standing guard watchfully with loaded Springfields, and Clay doubted any of the prisoners would test the responses of the guards. Clay walked up to one of those guards, who sported a corporal's stripes. The man saluted smartly.

"Corporal, I have a need to gather certain intelligence, intelligence most likely in the possession of Rebel cavalry. Do you have any prisoners from Forrest's command in there?

"Yeah, a couple of Johnnies brought in day before last," said the lanky man in the distinctive twang of Illinois.

"Please be so good as to bring them to me."

The corporal looked for a long moment at Clay, as if he were about to challenge the major's authority over the prisoners. Making up his mind, he finally shrugged and called to a nearby private. "Hey Burton, bring them horse soldiers we got two days ago out to me."

"Sure thing, Frosty," replied the private cheerfully. The formal, reserved Clay reflected disapprovingly that discipline seemed lax among units recruited from the West. In a few moments the private had brought two ragged figures out through the gate, saluted sloppily, and returned to his post.

"Here they be, Major. Two of that bastard Forrest's men that won't be raiding our lines again."

Clay studied the two. Both were lean and wiry. However, one appeared to be a lad of no more than sixteen years, whose eyes darted around like those of a hunted rabbit. The other, older man showed no fear, and favored Clay with a nasty, defiant smile. After a few moments, Clay abruptly asked "Were either of you with Forrest at Fort Pillow?"

The younger prisoner started, cast his eyes downward and replied in a small voice. "Yessir." The older man smirked and said "Waren't there. Was on leave." The young man glanced up, startled, but said nothing.

Clay ignored the older man. Instead, pale blue eyes glimmering behind his spectacles, he addressed the younger man. "Tell me what it felt like to kill all those men trying to surrender. Tell me how proud and valorous you felt."

The scared teenager raised his head further, but could not quite make eye contact with Clay. "Never felt lower in my life. Felt lower than catfish shit. Waren't glory. Couldn't believe the order . . . hell, didn't matter if they was darkies, they was Christians . . ." The youth suddenly sniffled, and wiped his eyes with a dirty sleeve. The older prisoner looked on with sneering contempt.

"How many did you yourself kill?" asked Clay in an emotion-less voice.

The teenager hung his head even lower and mumbled "Don't rightly know; waren't keeping count. Maybe . . . three, four."

Clay stared at the youth for a long moment, and then nodded slightly to himself; he was fairly certain that the boy had killed no one, and had probably fired wildly into the air so that his comrades would think he was participating in the butchery that had been unleashed at Fort Pillow. In a startling movement Clay stabbed a finger at the older man, and addressed the corporal. "Him. Tie his hands behind his back, then send this boy back to the pen."

The corporal stared at Clay for a moment. "Just what's this about . . . sir?"

"I am taking this prisoner for an interrogation. I wish to conduct it outside our lines and alone, as my methods are . . . unorthodox."

"Just hold on here," said the older Confederate. "I'm a prisoner, and you ain't got no right . . ."

With a swift movement the corporal smacked the side of the prisoner's head with the stock of his rifle. The older Confederate fell to the ground with a cry, clutching his wounded skull. The corporal reached into his tunic pocket and withdrew an ungainly pair of iron handcuffs, which he threw at the quaking teenager.

"Lock your friend's hands behind his back. Then you git back to the pen. Remember I can see you all the way, and if you take one step to either side I'll kill you sooner than I'd kill a dog in the road."

The trembling youth did as he was told, then nervously set off in the gloom, constantly glancing over his shoulder at the corporal, who did not even bother to look directly at him. Instead he roughly hauled the older Rebel to his feet, saying "Major, I reckon I know a place to cross the picket lines quiet-like. My boy is on picket duty there. He's a good boy, and will do what he's told. Follow me."

The three men began walking through the gloom single file, the prisoner between the corporal and Clay. They quickly left the campfires and bustle of the camp behind, but Clay noted approvingly that the older soldier seemed able to find his sure-footed way through the darkness with no difficulty.

"Halt! Who goes there?" came a voice suddenly from the darkness.

Instead of a password, the corporal replied "It's all right Zeke. It's Pa."

"Pa, what the hell you doin' out here? Ain't you supposed to be guarding the Rebs we took?" A half moon now shone in the sky, and in its pale light Clay saw a younger version of his lanky escort approach them, musket still at the ready.

"Major here wants to take this Reb bastard out past our lines, to put some questions to him private-like; figured it would be best if it was your patch he went through."

Clay drew his revolver. Pointing it at the prisoner, he said "See that tree to your right, about ten paces off? Go stand there, and do not move while I talk with these gentlemen." Muttering a curse, the prisoner did as he was told. Clay then turned to the two Federals. "The questioning I intend is of a . . . peculiar kind. I do not believe the prisoner will be coming back with me." With his free hand

Clay dipped into his pocket and extracted two twenty-dollar gold coins. "One for each of you, for the inconvenience of holding your tongues when there are questions about the missing prisoner."

Neither man moved to take the coins. The older one said "Your money ain't good here, Major."

Frowning, Clay asked "Does that mean you intend to report this to your officers?"

The older man did not respond. After a moment, the younger spoke up. "That ain't what Pa meant. You see, that bastard yonder is one of Forrest's boys." He paused for another moment, and then continued.

"You see, Major, when Uncle Abe called for volunteers a whole passel of men from our little neck of Illinois joined the same regiment; sometime several men in the same family. When Pa and me joined up, my younger brother Jacob joined up too, even though he was only seventeen. Both me and Pa tried to talk him out of it; two in the same family seemed enough. Jacob wouldn't listen. He was always holding on about the sacred duty to free the niggers, and that he would never have a better chance to do God's will. Family had been saving up to send him to college; he had more brains than the law should allow, always having his nose in a book, and it was clear he wasn't cut out to be a farmer. Still, he said college could wait, and that this was the opportunity of a lifetime. When the call went out for officers for them new colored regiments, he went for the interview, and got jumped clean up to lieutenant; not many white men wanted to officer darkies, even for promotion. Pa and me would rib him about being promoted over us; but we was really proud to bustin' of him. Got one letter from him after he left for his new regiment, and he said the new darky recruits were shaping up just fine. Said he was even organizing reading classes for the runaways in his company, as he believed a black man with a book in one hand and a gun in the other would really be going places. Last thing in his letter was that after a few more weeks of drill and practice at Fort Pillow, they would be ready to leave off garrison duty and see some real action."

None of the three said anything for a few moments, the weight of the Fort Pillow massacre hanging palpably in the air around them like a cloud. Finally, the young sentry spoke again.

"So you see Major, your money ain't good here. You take as long as you need to do what you need to do. Pa and me will be waiting here when you get back."

Clay said nothing. In the light of the rising moon he could clearly see the hard, granite-like set of the older man's face, as well as the wet trickles coming out of the corners of both eyes. After a moment he pocketed the two coins, turned around, and marched over to where the surly prisoner stood waiting.

"Turn around and start walking," Clay announced. "Make any sudden move and I will shoot you in the leg." Growling an obscenity, the prisoner began to pick his way over the uneven ground leaving the Federal lines, while the more sure-footed Clay followed closely behind him.

The pair had been walking a quarter of an hour, the lights of the Federal encampment behind them faded to nothingness, when Clay suddenly announced "Halt. This is far enough. Turn around." As the prisoner turned, an uneasy look now on his face in place of the previous arrogant smirk, Clay holstered his revolver. Then he produced a Bowie knife from where it had been secreted under his tunic.

An expression of genuine fear now on his face, the prisoner nervously licked his lips. "Ah, Major, ain't no need to go on with this anymore. You tell me what you want to know, and if I can, I'll give you the answer."

Unexpectedly, Clay giggled; coming from such a solemn officer, the sound was terrifying. "You need not concern yourself with that. There is no knowledge in your possession of interest to me."

"Then what the hell is this all about?" the Rebel asked loudly. He found himself hoping that there was someone, Confederate or Federal, out in the darkness that would hear his voice and come to investigate. He strained to hear the sounds of any passer-by, but all he could hear were the chirpings of crickets, and the distinctive hooting of a flock of whippoorwills. In the midst of his unease he still had time to think the latter odd; those birds should have flown north weeks ago.

Clay began to speak, as if musing to himself. "I am sure this is not what Father wanted. He hoped that what Grandfather von Juntz had done could be diluted, diluted through his own blood, so that good could be done for the Republic he loved while the darkness was kept under control. What he did not know was the desire would always be there, the . . . hunger. He did not anticipate how many opportunities there would be to justify the darkest deeds, calling on the foulest things, in the name of some greater good. He could not have known that I would call upon things which should not be called, and never be sure if I did so for the good of others or to satisfy my . . . craving."

"What the hell are you babbling about?" blurted the prisoner. "You drunk or what?"

Clay giggled again. "No, my friend. It would have been better for you if I were. Better still that you had stayed away from Nathan Bedford Forrest. You see, the living person I care most about in the world is about to suffer a loss, and I would spare him that loss. That person's friend is dying, and medical science can do no more. However, as the Bard once said, 'There are more things in heaven and earth than are dreamt of in your philosophy.' There is help I can call upon, help that may choose to grant a request for intervention, in a way that the narrow-minded pedants of science refuse to acknowledge exists. However, those forces demand a price, a tribute, in exchange for their help. What I am about to do will break a solemn promise I made to General Grant, and that weighs upon me; breaking such promises is dishonorable, and Clays strive to uphold their honor. It will make no difference to you, but I truly wish that I could obtain this assistance without doing what I am about to do, and truly wish that it would not stain my family's honor, or that it would give me . . . pleasure."

Clay began to tremble all over, as if snakes squirmed under his skin, and began advancing on the Rebel with the Bowie knife. Wide eyed, the prisoner turned to run, but tripped over a rock and fell hard, the handcuffs preventing him from breaking his fall. From somewhere in the darkness, a flock of whippoorwills began hooting in unison.

Father and son started as the screaming began, and stared intently into the darkness that had swallowed Clay and his prisoner. Distance made the screaming faint, but the agony and terror came through as clearly as if the screamer stood beside them. After the horrible sounds had continued for about a minute, the younger man started to move toward the sounds. His father seized his shoulder with a grip of iron.

"Let it be, Zeke. Let it be." The younger man was about to protest when the distant screaming ascended to an impossibly high note of terror, then was suddenly cut off as if a door had slammed.

With a note of fear in his voice, Zeke asked "Pa, what the hell was that major doing?"

"Don't know, don't care. Whatever his own reasons for doing whatever he done, it was a bit of payback for your brother. A very little payback."

The two men peered into the outer darkness for some minutes, until they heard the sound of soft footsteps approaching. "Who's there?" blurted the younger man nervously.

A shadowy form emerged from the darkness, and in the pale moonlight resolved itself into Alphonso Clay. Even in the dim light the soldiers could see the vacant, numbed expression on his face, the wooden, mechanical way in which he walked. He did not look at the soldiers, nor did he alter his pace, but as he passed them he murmured "I very much fear the prisoner bolted, and eluded me in the dark. I can find my own way back."

Father and son watched the major walk leadenly toward the lights of the main encampment. After a long moment, the older man said "Zeke, you don't have nothin' to do with that major ever again. He's not a good man to have near."

"Yes, Pa," said the younger with nervous sincerity.

Ambrose Bierce suddenly began thrashing wildly about, uttering agonized, animal-like sounds. Lot dropped his Bible, rose to his feet, and tried to restrain the wounded man, calling "Help here, help! For the love of God, help!" The exhausted Dr. Fetterman rushed up, followed closely by Duval.

Helping to hold Bierce down, through gritted teeth Fetterman said "These convulsions mean your friend's death is imminent. Prepare yourself." Behind the doctor Duval stared with fascination at Bierce's wild, mindless motions.

Suddenly, the young captain arched at an impossible angle, only the back of his head and his heels touching the cot; then with an agonized cry he collapsed limply. Releasing his hold on his friend, Lot audibly sobbed. Dr. Fetterman rested his hand sympathetically on the lieutenant's shoulder and was about to say something comforting when the form on the cot shuddered and suddenly drew a lungful of air. After a few irregular breaths his respiration became normal; in a few more moments, to the astonishment of all three witnesses Bierce began to snore softly. An amazed Fetterman watched Bierce's complexion return to normal. He then gingerly felt the lieutenant's forehead.

"The fever is gone," he said wonderingly. "I cannot explain this. If it were not for the nature of his wound, I would swear this man was on his way to recovery."

"Is it possible?" asked Lot in a low voice. "Has the crises passed?"

"I hardly know what to say. I have neither heard nor read of such a recovery. Miss Duval, I respect your knowledge of head wounds. What say you?"

Duval drew up to Bierce, struggling to overcome the unaccustomed dread of the unknown. If there was one thing she understood, it was death, and she had *known* Bierce would die once the fever had set in, as sure as the sun set in the west. She felt first his forehead, then the throbbing artery in his neck; the forehead was cool, the pulse strong and regular. "God be praised, I believe he may live. It is a miracle." Duval had a look of pious joy on her face. However, carefully hidden in her cold heart was an uneasiness that was close to panic; Bierce was recovering for no reason she could imagine, and that lack of reason gave rise to unaccustomed fear in her breast.

Suddenly the tent flap was thrust aside, and the darkness vomited into the tent Alphonso Clay, the strangest of expressions on his face. All noticed it, but none could exactly describe it. Lot, who tended to Christian mysticism, later decided it looked like his friend had something subtly added to or subtracted from his soul.

Clay strode over to Bierce's cot, and spoke without preamble. "How is he?" The voice was perfectly normal, in weird contrast to the disturbing expression its owner's face carried.

As if to answer his question, the captain's eyes slowly opened; Fetterman stood frozen in amazement, while Duval hissed her surprise. At first the eyes were unfocused, but they quickly gained a spark of alertness. Bierce looked at the figures gathered about his cot, and his gaze settled on Jeremiah Lot. Then to the utter amazement of all, he spoke in a faint voice.

"I'll be damned. Lieutenant Sambo. Guess I'm alive after all. If there is an afterlife, I know where I'm headed, and Hell could never hold a Bible-thumper like you." A faint, wheezy laugh escaped his lips. "Say, I'm so dry I could actually drink water, providing nothing better is available."

Despite the tears in his eyes, Lot was smiling. "Ambrose, be sensible. You know water is what you need now, not alcohol. Why do you act as if you hate it?"

"I cannot abide putting the substance in me, normally. I understand fish fornicate in it." Another wheezy laugh escaped the wounded captain; meanwhile, Fetterman had located a water bottle, and began gently raising Bierce's head so he could drink the liquid.

After the young captain had taken a number of careful sips, Fetterman lay his head back down, and asked "How do you feel? Please describe everything."

"My head aches as if I had drunk a gallon of monumentally bad liquor the night before."

"Not surprising, Ambrose," said Lot. "You have been shot through the head."

Bierce muttered an obscenity, and started to raise his hand to his bandages.

"Please do not do that, Captain Bierce," said Duval briskly, grabbing his hand and firmly placing it in its original position. "Lieutenant Lot has been here for a day, without rest or food. If you relapse, his sacrifice would have been for naught."

Bierce slowly focused his eyes on the black officer. "You were here all that time?"

Lot looked embarrassed. "Dr. Fetterman, Miss Duval and the

orderlies were too busy caring for others to stay by your side, but it didn't seem right to not have someone here."

Bierce winced with pain. "Guess I was damn lucky, to have a bullet bounce off my skull like that."

"Lieutenant, you are luckier than you know," replied Fetterman. "It penetrated the brain, in-and-out. Miss Duval undertook to repair the wound. If you live, it is due to her."

Bierce focused his eyes on the nurse and frowned, remembering her reaction to the horror that a cabin near Knoxville had contained. Her response there did not seem consistent with an angel of mercy.

"I then thank you for your skill, madam," he said slowly.

"Show your thanks by getting some rest," she responded brusquely. "You are far from out of the woods, and having all these people excite you could cause a relapse."

Clay, who had observed events silently, now spoke. "Miss Duval, gentlemen, I believe the captain does indeed need rest and quiet. Be that as it may, there are some brief questions I need to ask him in private. Miss Duval, if you will all leave him in peace, I promise to stay only a few moments to ask those questions."

Duval was about to answer in the negative when she checked herself, remembering her long-term plans for Clay. Instead she said "Very well. But only the major, and only for a few minutes."

Clay looked at Lot. "Go get some rest. You are exhausted, and there will be much to do tomorrow."

Lot, Duval and Fetterman quickly murmured best wishes and good night to Bierce, and moved off. Only a few wounded men in nearby cots could overhear Bierce and Clay now; and those that were awake were concerned with their own injuries, and in no condition to concentrate on a conversation that did not involve them.

Bierce looked intently at Clay. "So to what do I owe this visit?

Do not misunderstand me, I know that both of you, especially Jeremiah, are among the very few in this life who care whether I live or die, but last I heard you were on Grant's staff way up in Virginia, helping him weed out criminals and Copperheads who had found their way into the Army of the Potomac. I know your sense of duty too well to flatter myself that you would abandon that to hold a wounded friend's hand."

Clay looked down on the frail looking Bierce for a long moment before deciding that he was strong enough for the story and what it implied. "Miss Duval repaired the entry and exit wounds in your skull. I must admit that her skill is astonishing, given that this conversation is taking place. In any event, the bullet that struck you just penetrated the skull on its way out, and was recovered from under the skin by her. It came from a .44 caliber revolver, almost certainly either a Colt or Remington, and she is convinced that it was fired deliberately at you by someone on the Federal side. She sent a telegram to Grant to that effect."

The shock was apparent on Bierce's pale features. "That's not possible. Some Johnnie must have picked up a pistol from a dead Union officer, or some shot from our side went wild. Why would anyone on our side want to shoot me?"

"Why indeed. It is of course possible for Confederates to have captured Union sidearms, despite their preference for .36 caliber Colts or .42 caliber LeMatts. However, it would seem that you were looking at the advancing Rebels when you were struck in the back of the head. Furthermore, Miss Duval correctly points out the short range of the Colt and Remington .44s, and believes that whoever fired the shot was close enough to clearly identify you, not only as a Union officer but by name, if they knew you to begin with. We must at least seriously consider the possibility that you are the victim of a murderous assault perpetrated by someone on our side, under cover of a battle. The question now becomes one of why. Do you have any enemies who might conceivably desire your death?"

Bierce became visibly moody, then made an effort to appear jauntily cynical. "Sorry, Clay. I cannot think of anyone who would care whether I lived or died."

"Stop feeling sorry for yourself," replied Clay impatiently. "Many people care whether you live, up to and including General Sherman. I want to know if there is anyone who would hate you enough to commit murder."

Bierce slowly shook his head; then Clay continued. "Then I must take as a working hypothesis that you possess knowledge which your assailant wished to prevent from being communicated to others. Can you think of anything that you know that another would consider worth killing for?"

Bierce frowned in concentration for nearly a minute. Finally he said "I truly cannot think what I know that would motivate such an attack. I had just seen with my own eyes that the Rebs were well-prepared to receive our assault, but by that time this was hardly a secret."

Clay frowned thoughtfully. "Well, you are far from well. Get some sleep, and we will revisit this issue when you are stronger."

Bierce's handsome features clouded. "I am very tired, but I do not want to sleep."

"Why is that?"

Bierce hesitated, as if embarrassed to say more. Finally he spoke, "Last thing I clearly remember was being slammed in the back of the head; the impact of the bullet, of course. Until I woke up just now, things are not clear. I have scraps of memory, impressions. Strange, disjointed images; obviously nightmares while I was unconscious, but I cannot seem to put them out of mind. Glimpses of strange things; what I remember makes me glad I do not remember more. Memories of strange buildings where . . . it's hard to describe . . . the geometry seemed all *wrong*, as if the angles of a square added up to something other than three hundred sixty degrees. Sounds insane, I know; bullet must have really scrambled something in my head." Bierce paused, unease written on his features. "And then the craziest thing of all. Remember I knew nothing of your being here; yet at the very end I heard a voice chanting something, something in a language I could not understand. And I would have sworn it was your voice doing the chanting, Clay."

Clay stared intently at the wounded captain for a long moment before saying "Of course you are going to have unpleasing memories. Very few have survived an injury such as yours, and it would be surprising if your injured brain had not given you unpleasant thoughts. However, these thoughts will fade with time. I suspect you will always have them, but they will not be such as to bother you. Sleep now as best you can. We will talk more on the morrow."

Unexpectedly, Clay patted Bierce's shoulder reassuringly. Bierce could hardly keep the shock off of his face; coming from Clay, this sign of human emotion was as unexpected as roses starting to sing.

With a few quick strides, Clay left the hospital tent. He hurried to a tree that he could see in the gloom, far enough from the scattered campfires that he was certain he would be unobserved. He braced his back against the tree, buried his face in his hands, and began silently to sob with the misery of a lost soul.

The covered army ambulance jounced over the uneven road. Lot sat on the driver's seat, doing his best to guide the tired horse around the worst of the potholes, all too aware that too many jolts could send the still-weakened Bierce back into the darkness that had almost claimed him. Oh, well, there was nothing he could do about the clouds of dust that the thousands of soldiers and horses preceding him at kicked up from the unpaved road. The canvas covering of the ambulance kept the worst of the blazing summer sun off the occupants of the ambulance, but did little to keep the choking dust from filtering in.

In the ambulance itself, Teresa Duval used some more of the scarce, tepid water to sponge Bierce's head and neck. She then offered him the last drops water that the vehicle contained to drink.

Having sipped the unappetizing liquid, Bierce said "Thank you, madam. There was a time when I despised water; now I fear that I am becoming an addict."

"I fear that is the last, Captain, at least until we get to Chattahoochee River. The whole army is about out of water, due to the drought hereabouts. Let us hope Johnston does not make a stand before the river, or the whole army will be in very serious trouble."

"I do not believe he will do so, Miss Duval," replied Bierce in his still weakened voice. "The Chattahoochee may be a wide river, but this time of year it is fordable everywhere, and the banks are shallow. The steep-banked Peach Tree Creek just outside Atlanta would make a much more defensible position. And if Joe Johnston has shown anything, he has shown that he has an excellent eye for the defense."

Suddenly they became aware of the sound of distant cheering, then of hoof beats rapidly approaching the ambulance. One of the side-flaps was lifted, and they saw Clay leaning far off his horse to hold up the canvas as his mount kept pace with the wagon.

"Why Major Clay, whatever does that sound mean?" said Duval.

"Our advance column has reached the Chattahoochee, and has found it undefended. Water will be plentiful from here on."

"Praise be to the Lord," said Duval piously.

Clay, who knew just how sincere that sentiment was, favored her with a tight, grim smile, then turned his attention to Bierce. "Captain, how are you doing?"

"Thanks to this angel of mercy, well enough. Headaches and dizziness, nothing worse."

"It is not good for you to be moving at all. Still, you would have been captured if we had left you behind, and I suspect Andersonville would be far worse for your health then the motion of this wagon."

"True enough. You do not hear me complaining."

Suddenly a distant, high-pitched voice interrupted their conversation. "Clay, is that you? Bierce in that wagon? Get your sorry asses over here! I want to see you both!"

Frowning, Clay let the flap of the wagon fall, and looked at the source of this voice. It seemed to be coming from somewhere in the river, which had just come into view. He spotted the shouting man. To the reserved Clay's shock, it was General Sherman, standing in the river up to his thighs, buck naked.

Clay glanced at Lot on the driver's box; his friend was a picture of shocked surprise. Suppressing an urge to smile, Clay solemnly commented "Lieutenant, better pull over to that clearing on the shore by the commanding general."

As Lot wordlessly complied, Clay trotted ahead to the unselfconscious general. He dismounted and saluted smartly while glancing around. He noticed that although a steady stream of soldiers were wading across the shallow river, all were stopping to fill canteens and water barrels, and some were taking advantage of an opportunity for a long-deferred bath, especially enjoyable in the hot Georgia sun. A few even mimicked their commanding general's lack of inhibitions. As Clay wrapped his mount's reins around a convenient branch, several passing soldiers cheerfully shouted in unison. "Howdy Uncle Billy! Parade dress today?"

"I don't give a crap how you rascals dress, so long as you keep Joe Johnston on the run," Sherman replied with equal good humor.

As a ragged cheer issued from the advancing soldiers, Clay approached the edge of the water, "Sir, Bierce is in the wagon, but he is accompanied by Miss Duval. You may wish to attend to the . . . informality of your attire."

"Hell, this is the first time I've been comfortable in a month," replied Sherman grumpily as he waded to the shore. Nevertheless, he gestured to an embarrassed aide standing nearby, who handed his commander trousers and a flannel shirt. He was just buttoning the latter when Lot brought the wagon to a stop before him. Without waiting for help, Sherman strode barefoot up to the side of the wagon and threw back the flap. Startled by the sudden appearance of the commanding general, Bierce attempted to raise himself on his elbows and salute.

"To hell with that nonsense, Bierce," growled Sherman with pretended anger. "You lie quiet; just wanted to see that you were all right with my own eyes. Army business kept me from coming in person, but Clay kept me informed, and I want you to know how happy I am that the army will not be deprived of your services. Soon as Miss Duval says you are up to a long rail trip north, north is where you are going, to stay as long as you want."

"Thank you sir," said Bierce smiling wanly. "Still, I should be fit for duty soon, and would prefer to stay with the army."

"Goddamn it Bierce, you've had your brains blown out, and want to stay on duty! Come to think of it, might not be a bad idea; having had a bullet go through your brain qualifies you to be a general."

Bierce laughed one of his unlovely, barking laughs. Sherman turned his attention to Duval. "And you, madam, you did the actual surgery. I am in your debt, as the army already is in your debt for many things."

"I am just an instrument of the Lord's," she replied humbly, letting no sign of her conflicting emotions show on her face. The praise fed her cold ego, but she knew that she could not explain Bierce's apparent recovery, and the compliment reminded her of that uncomfortable fact.

As if on cue, General McPherson galloped into view, followed by a number of aides and escorts. He came to a halt and saluted smartly. "General Sherman, sir, my advance scouts have reached Peach Tree Creek, and can see church spires in Atlanta. However, the Rebs are drawn up behind it in force. My men took a few prisoners, and they revealed disturbing news. Jefferson Davis seems to have lost patience with Johnston's careful retreats, and has sacked him. The new commander is John Bell Hood."

Sherman stood stock still for a moment. "Davis is a goddamn fool, and thank God for it. Of course Johnston retreated. What else could he do? We outnumber him near two to one. He would wreck his army in an attack; his only hope was to keep forcing us to attack him in defensive positions, rolling up casualties that might so shock the good people of the North that they would lose their minds and elect that goddamn traitor McClellan President in two months' time."

"Hood was appointed to attack, and attack he will," said McPherson. "He was always aggressive. Furthermore, he is so reckless that he might try something wild that we are not prepared for. I played quite a bit of poker with him, when we were on duty together before the war. I once saw him try to run a $500 bluff with nary a pair in his hand."

Sherman nodded. "I think you're right. We're going to see the elephant real soon. I want you to get the Army of the Tennessee brought up and dug in on our side of the creek as fast as you can. I'll do what I can to hurry up Thomas on your right; good man, but not as quick off the mark as you."

A troubled look on his face, McPherson replied "General, maybe it would be better if I handed over command to Logan. He's my senior corps commander, and very good. After how I . . . let you down, I'm not sure you should rely on me with so much at stake. Say I took leave to go north and get married. It's plausible, I have postponed it twice already."

Sherman looked up at the youthful general steadily for a few moments, then replied in a low voice. "General McPherson, I told you that . . . the other matter is closed. You were mistaken, and men died. I have been mistaken, and men died. That's war; no general's judgment is perfect all of the time. I still believe you are the best the Union's got, if something happens to Sam and me. If I thought you couldn't do the job, you would have been long gone. Now, get your ass out to the left and set up a surprise for General Hood!"

A look of melancholy gratitude on his face, McPherson saluted and led his staff splashing across the Chatthoochee.

Clay and Lot were standing in the shade of a tree, having just settled Bierce into one of the walled tents, watching Fetterman direct his staff in setting up the field hospital. Duval was nowhere to be seen. One of the harried orderlies said he thought he had seen her heading off toward where the military telegraphs were being set up, but he was not certain.

After a long silence, Lot said "There is really no reason to stay here. Miss Duval must have been mistaken. Bierce must have been shot by a Rebel with a captured Union pistol, perhaps turning his head just as he was hit; making it seem like he was shot from behind."

Moodily, Clay responded. "Perhaps. Still, that exchange earlier between Sherman and McPherson interests me. McPherson acted as if he had some great burden of guilt concerning his military judgment. Sherman has refused to tell me from whence came his information that the center of the line at Kennesaw was lightly held. I cannot help but wonder if it was from McPherson. I think that before we start on the long journey back we should . . ."

Clay was interrupted by the sound of dozens of cannon firing at once, thousands of rifles volleying, and the unearthly screech of the Rebel yell coming from numberless throats simultaneously.

"McPherson's judgment cannot be that bad," commented Lot over the noise of the battle. "Seems like he was right about Hood attacking immediately."

Clay nodded absently. "Since we have no immediate duties, let us find Sherman and ask if we can at least act as couriers, or in some other capacity. I really do not feel like staying back here in safety while good men die."

"My feelings exactly," said Lot, and both officers moved off to find their horses.

Sherman was found without difficulty, he was with Thomas, and both generals were dismounted and in the middle of the front line, with rebel bullets clipping twigs from the trees all around them. They saluted, and Clay spoke.

"General Sherman, General Thomas, is there any capacity in which we could be of use to you?"

The massive, Union-loyal Virginian replied for both generals. "I thank you for the offer, but we have the situation in hand. I can hardly believe Hood is flinging his men straight at my lines, especially as he can see that we are dug in and outnumber him. There is scarce anything for me to do; all my boys have to do is reload and fire."

"McPherson's having some trouble off to the left," added Sherman. "That's the only place where Hood tried anything clever, a feint and a flanking movement, but early reports indicate that even there he was sloppy and bungled it. So long as our boys keep their nerve, we can stand all day and let Hood destroy his army for us." Suddenly something to the right caught Sherman's attention and he frowned. Clay and Lot followed the general's glaze, and saw a lone private, probably someone who had lost his nerve and fled the front line, lying on the ground behind a thick tree, visibly quaking with fear; somehow in his terror he had not noticed the generals and their staffs behind him to his left. Sherman looked as if he were about to explode at the sight of cowardice, but then a grim smile crept over his face. He picked up a handful of pebbles from the ground, and starting walking toward the skulker. Casually he threw a pebble at the tree, which struck the trunk inches above the head of the shivering private.

"God save me!" the man shrieked at the top of his lungs, screwing his eyes tightly shut. Sherman threw another pebble, and heard the same shriek. He repeated his action a third time, and received the same response. By now Sherman was quite close.

"Hot and heavy fire, isn't it" said Sherman.

"Oh God, I don't know how any of us will live!" wailed the man, who then opened his eyes and looked over his shoulder, to see his commanding general. Terror of a different kind possessing him, he leapt to his feet and began running to the rear at top speed. A couple of aides made as if to pursue him, but a laughing Sherman said "Never mind, never mind. Shame will make him come back to his unit eventually. Who knows, when he calms down the shame may make him a good soldier."

Sherman was still laughing when a dust-covered major rode up and saluted. "Complements of General Logan, sir. He begs to report that although the Rebs got in among our troops in several places, the bravery of the officers and the men contained the breakthroughs, and eventually drove Hood's men back to their starting positions."

Sherman frowned. "Why are you reporting from General Logan? What is General McPherson's assessment of the situation?"

The aide could not look Sherman in the eye. "General McPherson behaved as a true hero. He was everywhere during the height of the attack, personally rallying the men if they showed signs of breaking, leading the reserves to where they were most needed. There was a dust up near a battery of Hooker's artillery; some of the Johnnies got in among the guns, and while the general was directing the counterattack he was shot. Sir, General McPherson is dead."

Sherman stared at the man with disbelief for the longest moment. Then, Sherman began uttering a series of mournful shrieks, tears streaming from his eyes.

Sherman's grief and anger had passed through the blustering stage; he now spoke with quiet, deadly precision. "Dr. Fetterman, we are not putting James into a nameless grave in Georgia."

In one of the hospital tents Sherman, Fetterman, Clay, Lot and Duval stood around the table that supported the lifeless body of the youthful general. Sherman continued speaking.

"Dr. Fetterman, you will come with me now. Several sutlers who attach themselves like leeches to this army are set up with embalming equipment; but some have better equipment and chemicals than others. I need you to come with me and canvas those parasites. I rely on you to tell me who can do the best job of preserving his remains. I want no horrible surprises when his fiancée sees him for the last time."

Fetterman silently nodded, and Sherman replied "Good. We will not be long. Please keep watch until we return." He looked down at the corpse and said enigmatically, "The South has taken another. Very well. I will begin taking from it." With jerky steps, he exited the tent into the evening twilight, followed closely by the army doctor.

Clay waited a moment before speaking. "Quickly. We will not have much time. Please help me take off his tunic and shirt, and turn him over." Puzzled and uneasy, Lot and Duval did as they were asked. In a few moments, the general's body was face down on the table.

"You both observed there was no exit wound in the front, so the bullet that entered the back must still be in McPherson. Miss Duval, I know that you are not made uneasy by such work, so would you please probe for the bullet and remove it? I would do it myself, but I lack your expertise."

Duval was puzzled as to why Clay wanted the bullet, but saw no reason to refuse his request. She grabbed several evil-looking tools from a nearby bag, and commenced her task. The squeamish Lot had to turn away; Clay watched with emotionless interest.

In less that five minutes Duval had located the bullet and secured it, drawing it from the corpse with unpleasant squelching sounds. She dropped the bullet into her hand, wiped it clean with a scrap of cloth, and took it to the nearby oil lamp for close examination.

Her eyes widened slightly, and she turned to Clay."How did you know?" she said to him with a combination of wonder and admiration.

"I did not know, only suspected. However, you appear to have confirmed my suspicions."

"What suspicions?" asked Lot.

Clay nodded to Duval, who answered "General McPherson was killed by a .44 caliber bullet, undoubtedly fired from a Union army pistol."

The three people stared at the lump of lead in the woman's hand, considering everything it implied.

CHAPTER 2

"HARDLY COULD THEY BE RESTRAINED FROM BREAKING OUT IN CHEERS . . ."

"You bastards," said Sherman in a quiet, controlled voice from the tent opening; it was somehow more frightening than his wildest shouts and wails. "I leave for one moment, and you mutilate this fine young man's body. Isn't a Goddamn Rebel bullet enough? Could you not leave the remains with some scrap of the dignity he held in life?" Behind the coldly furious commanding general stood Dr. Fetterman, who nervously plucked at the general's elbow in an ineffectual gesture toward restraining him.

In a motion so swift that it made Duval blink with surprise, Clay snatched the bullet from the palm of her hand and advanced toward the general, displaying the lethal piece of metal in his own open palm.

"This was done at my request; the others bear no responsibility. I feared that your esteem for the late General McPherson would cause you to forbid recovering the bullet still in him. No disrespect whatsoever was meant for a brave man who was murdered while defending his country."

Despite his fury, Sherman was too quick-witted to overlook the fact Clay used the word "murdered" rather than "killed". Sherman was already aware that Clay used language with unusual precision. Bright eyes narrowed in angry puzzlement.

"I know you well enough to realize you say nothing that is without purpose," said the general in the same icy, controlled voice. "However, I don't know what you are driving at. Enlighten me."

"Sir, I suspected that General McPherson may have been murdered under the cover of battle by a traitor in our midst. This bullet is a .44 caliber pistol round; just as Miss Duval indicated in the case of Captain Bierce; it is my belief that this bullet was fired by a Union officer, almost certainly by the same pistol wielded by the same man."

With quick, bird-like movements of his head, Sherman shifted his attention from the bullet to Clay's face to Duval and back to the bullet. He paused, then lifted his eyes to meet those of Clay and asked in the softest of voices "Is it truly your belief that James was murdered by a traitor wearing the blue?"

"Sir, I cannot be certain at this time; but I fear that is likely."

Sherman brushed past Clay to stand over McPherson's body. He was silent for a moment, and then began speaking as if to himself.

"He was the best we had, destined to be the glory of the army. Sam and I can do the job, but we are flawed, and probably aren't doing it as well as we should. I failed in banking before the war, and went a little crazy in Kentucky, till Sam took me in hand. Sam himself . . . well, he had that bad patch in the '50s. But James . . . nothing like that for James. Sailed through the Point number one in his class, and never looked back. Smarter than the law should allow, but was so charming you didn't mind. I know people say he was promoted too fast, that Sam and me made things easy for him. Don't give a damn what people think; young as he was, he was better than us, and getting better every day. Never set a foot wrong, except once; some days I almost hoped something would happen to me, so he could take over the army here and do things better."

"Sir, it was General McPherson who told you Johnston's center was weak, back at Kennesaw." Clay had made a statement, not asked a question.

Sherman's head jerked around violently. "How came you to know that? I've told no one!"

Clay shrugged slightly. "McPherson's offer to withdraw from the army, when combined with your admiration of him and your refusal to assign blame to anyone but yourself, makes it fairly obvious. You are, shall I say, usually intolerant of failure. Your tolerance in the face of the massive intelligence failure before Kennesaw could only come from a desire to shield someone for whom you felt the greatest respect."

"Felt country couldn't spare him. People like Hooker and Logan wanted his command and were already nipping at his heels, spreading tales of his inexperience, damn them. Well, I could hold them off and give James cover, what with Sam heading the army and my brother in the Senate. But if word got out that all those men died because he had believed some high-drunk nonsense . . . well, couldn't permit that. I can look after myself, with Sam and my brother covering my flanks; if I took the blame, at worse James would replace me if I were removed."

"I fear that General McPherson was used as an unwitting tool to provide you with disastrously bad intelligence," said Clay. "Although I am not personally in a position to judge, I will take your word for it that he was a skilled, intelligent officer. Unfortunately, that makes this matter even more serious. McPherson was in turn protecting someone he trusted implicitly. I can only assume someone of rank, someone deeply respected by the army at large, not just one of its officers."

Sherman stared for a long moment at Clay, shock warring with rage in his features while he thought of the traitor who had nearly destroyed Grant's army outside Vicksburg, the traitor who must never be named, to protect the country at large. Finally he said to Clay "I am not a policeman, Goddamn it. I know how to run and supply an army; but I don't know jack about how to go about smoking out such a bastard. You know this shit Clay. What do you suggest?"

"Lieutenant Lot and I are going to need unrestricted access to all your top commanders; I fear that one of them must be at the center of the matter. Although we will not reveal the fact that General McPherson's death was not the result of the fortunes of war, we will need to ask hard questions that an innocent man could regard as aspersions on his personal honor. We will need your authority and backing to compel cooperation from the more recalcitrant."

"Can't stop the army while this is sorted out," said Sherman moodily. "Have to keep the strategic initiative going."

"There is no need to do so. We can pursue our investigation while the army is in motion."

The flap of the tent was thrust aside, and a lean, slovenly civilian appeared. In his left hand he held a pump with a long India-rubber tube trailing to the ground; under his right arm he cradled a large wooden box that clinked as he moved, as if filled with heavy bottles. Sherman glanced at the civilian with an unreadable expression, saying to the others "Miss Duval, gentlemen, there is no further need for your services tonight. You may turn in for the night."

Clay and the others took the hint. Clay himself was the last to leave; as he lowered the flap of the tent, his final sight was of the civilian moving toward the table holding McPherson's body, while Sherman suddenly covered his mouth with his hand, as if to stifle a sob.

* * *

The following morning Clay and Lot encountered General Sherman again. Knowing that his temper was uncertain in the best of times, and that his grief over McPherson's death would not be quickly assuaged, they had hoped to avoid dealing personally with him for some time. However, the universe is ironic, and seldom takes account of personal preferences in its ordering of events.

After an unappetizing breakfast of hardtack and bacon, they had tentatively drawn up a list of officers to be interviewed. However, before formally commencing their investigations, they had decided to look in on Bierce. It was unfortunate that Sherman had independently decided to do the same thing, and still more unfortunate that a group of generals had tracked him down at the same time.

Clay and Lot entered the hospital tent only to find a furious argument was taking place between Sherman, Hooker, and Logan, with Thomas and Generals Oliver Howard and Jeff Davis watching uncomfortably. Sherman's back was to the cot on which Ambrose Bierce reclined, grinning from ear to ear; the three other cots in the tent were occupied by silent forms that lay dreaming under the influence of morphine.

"I do not deny that General Logan performed heroically after McPherson's death," Hooker loudly announced in his deep baritone. "Nevertheless, the Army of the Tennessee is mine by right! I have seniority in the rank of major general of volunteers. Furthermore, I also hold the permanent rank of brigadier in the regular army, while his commission will expire with the end of the war. It is insupportable that there is any doubt!"

Clay touched Lot's shoulder, and nodded toward the tent flap; it was obvious that they had intruded on a policy disagreement that did not concern them. However, before they could make a quiet exit, Bierce spotted them. In a strong, clear voice the wounded captain cheerfully announced. "Lot, Clay, I am so glad to see you! Don't leave; I believe that the generals will not be much longer."

Almost as one, the six generals turned their attention to the unexpected arrivals. Hooker looked as if he was about to explode at the interruption. However, before he could launch into one of his famously profane tirades he was interrupted by Sherman.

"Oh hell, let them stay. I'm not saying anything they can't hear." He then turned his glowering attention back to Hooker. "General, I am well aware of your seniority. However, the days of promoting strictly on the grounds of seniority are over. We damn near lost this war in its first two years, largely from letting Goddamn fools with seniority command better men. You are nothing more than a corps commander, a barely adequate one; and it would be murder of good men to jump you up to an army command . . . again."

Hooker's already florid complexion turned beet red at the unmistakable reference to his brief command of the Army of the Potomac. Bierce's smile became so wide it looked like it might reach past his ears. The darkly handsome John Logan smirked; but then Sherman turned his attention to Logan.

"Don't smile, General Logan," he said gruffly. "You're not getting the Army of the Tennessee, either."

Looking as if he had been slapped, Logan almost whined as he blurted out "But I'm the senior corps commander! There was my performance after McPherson's death! Doesn't that count for anything?"

"You did well enough, Logan. However, it was a matter of holding the line for half a day. There's more to being an army commander than holding the line. I'm giving the Army of the Tennessee to General Howard."

The handsome, earnest-looking general to the right of Thomas started, then stepped forward. "General, it is an honor greater than

I deserve. Are you certain this is for the best?" Only then did Lot notice that the empty right sleeve of his uniform that had been carelessly pinned to his chest. Of course, Clay had noticed that disability the moment they had entered the tent.

It was hard to determined who looked more enraged, Hooker or Logan. The later spoke first.

"Sir, you can't do that! He's not even from the Army of the Tennessee! What will the boys think when they see a Cumberlander promoted over me?"

"They will think that William T. Sherman is a bastard, and I can live with that. Howard is an experienced West Pointer, and you are not; I'll not hand an entire army over to an amateur." Sherman then turned to Hooker and spoke before the latter could launch a long-winded objection. "As for you, I think that your current assignment stretches your abilities to the limit. To the limit, sir."

Clay had often heard someone referred to as "exploding with rage." Until this day he believed it to be a metaphoric expression; but watching Hooker's face redden to the point it nearly turned purple, he wondered if he was going to see it literally happen. Hooker seemed to struggle for words to express his outrage, and it was some seconds before he could rasp a reply.

"General, in case you are not aware, General Howard is my senior division commander. My subordinate! You are jumping him over me sir! The man whose 11th Corps went to pieces at Fredericksburg, and let Jackson take me in the flank!"

"It was your sloppy dispositions and indecision that allowed Jackson to take you in the flank. As for Howard's 11th, his boys were mainly Dutchmen who had never heard a shot fired in anger before that day. This campaign has already allowed him to prove that when given experienced, steady troops General Howard is a superb commander."

Literally quivering with rage, Hooker shouted "Damn you! I will submit my resignation this very afternoon!"

With no notable pause, Thomas replied "Your resignation is accepted—gladly." Hooker's immediate commander stared with calm dignity at his just-fired subordinate. Hooker balled his hands into fists, and actually looked as if he would attack the commander of the Army of the Cumberland.

"That's fine with me," snapped Sherman. "I think that with the consent of General Thomas, I'll give your command to General Slocum." For a moment, one could literally hear a pin drop in the hospital tent. The whole army knew that Slocum so despised Hooker that he had agreed to become one of Thomas' corps commanders on the express condition that he would have no personal dealings with Joe Hooker. Giving Hooker's command to Henry Slocum would be the final insult.

Although everyone else in the tent was focused on Thomas and Hooker, appalled at the spectacle and fearing the outcome of the next few moments, Clay had focused his attention on General Jeff Davis, standing on Thomas' left. The emaciated Davis had the body of a very sick man; but Clay noticed that his steady, dead stare was locked on Hooker, and that he had quietly unsnapped the flap of his holster. Clay suddenly remembered that two years previously Davis had shot to death his own commanding officer in a personal dispute, and had only evaded a court martial through obscure, behind-the-scenes political manipulation on his behalf. Clay briefly wondered whether he was about to see history repeat itself. Hooker had not noticed Davis' actions, which was just as well, thought Clay; Fighting Joe was a man of many and serious flaws, but physical cowardice was not among them. With what appeared to be a titanic effort, Hooker seemed to bring himself under control. He stormed out of the tent, shouting over his shoulder "None of you have heard the last of this!"

Thomas was the first to break the silence. "I have wanted to do that for a long time, but needed some reason, Joe Hooker is one of the pets of the Radical Republicans in Congress, and there would have been hell to pay without some good excuse. His offer of resignation is that excuse. We cannot have officers threatening to quit every time they are denied promotion." He did not mention the fact that he continued to serve uncomplainingly after Sherman was promoted over his head.

John Logan had been a congressman before the war, and expected to go much higher after it; he was not accustomed to humbling himself to anyone. Nevertheless, under the burning ambition was genuine patriotism. Forcing himself to look straight into the eyes of the one-armed General Howard, he said "General, my outburst and . . . disappointment was not directed at you, at a man, or commander, but at the situation. I, of course, will abide by General Sherman's decision, and will serve you to the best of my ability. However, if you feel that in light of my . . . freely expressed opinion you would be more comfortable with a new commander for the 15the Corps, I'll understand it. I will make no fuss. '*Unlike Joe Hooker's*' was the unspoken thought.

Howard was a rigid but genuine Christian; Logan's frank statement was the best approach toward healing any incipient breach between the two generals. "General Logan, the 15th Corps has proven itself to be the backbone of the Army of the Tennessee time and time again, due in no small part to its commander. It would be a privilege to have you continue in the role you have filled so well." The tension palpably drained from the room; only Clay noticed General Davis unobtrusively fasten the flap of his holster back into place.

Sherman nodded approvingly at the determination of the two generals to work in harness. "Well, gentlemen, it was not my intention to burden Captain Bierce with the squabbles of high command.

He needs rest to complete the recovery from his head wound; I suggest we leave him to his visitors." Sherman exited the hospital tent with his quick, bird-like walk, followed by the other generals while Clay and Lot snapped formal salutes. Davis was the last in line; as he passed by Clay he turned his head and briefly favored him with an once-over from those cold, dead eyes.

The two friends walked over to Bierce's cot. Bierce looked pale and tired, but surprisingly well for a man who had taken a bullet through the brain. "Glad you were in time for the show," said the young scout cheerfully. "It was a welcome change of pace. The pious Miss Duval does not want me to read yet, much less write. And as you can see, my tent mates are not precisely sparkling conversationalists." He gestured vaguely to the inert forms occupying the remaining cots.

"Where are Doctor Fetterman and Miss Duval?" asked Lot.

The smile suddenly left Bierce's face. "As you can surmise, this tent is for those requiring nothing but quiet. There are many demands on Dr. Fetterman's time; he is not negligent, just giving his attention this morning to other tents where more active treatment is required. As for Miss Duval, I believe that in addition to duties in the other hospital tents, she is spending some time at the telegraphy office. Very devoted to her mother, back in New York; seems to be sending wires virtually every day." He turned his head to look straight at Clay, and cocked a cynical eyebrow.

"So you believe there is something more involved than messages to a parent?" asked the blond major.

"Don't you?"

The faintest of smiles played about Clay's lips. "I do, as a matter of fact."

Bierce suddenly turned completely serious, jaunty cynicism shed like a cloak. "Listen Clay, be careful around that one. She isn't what she seems, and . . . well, just be careful."

With mock surprise Clay responded "Captain, I am shocked. How can you harbor suspicions concerning the woman who saved your life?"

Bierce closed his eyes, feeling even wearier than before. He remembered how he owed his life to Teresa Duval's medical skills; but he also remembered a shabby cabin outside Knoxville, and the shocking way she had responded to the horror it contained. Without opening his eyes, he said, "I don't think she means you or the Union harm; just don't stand in her way. That goes for you too Jeremiah. Now, if you don't mind, I'm suddenly very tired. Do appreciate the visit, but . . ." He was asleep, having never completed the sentence.

"He is still in danger, isn't he?" asked Lot.

"Yes, yes he is." Avoiding looking at his friend, Clay continued. "Nevertheless, you can be confident he will recover, more or less, providing he has rest and quiet. Now, let us go find General Davis."

"We start with him? Why?"

"My initial inquiries show that neither Sherman nor Thomas know quite where General Davis was at the height of the assault at Kennesaw Mountain. Very strange, given how central his troops were to the assault. Besides, we are looking for a murderer, and General Jeff Davis brings an interesting quality which recommends him to me as a suspect."

"What is that, Alphonso?"

"Oh, he is already proven to be a murderer."

Sitting in the camp chair before a table placed outside his command tent, General Jeff Davis looked even more emaciated than when he was standing. His skin had the appearance of yellow parchment, more appropriate to a three-day corpse than a living man. Even his eyes seemed to belong to a corpse, appearing to reflect no light whatsoever. Still, his voice was firm enough, which he demonstrated after Clay had introduced himself and Lot. Turning his dead eyes on the young Lieutenant, he said to Clay "Sherman told me you would be asking some questions, and I was to answer. Still, I don't talk to niggers, except to tell them to empty the slops. Tell that one there to wait over yonder; I only talk business with white men."

Jeremiah Lot found such insults hard to take at the best of times; from a general officer of the United States, it was intolerable. He had opened his mouth to reply when his cousin rendered any reply superfluous.

"General Davis, you have insulted an officer of the United States, an officer to whom I am bound by the strongest obligations, furthermore an officer whom I suspect is your superior in intelligence and character. If you were any kind of gentleman, and not the Hoosier cracker you obviously are, I would call you out for that remark. As it is, repeat the offense and I shall horse-whip you in front of the camp."

Davis leaped to his feet, hand resting on the flap of his holster, a spark of animation finally showing in his eyes. "You bastard! I should . . ."

"Should what, General?" interrupted Lot. "Shoot Major Clay like you shot General Nelson, back in Kentucky? I think not. Your friends in Washington would not save you a second time."

Davis turned his attention to Lot. "So, you know about that. Nelson insulted me, and I killed him. No nancy-boy dueling nonsense. That bastard humiliated me in front of my own men. He died for it."

"Yes sir, you killed a brave man who helped rally Kentucky to the Union when there were not many there standing with the Union," responded Lot.

"Your friends noted your genuine bravery and ability in command, qualities sadly lacking in our generals at that stage of the war, and decided to quash the court martial against you," added Clay. "However, both Lieutenant Lot and myself report directly to General Grant, and through him the President. They would make sure that nothing would save you from the firing squad this time, should something . . . untoward happen to either Lot or myself."

Davis' eyes bored into Clay. "You think I'm scared of you? Wasn't scared in Mexico. Wasn't scared at Fort Sumter, when frenchie Beauregard sent the cannonballs flying thicker than flies. Wasn't scared at Chickamauga. And I'm not scared of you."

Clay contemplated Davis for a moment. He now realized that there was before him a man in constant pain, a slowly dying man, a man who flung himself into battle because only by risking death and inflicting it on others could he feel even momentarily alive. A man who had his uses while the Union struggled for its life.

"Sir, I realize that you are one of those who think this bloody conflict is simply about preserving the Union, and not about bringing dignity and freedom to the black man. I will not argue the point. However, I will insist upon this: either apologize to Lieutenant Lot, and treat him with the respect due his rank, if not his person, or I will break you from the army. Do not doubt that I have the power. I would prefer not to use it; but I will if need be. You will then be unable to participate in the battles to save this country; unable to do anything save look on while resting quietly and in peace."

Davis looked back and forth at the two men before him several times. Gradually the fire in his eyes died, and they reverted to their normal dark, lifeless appearance. Moving his hand away from his holster, Davis turned at last to Lot and said with apparent effort, "Lieutenant, I forgot myself just now. I . . . apologize for my rudeness and . . . ask . . . your forgiveness."

"Sir, your apology is accepted," replied Lot, with as much sincerity as the apology itself.

"Now that the air is cleared, I would like to ask you a few things, sir," said Clay quietly. "Would you care to be seated?"

"I'll stand," replied Davis abruptly.

"Very well. What was your opinion of how the engagement at Kennesaw Mountain was conducted?"

Davis stared at Clay for several moments before replying. "Ain't my place to comment on that. That's the job of Sherman and Thomas."

"Not the job of McPherson as well?" asked Lot. "You refer to General Thomas, who is one of the two army commanders, but not to General McPherson. That seems odd, given that your division was in fact in direct contact with McPherson's flank."

Davis turned his attention to Lot, with some obvious effort. "George Thomas knows his business; showed that long before this war, in Mexico and the frontier, and has continued to show it ever since. McPherson . . ." Davis suddenly cut himself off.

"McPherson did not quite have the experience of Thomas?" Clay supplied.

"Think what you like about me speaking ill of the dead," Davis suddenly replied. "McPherson was a pretty-boy desk soldier, a pet of Grant and the abolitionists. He came out of the academy in '54, and went into a series of cushy engineering assignments, while I already had eight years of combat experience, winning my commission in the field at Chapultepec, not in a classroom!" Again Davis grimly clamped his mouth shut.

"So you had difficulty working with a superior you considered your inferior in experience and ability?" asked Lot.

Davis' dead eyes flickered to life briefly. "Don't you ever accuse me of forgetting my duty to my country, or you will not have the opportunity to regret it," he responded in a low voice. Making an obvious effort to control his deadly temper, Davis continued. "I have never let my feelings interfere with my duty. When General

Thomas said I was to support McPherson, I did everything in my power; even gave him Colonel Kitching, Hooker's artillery commander, who was supposed to be added to my division, along with every cannon of my own that I could spare, without even being asked."

"Let us leave Kennesaw aside for the moment," said Clay. "Did you happen to observe General McPherson's death during Hood's attack?"

A spark of unpleasant animation came to Davis' eyes. "What you mean is did I kill the pretty-boy."

Clay looked appraisingly at the emaciated general. "No one has mentioned murder."

Davis spat out an obscenity before replying. "Why is it all you college boys think that everyone who ain't been to college is stupid? I've heard of you, Major Clay. Heard rumors of what you do for Grant, and how you leave a trail of broken careers wherever you go. And now you're here asking me what I think of McPherson and whether I saw him die. Don't take a college boy to figure out where you're heading."

Clay looked at Davis with grudging respect. "I would suggest you keep your surmise concerning McPherson's end to yourself; we would not want to start rumors that would rot morale."

"Fair enough; I see the point. Anyway, didn't see him fall. Did catch glimpses of him from time to time, but didn't pay much attention; my own division was having a pretty hot time." Davis paused, then almost unwillingly added "He was brave enough, I grant him that. Didn't wish him dead, if that's what you are thinking."

"Would you know of anyone who would wish him dead?" asked Lot gently.

Davis wheezed a very unpleasant laugh. "You could take your pick. Just about any officer older than forty who saw Sherman's pet pin two stars on each shoulder. Maybe they wouldn't actually do it, but they sure must have thought of doing it from time to time."

"I appreciate your candor," replied Clay. "We have taken up enough of your time for now. Please remember to keep our conversation private." Clay and Lot both saluted Davis, who sourly returned the gesture. The general then half-sat, half-collapsed into his camp chair, looking more like a corpse than ever, not even bothering to look at his two visitors as they turned and walked away.

"What do you think? asked Lot as soon as they were out of earshot.

"He is certainly capable of murder, and bore no love for McPherson. However, murder by stealth does not seem to be his style; he shot the unarmed General Nelson in front of two witnesses. We should keep him in mind, but enquire further."

"Enquire of whom?"

"To start, of General Hooker. He is taking the train north as soon as he can pack his kit; and I would dearly like to have a talk with "Fighting Joe" before he is out of our reach."

In contrast to the isolated, brooding calm of Davis's tent, Hooker's large command tent was a scene of crowded commotion. Young officers in immaculate uniforms were hurriedly filling a number of large trunks with a variety of objects, some of which clinked and gurgled. Both Clay and Lot visibly started at the sight of an attractive young woman lounging on a cot at the far side of the tent, who boldly stared at them as they entered; although her dress was of expensive and demure muslin, it was obvious that "she was no better than she should be." In the center of the commotion the tall, handsome Joe Hooker stood directing the packing, casting frequent, appreciative glances at his female guest. Clay and Lot caught the general's eye, and saluted.

Hooker frowned, and then said "I remember. You two were in the hospital tent. Well, what do you want?"

"General, I have been given a special task by General Sherman," said Clay. "I would suggest that you ask your staff to leave while we discuss that task." Suddenly, one could have heard a pin drop in the tent; none of the staff officers had ever heard anyone be that peremptory to Fighting Joe.

"And just who the hell are you to give a major general orders?" replied Hooker loftily.

"Major Alphonso Clay and Lieutenant Jeremiah Lot, on detached duty from General Grant's staff, at your service, sir."

Hooker's pale blue eyes darted between the two officers, and then settled on Clay. "Clay. Are you the Clay who has been with Grant since Vicksburg, the one who in New Orleans had . . . some trouble?"

Clay bowed slightly. Hooker seemed lost in thought for a moment, and then abruptly said to his staff, "Out. All of you out. Arrange my baggage on the train as best you can. You can finish cleaning up in here after I'm done with these . . . guests." The various staff officers scurried to comply with the imperious Hooker. However, the woman in the corner rose languorously from her cot and glided up to Hooker, placing her arm lightly on his.

"Joe, you don't mind if I stay?" she asked in a husky voice.

"Yes, I do. Go get yourself settled on the train. Make sure that we're guaranteed some privacy; it will be a long ride north." Suddenly he slapped her on the rump, and smiled. The tart gave him an angry glance and left, seeming to walk as slowly as possible.

While watching this display, Clay suddenly remembered what a cavalry officer named Francis Adams (of the Boston Adamses) had told him about a visit the snobbish young New Englander had made to Hooker's headquarters during the latter's brief, disastrous tenure at the head of the Army of the Potomac. The grandson and great-grandson of Presidents had sniffed that Hooker's head-quarters was a combination of barroom and brothel, where no gentleman cared to go and no lady dared to go. At the time, Clay had dismissed the comment as a product of insufferable snob-bishness. Now he realized Adams may have made a valid point.

Now that they were alone, Hooker turned his undivided atten-tion to his visitors. "Listen, if you are here to tell me not to raise a fuss about being passed over, you're wasting your time. Don't care that Sherman has Grant as a friend, and a brother in the Senate. I have my own friends in Congress; Thad Stephens, Ben Wade, Charles Sumner, to name three. They'll trump any moves by Sherman, and raise such unholy hell that Lincoln will have to overrule Grant, and do the right thing."

"We are not here to concern ourselves with your wounded self-esteem." Lot noticed that Clay's voice had adopted the exag-gerated, superior drawl that displays of arrogance always seemed to induce; any arrogance aside from his own, that is. "We are concerned with the circumstances surrounding the death of General McPherson, not the consequences of that death."

That seemed to bring Hooker up short. Frowning, he replied, "Just what the hell do you mean, 'circumstances surrounding'? Circumstances couldn't be clearer. He caught a bullet while leading his men. Not a bad way to go; hope when my turn comes, it's something like that."

Lot stared carefully for signs of hypocrisy on Hooker's face, but saw only sincere admiration for the manner of McPherson's end. Then he asked, "Did you witness the moment of his death yourself? Grant and the president will want to know every detail."

Hooker seemed to ponder the black lieutenant's question before responding "I suppose I did, though I didn't realize it at the time. My 20th Corps was supposed to be in contact with McPherson's flank, but the idiot said lead brigade commanders weren't pushing their men enough, and had left a gap an army could have walked through. I was screaming at the top of my voice at the lead brigades to join hands with McPherson's boys while scribbling orders for other brigades to come up and take their place in the line. Anyway, caught a glimpse of some mounted officers having a dustup with Reb skirmishers near my artillery. Saw one of them go down. Must have been McPherson. I appreciate a brave general as much as the next man; but being that far out ahead of his boys was just plain stupid. Your example to the men is useless if you get killed in front of them; worse than useless. Anyway, he's dead, and Sherman's denied me the command that's rightfully mine. If you have no further fool questions, I've a train to catch. Sooner I'm in Washington, sooner this injustice will be put to right . . ."

A medium-sized, stocky officer of about forty appeared at the tent flap. He saluted smartly and said "General Hooker, my deepest apologies for interrupting. However, the departure time for the northbound train has been moved up, so the track will be clear later on for a supply train coming south. We really need to finish packing your kit." There was a slight pause, "Sir, if you would like, I will come north with you. I've been with you since the beginning, and have seen you dealt with unfairly repeatedly, but this takes the prize. I could hardly stand to answer to officers that have treated such a great hero so shabbily."

Clay looked at the new arrival, expected to see the subtle signs of sycophancy. However, all he could detect was admiration that approached hero-worship.

"No, Colonel Kitching, you are the best artillery commander in this army, and if you left with me my enemies would accuse me of trying to sabotage the Union forces," replied Hooker. "Stay here. I will be back soon, with plenty of promotions for those who have shown their loyalty and the boot for those who have not."

Several low-ranking officers peeked over Kitching's shoulder, obviously anxious to scurry in and finish their general's packing. Clay returned his attention smoothly to Hooker. "I believe our business is finished. However, with your permission, I would like to talk to the colonel for a moment outside, where it will not interfere with your . . . preparations."

Frowning, Kitching looked to Hooker, who with a wave of his hand said "Oh, go talk to them, Kitching. Don't need you for the packing business, and besides, they are a couple of Grant's minions. Best to humor them." Wordlessly, Kitching formally saluted Joe Hooker, spun on his heel, and led Clay and Lot out of the tent and under a nearby shade tree. He then turned to face the two investigators. "Well, what is it? You here to try to get more dirt on Fighting Joe Hooker." Frank hostility emanated from the artillery officer.

Clay decided that adhering to a diplomatic falsehood would be easier. "General Grant is concerned about friction in the command structure out here, and sent us to see if matters were as strained as rumor would have it. However, the death of General McPherson has reordered our priorities. General Grant is a sentimental man, and was very fond of McPherson. Without any doubt, he would want to hear every detail of his last moments. I understand you may have been one of the closest officers to him when he died. What can you tell us about that tragedy?"

Colonel Kitching frowned, as if working hard to remember. "Didn't see anything at the time. That's not surprising. Either of you ever serve in an artillery battery? No? Well, there's nothing closer to hell on earth than an artillery position in the middle of a fight. You load, aim fire; then run the gun back out and do it all again and again. And if you think one cannon can make a big noise, try three or four batteries going off all the time; and once every while a Reb shell hits a gun or caisson, which explodes with a sound like the end of the world, likely as not blowing little bits of men and horses into your face . . . Never met an artilleryman who had good hearing past middle age, or one who didn't have a strong stomach. Anyway, everyone was keeping their heads down while Hood's madmen seemed to be coming at us from every direction, only looking up to correct aim. And I was even busier than my men, running back and forth along the line, redirecting batteries constantly as new targets presented themselves. I wasn't wasting time looking around for what other officers were doing, and wouldn't have seen the shot that killed him anyway. Anyway, that's all I can tell you." He looked at Hooker as the general proudly strode out of his tent toward the railhead, followed by a gaggle of young officers puffing under the weight of their commander's luggage. "Now, I must leave you. Joe Hooker is the greatest man I have ever known, and I will see him off." With a sloppy salute, Kitching turned on his heel and hurried after his adored chief.

"That was . . . intriguing," murmured Clay. "Well, let us see what we can learn from McPherson's staff officers. They were with him when he died, and should have seen everything."

"They should have seen everything," muttered Clay with savage emphasis as he entered the tent where Ambrose Bierce lay recuperating.

"Be fair, Alphonso," said Lot soothingly. "Everyone agrees that it was utter chaos at the moment McPherson was shot. An enemy regiment had approached through a slight ravine up to our lines, and had made a sudden dash. Our line was broken in several places, and a few even got in among Kitching's guns. It was suicidal, of course; one lone unsupported Reb regiment could not break the whole line. However, you have to imagine how it seemed. Horsemen and foot-soldiers, blue and grey, all mixed together, rifles and cannon firing every which way, smoke blurring everything . . ."

"Afternoon Major, Lieutenant," interrupted Bierce in a weak but cheerful voice. "Clay, I have to say that this is the closest I've ever seen you to losing your temper—at least without someone about to die. What has gotten under your skin?"

"General McPherson was surrounded by at least six aides at the moment he was shot, and not one of them noticed a thing, at least until the general toppled from his horse. Not one! Staff officers that unobservant have no business around a headquarters. They should be stripped of their rank and fed into the line; stopping a bullet is about as useful as they can be."

Bierce frowned slightly in puzzlement. "Why the hell does that matter, Clay? McPherson is dead and proclaimed a martyr. End of story. The details are of no earthly use to anyone."

Lot looked questioningly at Clay, who after a slight hesitation nodded.

"Ambrose, you already know that we suspect you were shot by a traitor. What we now suspect is that the same traitor murdered General McPherson under the cover of Hood's assault."

Bierce's face assumed a melancholic expression. "I see. I won't insult you by questioning your conclusions; not after Vicksburg and Knoxville. So sad. McPherson was miles ahead of most of the incompetent butchers in our command. Bad enough to die facing an open enemy in open battle. To be killed by a skulking traitor. . . Anything I can do to help?"

"Don't be foolish," said Lot. "You are weeks, if not months, from full recovery. You duty is to do nothing but rest until that recovery is assured."

"Excellent advice," said Teresa Duval from the opening of the tent. She strode in, saying "Thank you gentlemen for reinforcing my excellent instructions to Captain Bierce. In fact, when he is strong enough, I will try to get him a priority billet on a north-bound train, so that he may complete his recovery in more restful surroundings than an army camp in the field."

Clay bowed slightly to Duval, the slightest trace of an ironic smile on his face. "A pleasure as always, Miss Duval. And how is your mother?"

Duval hesitated slightly. "I do not receive many messages from her. She prefers to receive them from me. I am better able to afford the charges."

"I was not aware that the military telegraphers were in the habit of charging, even for those civilians who use their services," replied Clay.

Hiding her irritation at her slip, Duval responded. "I mean, they would charge her at her end, but do not charge civilians in the field at all."

"I see," commented Clay with a hint of mockery in his voice that both irritated and intrigued Duval. "In any event, have you been able to make arrangements for Captain Bierce to be taken north for his recovery?"

She shook her head, a frown of sincere irritation on her face. "General Sherman has ordered that for the time being no wounded be transported on the line. General Forest's cavalry is very active, and has even derailed two trains. Only fully capable, fully armed soldiers are permitted until greater security can be guaranteed."

"Surely not even Forest would molest the wounded and sick," interjected Lot.

"The man responsible for the Fort Pillow massacre is capable of anything," replied Clay abruptly. "In any event, there is a pressing need to get Captain Bierce and the other wounded out of field conditions and into more permanent, healthful surroundings. If only General Sherman would make haste and take Atlanta."

Duval seemed to be mulling over whether to speak further, then abruptly said "You may not have long to wait. While I was with the telegraphers I happened to overhear several staff officer's talking about the latest movements. It looks like tonight General Howard's command is to move toward the last railroad into Atlanta we haven't cut. At the same time, the long-range cannon will continue the bombardment of the town center that has already begun; then the moment the Rebs start to respond to Howard, General Thomas' men will smash straight through into Atlanta. We may very well have the town and Hood's army by noon tomorrow."

"Why do you believe that"'? asked Clay curiously.

Duval uttered one of her silvery, chilling laughs. "Isn't it obvious? After his losses of the last week, Hood must know he'll be destroyed if he stays in Atlanta; he doesn't have the slightest chance of winning a stand-up fight with Sherman's entire army. He is probably evacuating as we speak along the railroad. Howard will cut it to find that his prey has already escaped the trap."

Clay looked at Duval with grudging admiration. "An astute analysis, Miss Duval. My opinion on such matters is of no value. However, we will know if you have correctly analyzed the situation by tomorrow."

Clay and Lot were settling into their tent shortly after midnight when suddenly the night began to fill with the sounds of hoarsely shouted orders, bugle calls, and neighing animals. Dimly lit figures dashed about seemingly at random, on foot or horseback. Clay snatched the arm of a passing corporal, and shouted "What has happened? Are we under attack?"

"Hell no, sir," said the young man in a voice pitched high with excitement. "Scouts report Hood is pulling out of Atlanta before we cut the last railway. Sherman has told Slocum's corps to go right into town, right now, while the Army of the Tennessee is to set out to catch Hood on the hop. One-arm Howard better be quick; looks like the Rebs are truly heading for the hills. Excuse me, sir; my colonel will skin me if I ain't there when we start marching." With a hurried salute, the excited young soldier disappeared into the confused darkness.

"If the army is on the move, so will be the wounded," commented Lot. "They dare not be left behind, to the tender mercies of Forrest's cavalry. We had better go to the hospital and make sure that Ambrose is handled as gently as may be."

Impatiently Clay started to say that Ambrose Bierce was not the only wounded soldier at risk, but a glance at the concerned face of his friend stopped him. "Of course, let us attend to him. We can always pack our own gear at the last minute."

Shouldering their way through masses of hurrying soldiers, barely evading galloping teams of horses hauling cannon or caissons, they quickly found Bierce's tent. To their surprise, they saw that almost all of the medical supplies and equipment were already neatly packed and loaded in wagons outside the tent complex, and that Fetterman and Duval were gingerly carrying Bierce out the front of the tent toward the lead wagon.

"Dr. Fetterman, you have my admiration. I can scarce believe you have organized things so efficiently in such a short period of time. May Lieutenant Lot and myself help you transfer the other wounded to their transport?"

"No need," replied Bierce weakly from his stretcher. "I'm the last.

"Don't compliment me," said Fetterman, grunting under the strain as they leveraged Bierce gently into the bed of the lead wagon. Clay noted that Duval held up her end of the load with no sign of strain. "Miss Duval has organized the supplies and the patients wonderfully, actually assigning them numbered wagons in advance, and making sure that our orderlies kept the wagons at the ready.

"Miss Duval is a woman of many talents," said Clay. Duval glanced sharply at Clay, that was the first compliment he had paid her that had not been laced with subtle sarcasm, and she found the sudden lack of mockery as disturbing as she had previously found its presence.

"Many talents, and hidden depths," said Bierce weakly from his prone position between stacks of medical supplies.

"Captain Bierce, Lieutenant Lot, despite Miss Duval's efficiency, we can always use extra hands. Besides, Atlanta is likely to be in confusion now, with rioters and deserters from both sides on the prowl. I would deem it a great favor if you would accompany us, if you do not have duties elsewhere."

"Of course," responded Clay. It will take Lieutenant Lot and I just a few minutes to pack our gear and saddle our horses. We simple could not allow wounded heroes to be put at risk—or a helpless, defenseless woman." Lot thought that he saw Clay wink at Duval as he said this; but the nearby lamps were flickering in the murky darkness, and he decided it had just been a passing shadow.

It was shortly before first light when the wagons of the medical corps rumbled into Atlanta proper, embedded in a moving column of blue soldiers who nervously awaited a surprise attack that did not come. Fetterman held the reins of the lead wagon, while Duval sat primly on the seat beside him. The mounted Clay and Lot flanked the lead wagon, Clay on the right, Lot on the left. The gas streetlamps had failed, but the darkness was not complete; aside from the occasional lamp or torch that the tramping soldiers surrounding them held, a group of burning buildings in the distance threw a lurid illumination over the army column.

Duval looked at Clay, who had ridden silently beside the wagon for some time. Occasionally his spectacles caught the red glow of the distant fire, giving him an unearthly appearance. Deciding to break the silence, she said "Major, you seem to have something on your mind. May I know what concerns you?"

Clay turned his head and seemed to consider her as his horse kept pace with the wagon. "I was thinking of the many trips I had made to Atlanta, before the war," he finally responded. "This is Peachtree Street, the stretch where the people of quality lived." He gestured to the homes that lined the street, all dark, many in ruins from random artillery shells. "The people here had lives of grace and beauty, and threw it all away in a fit of pride and arrogance. I doubt they will ever retrieve those lives."

Clay's melancholic mode disturbed Duval for no reason she could easily identify. Trying to change the subject, she pointed to the buildings that burned in the near distance. "Since you are familiar with the town, can you tell me what is on fire over there."

Without pause Clay replied "Those are the railroad yards, and the associated warehouses. Every major railway in the Deep South meets here. Movement of large numbers of Confederate men and supplies is now going to be virtually impossible in half the Confederacy."

"Why would General Sherman burn them?" Duval asked curiously.

Clay giggled, a sound that disturbed Duval's nerves, nerves that were unsettled by very little. "Not Sherman, I assure you, Miss Duval. Hood himself, without a doubt. Those warehouses must be filled with supplies the Rebs had carefully gathered up and horded. Now that they had to retreat in a hurry, there was nothing left to do but burn them all."

Silently, several of the buildings they were watching seemed to leap into the air and disintegrate; a second later, the air was filled with an ear-shattering series of explosions. Involuntarily, the hospital train and all the soldiers surrounding it came to a halt and stared at the spectacle as burning timbers seemed to sail to the very skies before falling to the ground. A feeble Ambrose Bierce lifted a flap of the wagon's canvas cover, spiting out an obscenity and then asking "What the Hell has happened?"

"It would seem that General Hood was not able to take all of his explosives with him," replied Clay, a grim smile on his lips. "That should make General Howard's task somewhat easier, at least." Clay peered at the flaming ruins of the rail yard, and then spotted a remarkable sight. Dangerously close to the fires, threatened by secondary explosions at any instant, a man led a horse attached to a buggy through the hellish scene; some garment covering the animal's head to prevent blind panic. As nearly as Clay could tell, a lone woman occupied the buggy itself. Obviously refugees trying to slip past the Federal army before it was too late. Suddenly Clay's view of the refugees was cut off by a nearer sight. William Tecumseh Sherman was approaching the wagons, his unmistakable profile illuminated by the flames in the distance. Behind him trailed his staff, which seemed unusually subdued by the destruction around them.

"Clay, Fetterman, Lot, Miss Duval," Sherman said without preamble. "Here we are. Here we are at last. Glad to find you. Wanted you with me; especially wanted Bierce."

"I am flattered, sir, but why?" said Bierce, propping himself up on the back of Fetterman's seat. "I am sure you have a lot to do right now."

"Quite a lot Bierce, quite a lot. Couple of my aides have gone up to city hall with Slocum and corralled the mayor. He wants some high-falutin' surrender ceremony. Thinks he's delaying us in chasing after Hood; doesn't know that Howard is already hot on his tail. Still, it is a big thing to have Atlanta in our hands, and . . . damn it Bierce, I wanted you to be there!" In the slowly growing light of dawn, Sherman looked angry at himself for expressing a sentimental thought. "Anyway, there's a big public park in front of city hall where the medical corps can set up, so you might as well tag along."

Sherman looked at the milling soldiers around the wagons and addressed them in a loud voice. "What are you waiting for, you saucy bastards? You've wanted to see downtown Atlanta for four months, let's go take a gander!" With a full-throated cheer the column began moving again, Sherman ramrod straight in his saddle, eyes straight ahead. The soldiers around him had suddenly lost their weariness; smiles could be seen everywhere, laughs heard everywhere.

Duval said softly to Clay as they proceeded. "How do you think he does it? These men love him. A man who has sent thousands of their comrades to their deaths, a man who is, let us be blunt, half mad. How does he do it, Major?"

"I truly do not know, Miss Duval," Clay responded thoughtfully. "As far back as history goes, there have been leaders who can reach out mystically to those they lead. Some have used their influence for good, many more for evil. It will be interesting to see which one Sherman will be."

By the time they reached city hall, a charming building in the Greek Revival style, the morning sun was peaking over the horizon. Showing no sign that he had been twelve hours in the saddle, Sherman leapt from his horse and bounded up the steps where the mayor, a portly, sweating man, stood flanked by General Slocum and another officer who Clay recognized with surprise as Colonel Orlando Poe, who had played such a key role in the events at Knoxville. Clay turned and saw that Lot had already dismounted, and was gently helping Fetterman and Duval seat Bierce on the driver's seat, where the invalid could clearly observe the surrender. Clay turned back to the front of city hall, and observed that the mayor was reading something from a lengthy document that he held with both hands, while Sherman looked increasingly impatient. Curious to hear exactly what was being said, Clay quickly dismounted, tethered his mount to the wagon, and shouldered his way roughly through the crowd of festive soldiers who were the main observers, Atlanta's citizens seeming to have become invisible. As Clay approached the steps, he began to understand snatches of the major's speech, which seemed to be a long-winded defense of the Confederacy combined with a plea for mercy. Clay had pushed his way to the top of the steps in time to hear Sherman say, "Goddamn it, are you surrendering, or do you want me to tell these boys Atlanta is still a town in rebellion and turn them loose?"

Visibly quaking, the mayor replied "General Sherman sir, Atlanta is yours. We beg that you use us kindly."

Sherman than gestured to Poe, simply saying "Now." In his turn, the imperious-looking Poe pointed to two privates, who carried between them a large folded object. They stepped over to the city hall's flagpole, from which the Stars and Bars had already been removed. Reverently they unfolded the object, to reveal it as a large American flag. Quickly they attached it to the cord, and raised it the sky, where a morning breeze caused it to wave and snap majestically. The flag was saluted by the privates who had raised it, then by generals Sherman and Slocum, then by all of the other soldiers gathered before the beautiful building. Then, somewhere out in the vast crowd of soldiers, as single voice broke out in a cheer. More voices joined in, and soon the air was filled with the sound of thousands of wildly cheering soldiers, cheering not only the victory of their country but the fact they were alive to witness that victory.

Clay had aggressively wormed his way onto the city hall's porch, so despite the pandemonium he was close enough to hear a soldier approach Poe and shout "Sir, the line north is up and running!"

Poe nodded dismissively, then moved over to Sherman. The engineer saluted and said loudly "Sir, the telegraph line is operational. What message do you wish sent to Washington?"

Sherman turned his bright eyes on his chief engineer. "Take a telegram, Poe." The colonel swiftly drew a notebook and pencil from a tunic pocket and looked at his commander expectantly.

"Date it . . . hell, what is today's date, Poe?"

"The second of September, sir."

"Very well." Sherman looked thoughtful for a moment, then suddenly smiled. "Say 'Atlanta is ours, and fairly won.' That should set the right tone for those bastards in Washington."

Poe finished jotting the message, put the notebook away, then strode to the front of the steps and held up his hands for silence. Surprisingly, the boisterous crown immediately quieted. Then Poe proclaimed in a voice like a trumpet "You should all know that Major General Sherman is telegraphing to Washington 'Atlanta is ours and fairly won'!"

The crowd of soldiers seemed to go insane with joy. The cheering that had gone on before seemed as nothing compared to this. Clay looked at Sherman smiling down on his soldiers and suddenly knew the secret of charismatic leadership: it was in loving those you led, and letting them see that sincere love.

Clay suddenly felt dampness on his cheeks. Frowning, he looked upward expecting rain, only to see the Stars and Strips waving in an absolutely clear early morning sky. Suddenly he realized they were tears—tears of joy. Angrily he wiped them away.

CHAPTER 3

"SO WE MADE A THOROUGHFARE FOR FREEDOM AND HER TRAIN . . ."

Clay and Lot waited outside the office Sherman had established in what had been the mayor's headquarters in Atlanta City Hall, sweltering in the heat of a Georgia September morning. Lot sat rigidly at attention, never having lost his uneasiness around those with stars on their shoulders. However, his posture was nothing compared to that of Clay's, whose ramrod-straight spine at no place touched the chair's back; his posture had nothing to do with unease around high rank, and everything to do with his uncompromising sense of decorum. From behind the closed door to the inner office came the muttered sound of voices, occasionally punctuated by a fierce "Goddamnit!" in Sherman's high, fluting voice; each curse made the nervous aide at the desk to the side of the door visibly start, and shuffle the papers on his desk more frantically.

"You really think nothing can be gained by staying a little longer?" asked Lot, more out of a desire to distract himself from the commotion emanating from the General's office than any real curiosity.

"I am afraid not, Jeremiah," Clay responded. "We are at an impasse; I fear more time spent here will bring us no closer to the murderer. Meanwhile, we could be more productively employed in Grant's headquarters. Petersburg should have been taken by now, and Richmond not long thereafter; I suspect the General will need our assistance in determining why that is not so."

The door to Sherman's office flew open, and Colonel Orlando Poe, chief engineer of the Military Division of the Mississippi, stormed out, his proud, arrogant face contorted by equal measures of anger and frustration. He paused briefly upon noticing Clay and Lot, bowing slightly. "Gentlemen. I am pleased to see you again. Perhaps you will find the General in a more reasonable frame of mind than have I."

Lot stood up with Clay, who returned the bow. "I see congratulations are in order," replied Clay. "When we were in Knoxville you were a humble if able captain. From captain to full colonel in less than a year is quite an achievement; you are to be commended."

"Commended!" Poe snorted with disgust. "I have earned each step in the promotion, and continue to pay for it. I no sooner repair a bridge or culvert on our railroads than Forrest burns them up, sometimes destroying entire trains in the process. And Sherman will not give me the power to bring Forrest to heel! Well, gentlemen, you must excuse me; if I don't get some bridges built, this army will go hungry." Head erect, dark eyes flashing with anger, Poe strode out of the building.

"Uh, General Sherman will see you now, sirs," announced the young aide without making eye contact, his face flushing with embarrassment at witnessing such behavior by superior officers. The two friends entered the office and saluted formally.

"Close the Goddamn door!" growled Sherman. Clay shut the door, then he and Lot seated themselves in chairs before the cluttered desk. "Hate closing the door in this Goddamn weather, but the kinds of things you bring to me usually isn't for every pair of ears." The lean general mopped sweat from his face with a dirty handkerchief, casting a longing glance at the open window, where the lace curtains remained motionless in the absence of the slightest hint of a breeze.

Clay came straight to the point. "Sir, my investigation has made no progress. I can identify no probable subject for the murder of General McPherson, or even an unambiguous motive, for that matter."

Sherman reflected moodily for a few moments before asking "Couldn't it be just possible that both Bierce and Mac caught random bullets? That it is a coincidence after all?"

Clay did not hesitate before replying. "I think it is unlikely, but not impossible. I have erred before in my analysis, but, even if I have not erred, the criminal seems to have left too few clues to be traced. If he is wise and commits no further atrocities, he may be safe forever."

"So you recommend that we do nothing and hope for the best?" asked Sherman. "That doesn't sound like you, Clay."

"I take no joy in leaving a job undone, sir. However, the Union does not have the resources to spare on hopeless causes. With your permission, we will just visit Captain Bierce before packing our effects."

Mopping his forehead again, Sherman said "Guess you know best about this kind of thing, Clay. Well, let me come with you to see Bierce. Need to get out of this room for awhile, anyway, even if it isn't any cooler outside." Sherman abruptly stood and without further comment strode quickly to the door and threw it open. He ignored the hasty salute of the nervous aide, and went quickly out the entrance of City Hall, leaving Clay and Lot to keep up as best they could. One look at Sherman's brooding, angry countenance convinced the two friends that idle conversation was not desired, and they accompanied the General in silence to the hospital tents laid out neatly in the park across from City Hall. Barely acknowledging the salutes of the soldiers he passed, Sherman led his party to the tent housing Bierce and a few others. As he reached the entrance he suddenly noticed Doctor Fetterman, approaching hurriedly from the right. The slightly-built physician breathlessly saluted and said "General, an unexpected honor. How may I help you?"

Nodding to Clay and Lot, Sherman replied "These officers will be leaving shortly, and wanted to say their goodbyes to Captain Bierce. Thought I might poke my head in as well. Is he continuing his recovery?"

"It continues to amaze me sir, given the nature of his wound. In fact . . ."

From inside the tent a horrible strangling sound interrupted the doctor. Frowning, Fetterman said, "Excuse me. Some emergency," and entered through the large tent's flap. After only a moment's hesitation, Sherman also entered, followed by Clay and Lot. The scene inside astonished all four of the new arrivals.

Ambrose Bierce was kneeling alongside his cot, a small pool of reeking vomit in front of him. Clutching him from behind, arms wrapped around his stomach, was Teresa Duval, hissing in a distinct Irish brogue "Bring it up, bring it all up, you stupid bastard!" Then to the shock of the witnesses, she interlinked her fingers into a single fist, and viciously rammed the young captain in his stomach. With an agonized sound a small explosion of vomit burst from Bierce's mouth, joining the pool on the ground. Sherman and Lot were literally shocked speechless, but not Clay. Taking two small steps forward, in a tight, controlled voice the blond major said "Miss Duval, I demand an explanation for this assault on Captain Bierce."

Duval glanced up, and spoke in a voice now showing no trace of Ireland. "Do not be a fool, Major Clay. The Captain has been poisoned with laudanum. When I realized this, I administered an emetic and, ah, helped him to vomit out the portion not yet absorbed into his body. Now please assist me in helping the Captain walk. He must not be allowed to sleep until we are assured what entered into his system is not fatal."

"Poisoned!" exclaimed Sherman. "But how . . ."

"Major!" interrupted Duval sharply. "If you want your friend to live, help me keep him active."

Clay smoothly took Bierce's left arm, while Duval took his right. Together they raised the young scout unsteadily to his feet and began walking him about the tent in small steps. Bierce's face was deathly pale, his eyes fluttering. Fetterman peered closely at Bierce, then said "You are right, Miss Duval. He shows the symptoms of opium poisoning. We must keep him awake until the crisis passes. Lieutenant, be so good to find the nearest camp with coffee brewing and bring it here." Lot hurried to comply. Meanwhile, Bierce had begun to mutter, "Need . . . lie down . . . sleep few . . . minutes."

"You will get a chance soon, Captain," Duval replied firmly. "Right now we need to make you a bit better."

"How did this happen?" demanded Sherman.

"I had just finished changing the linens of the artillery sergeant in the corner and was passing the Captain's cot on my way to taking them to the laundry tub when I glanced at Bierce. His color was wrong for someone on his way to healing. I stopped, and noticed his breathing was labored, his pupils dilated wide. I suppose laudanum was in my mind; I had just dosed the artilleryman to keep him quiet while his stump began to heal. Anyway, I sniffed his breath, and detected its distinctive scent."

"Just how did the Captain come into a large dose of such a dangerous drug?" asked Clay, the blue eyes behind the spectacles seeming to glimmer with a light that made Duval nervous for no reason she could name.

"Wrong . . . didn't take . . . lau . . . laudbubm . . ." slurred Bierce. "Jus a little . . . little bit of John Barley . . . Barleycorn . . . damn rotgut . . . got a kick on it . . ." Bierce's head lolled and eyes closed. With brisk economy Duval slapped his face twice, and Bierce jerked awake.

"Why . . . angry . . . no cause . . . Clay's . . . want." Clay frowned at the enigmatic comment; but before he could make any response Lot appeared at the entrance to the tent, a tin cup in one hand, a pot full of steaming coffee in the other.

Pouring into the cup as he approached, Lot said, "Here Ambrose, drink. Drink as quick as you can."

The woozy young captain swallowed one mouthful, grimaced, and mumbled "Coffee . . . hot . . . need some more from my flask . . ."

"Damn your hide!" said the religious Lot, resorting to what was for him extreme language. "Forget liquor! You nearly died; keep drinking coffee until you are fit to burst!" Mumbling incoherently, Bierce nodded and continued his slow shuffle around the tent's interior while sipping the brew. After two cups, Bierce looked noticeably more alert and had ceased staggering. Clay released one of Bierce's arms, motioning Duval to do the same.

"Lieutenant, take the captain out for a walk in the open air. Keep an eye on him, and keep the coffee flowing. The rest of us have some . . . business to transact." Nodding wordlessly, Lot led the dazed but recovering Bierce out into the air.

As soon as they were gone, Sherman was able to maintain his silence no longer. "Goddamnit Clay, what has happened here? Poisoning? Fetterman, if your people have been making mistakes like that, I'll have your guts for garters!"

With quiet dignity the doctor replied "Sir, I have made many mistakes in my career, but overdosing patients with dangerous drugs has not been among them. Nor would any on my staff make such an error. Miss Duval, is it possible that the captain has an, ah, private weakness? There are a few opium fiends in the army, and laudanum can be freely purchased from the sutlers."

Duval was staring through the glass door to the supply cabinet. She did not answer immediately, but instead opened the door and removed a small brown bottle. Frowning, she hefted it, then uncorked it and peered intently inside. "No, doctor, I do not believe Captain Bierce overdosed himself," she said finally. "I have known him for some time; his vices are public and unconcealed, and do not include addiction to the poppy. I gave him only moderate doses during his recovery, and he never asked for more. Further, thievery is not among his vices."

"Thievery?" asked Sherman, frowning.

"He is too proud to stoop to theft, especially of army supplies," she responded. "When I last dosed the artilleryman in the corner, I left this bottle of laudanum two-thirds full; it is now nearly empty." Her eyes darted to the small pile of personal possessions Bierce kept at the head of his cot. She leaned down and picked up a battered hip-flask that was in plain view. Unscrewing the cap, she sniffed deeply, then turned to Clay, handing the flask to him. "Major, smell this," she said.

Clay sniffed at the flask, and frowned. "You are correct, Miss Duval. Laudanum. Its slight, sweetish odor is just barely detectable under the stronger scent of the, ah, inexpensive whiskey Bierce favors; he would be unlikely to notice. The obvious question is: How came the drug into the flask? Only someone whose presence would be unremarked in this tent would have the opportunity." As he capped the container and placed it in an inner pocket of his tunic, Clay focused his pale blue eyes on Duval. "You seem unusually conversant with tincture of opium, even for a nurse."

Duval met his stare without flinching. In a near-whisper, audible only to Clay, she said "I had the ability to kill Bierce at any time since he came to my care, and in any number of ways that would have seemed natural. Why would I wait until he was nearly recovered, or be caught in the act of helping him vomit?"

"What was that?" asked Sherman crossly.

"It is of no importance," replied Clay. "Think carefully, Miss Duval. In the last few hours, who came into this tent who might have meddled with Bierce's liquor?"

"I only saw some officers from the artilleryman's battery, come to check on his progress," she replied without hesitation. "However, that signifies little; I came and went many times during the last few hours, and someone with nerve enough could have come and gone during my absence."

Clay cocked his head to one side; his eyes unfocused for a few moments. Then abruptly returning from wherever his thoughts had taken him. "General, with your permission I believe the lieutenant and I will stay after all. The murderer is still active, and not content to lay low; this must take priority over other activities where we could be of use. However, I must ask that an armed guard be placed on this tent until transportation north can be arranged for Captain Bierce, and further that he be accompanied by an armed escort until he is well away from your command. He is in mortal danger, and little able now to defend himself; the Union owes him some protection, in view of his many daring services."

"I'll start cutting the orders today; he will be on a train north day after tomorrow at the latest." Sherman's face had taken on the wild, crazed look that always presaged the rare times when his anger threatened to spiral out of control. In his mind he saw not Ambrose Bierce, but little Willie in the moment of his death. '*God damn the South to Hell!*' he thought; then realized he had spoken aloud. "I will have sentries posted in this tent within the hour." Giving the impression he had reached a decision about another matter as well, Sherman spun on his heels and left the tent without further ado.

"That was strange," muttered Fetterman. "I wonder what it means."

"It means trouble for the South and for traitors," replied Clay, an odd eagerness in his voice.

The following morning an aide ushered Clay and Lot into Sherman's office. The general barely glanced up as the aide closed the door, then looked down to his desk and continued scribbling signatures on a series of documents on his desk.

"You summoned us, sir," said Clay.

"Thought you would like to know I'm putting Bierce on a train going north this afternoon, along with a protective guard. He will soon be out of danger, and able to complete his recovery in peace."

"We appreciate this," replied Lot. "However, would it not be wise to confirm with Dr. Fetterman that it is safe to move Captain Bierce?"

"Doesn't make a difference," replied Sherman gruffly. "Starting at dawn, I've been sending trains north as fast as they can be loaded with the wounded and with soldiers intended to defend Nashville. Bierce will be on one of the last trains, before we start tearing up the railroad."

Clay seldom allowed surprise to show on his features, much less shock; this was one of those rare times. "Sir, you are going to destroy your own railroad?" he asked incredulously.

"Can't bring Hood to battle. Howard keeps after him, and Hood keeps slipping away like some Goddamn Injun. Not Howard's fault; he's a good general. Rebs just travel too damn light, and always stay ahead of our boys. Howard sees what Johnnie Hood is up to as well as I do. Wants us to follow him away from Atlanta, from the Georgia breadbasket, and up into those barren Goddamn highlands again, while the good people of Georgia harvest the grain and raise the cattle the Confederacy needs to keep going. He also keeps Forrest and that other Reb cavalry general, Joe Wheeler, threatening that lone railroad back to the North. Trying to starve me into doing something desperate and foolish." Sherman signed the last paper, and suddenly leaped to his feet. "Well to Hell with that! Hood and Forrest are going to see my army do something desperate all right, but not what they expected. I'm sending back to Nashville all the wounded, all the tired and clapped out troops, along with General Thomas. He'll have time to whip them into shape. Those fellows, especially when Northern reinforcements arrive, should be able to hold Nashville if Hood and Forrest make a stab north. I'm going to divide the remaining army into two wings, one under Howard, the other under Slocum. We will burn this town, and then take a little stroll down to Savannah, destroying everything of any military significance along the way."

Recovering from his initial shock, Clay nodded approvingly. "I see. You are taking a leaf from General Grant's book, the same tactic he used at Vicksburg. Keep your army moving and live off the land, leaving the enemy to flail about, vainly trying to cut supply lines that no longer exist. I assume this is not a spur of the moment decision."

Sherman focused his bright, bird-like eyes on Clay. "That's right. Sent a message in code to Sam a week ago, telling him I thought it would be the best way to proceed. Back came word from Sam, saying the risk worried him, but if I thought I could do it, go ahead. I think I can do it. Scouts say there isn't much except Georgia militia and Wheeler's cavalry between us and the sea; and I don't care if it rains Goddamn militiamen! My fellows can take care of the sort of old, feeble and unblooded remnants that will be in the militia."

Lot hazarded a comment, "What if Hood goes north into Tennessee? If Thomas cannot hold him, he could end up on the Ohio."

Sherman glared at the black lieutenant, and replied "If Hood will agree to go to the Ohio, I will give him rations! My business is in the South. Any damage he could do up there is temporary, and will be easily rectified by the resources of the North. Any damage I do down here is permanent."

There was a hesitant knock at the door. "Come in!" growled Sherman abruptly.

The timid aide stuck in his head. "General Sherman, sir, Mayor Calhoun is demanding to see you. It is about your letter to him concerning, ah, evacuation of Atlanta . . ."

A tall, portly man dressed in white linen shouldered his way past the aide, waiving a document. "General Sherman, this is outrageous! This is barbarous! I demand you revoke this inhuman order!"

"Shut the door on your way out," said Sherman to the aide, who withdrew with alacrity. Deliberately not offering his guest a chair, Sherman sat down. "Mayor Calhoun. May I introduce you to Major Alphonso Clay and Lieutenant Jeremiah Lot, valued officers visiting from General Grant's headquarters."

Calhoun only glanced at Clay, but his gaze lingered for a long moment on Lot, the mayor's lip curling in a combination of disgust and rage at the sight of what he feared most: a black man in a position of authority. Then with an effort he turned his attention back to Sherman's grim visage. "Sir, I demand you retract this barbarous order!"

Without taking his eyes off Calhoun, Sherman addressed Clay and Lot. "Gentlemen, you may be puzzled as to just what the good mayor is talking about. You probably haven't heard yet, although I am sure copies of what the mayor is holding in his hand will be in every regiment by nightfall."

"May I ask what the document contains?" asked Clay.

"Your General has ordered the destruction of Atlanta!" exploded Calhoun.

"I have issued an order to Mayor Calhoun and his council, instructing him to evacuate all civilians from Atlanta."

"All?" exclaimed Lot with surprise.

"All," replied Sherman firmly. "No exceptions. The old, the young, the female, the infirm. All must be gone by tomorrow night."

"And if we refuse to leave?" asked the appalled mayor.

"That would not be advisable, Mayor Calhoun. I intend to burn every public building, every improvement, and every factory. I intend no deliberate violence to private residences. However, the weather has been so hot for so long that you know as well as I it will inevitably spread to people's homes. Better they leave now with some dignity and in some order, rather than screaming into the night with only the clothes on their backs."

"All of the civilians? All of them?" said Lot, whose Christian soul was appalled.

"Without exception. The use of Atlanta for any civilian purposes is inconsistent with the conduct of this war."

"Think of the suffering this will entail," exclaimed Calhoun. "This is inhuman!"

Without warning, Sherman jackknifed out of his chair, rounded his desk, and came nose to nose with the furious mayor. "Goddamn you, my order is not designed to be humane! Peace is what this country needs, not Atlanta, this country! I know about the food and manufactures your city has sent to kill my boys, and Sam Grant's boys. I know how you all, men, women and children, exult in the death of the brave soldiers fighting to preserve this sacred Union. Your people are fortunate that I let them go with their lives!"

The mayor drew back slightly, shocked at the abyss he glimpsed in the wild eyes of the general. With some visible effort, Sherman calmed himself and continued to speak.

"My plans make it necessary for all of your citizens to go away. All I can do is offer my army's services to make their exodus as easy as possible." A shadow passed over Sherman's face, and his voice became tinged with melancholy. *Willie!* "You cannot qualify war in harsher terms than I. War is cruelty, and you cannot refine it, and those Southerners who brought war into our country deserve eternal damnation. You might as well appeal against the thunderstorm as against the hardships of war. I will conduct this war for peace and Union, and destroy whatever is necessary to achieve that goal."

The anger had drained out of Calhoun, to be replaced by acute fear; the widening of his eyes showed that despite hearing all the horror stories of Yanks he had never dreamed of such terrible implacability. The paper slipped from his fingers, which now trembled slightly. Sherman saw the fear he had engendered, and smiling sadly, continued in a different tone.

"When peace comes, I will share with you my last cracker, and shield with my very life your homes and families against any threat from whatever quarter, but now you must go, all of you, and find shelter away from the business of this army, until the mad passions of men cool down and allow Union and peace to settle once more over Atlanta. Now go! Tomorrow the destruction begins, and you have much to do for your citizens before then."

Calhoun opened his mouth as if to say something, then closed it. With obvious effort at preserving his dignity he bowed ever so slightly and swept out of the office, banging the door behind him.

"My congratulations, sir," said Clay. "It is long since past due to show traitors that the wages of treason are the loss of everything they value, and that it is the purest mercy if they are left with their very lives." A disturbed-looking Lot opened his mouth as if to say something, but seeming to think better of it, his mouth snapped shut.

Sherman shot a suspicious glance at Clay, wondering whether the major was flattering or mocking him. He could detect only sincere admiration in Clay, which disturbed Sherman for no reason he could easily name.

"It has to be done," said Sherman gruffly. "It will be risky enough to leave Hood and Forrest on the rampage behind us. I cannot leave a transportation and manufacturing center like Atlanta in our rear. Besides, it will strike at the women."

"The women?" echoed Lot, disbelief in his voice.

"Of course," Clay replied for the general. "Southern women have been encouraging their men to maintain this war, cheerfully urging their husbands and sons toward treason and death, while they sit peacefully at home and read of glory in the illustrated papers. Now, the women of Georgia are going to see something of the war they so support; real war, war with mud on its boots tramping through their parlors. They will bravely send their men to death and mutilation, but will howl for peace when their live-stock is taken from them and gardens trampled."

"Alphonso, it cannot be necessary to go as far as this," said Lot.

"It is," replied Sherman grimly. "And if we do not make an end to the rebellion in this campaign, next year they will not be complaining about losing their homes, they will be pleading in vain for their very lives. If need be, I will create a vast silence and call it peace." '*Willie!*' echoed silently in his head.

Although there was not a cloud in the sky, a shadow seemed to pass over the room.

Ambrose Bierce had finished pulling on his boots and stood up. Too fast; a horrible wave of vertigo overcame him, and with a stifled moan he collapsed back onto the cot. Teresa Duval frowned disapprovingly, and then steadied him with one hand while she held his chin with her other, peering intently into his eyes.

"I warned you, Captain, take everything slowly. You should not even be walking. I will call for a stretcher and some orderlies."

"No," growled Bierce through gritted teeth. "I will not be an invalid anymore. I can walk to the depot, and will do so."

A small, chilling smile played briefly across Duval's lips. "Very well, Captain. It will be your funeral."

The nausea had passed for the moment. Bierce looked up at Duval, and unexpectedly said "I don't believe I ever properly thanked you for saving my life."

"Nonsense. It was my job. Besides, your own constitution saved you as much as my nursing. Before you, if anyone had ever told me a man could survive such a wound I would have called him a liar. No, no thanks are needed. My reward will come in other ways."

"Such as Alphonso Clay." murmured Bierce. He locked eyes with Duval, and began to speak in a low yet firm voice. "I know something of what you are and I shudder at the thought of the things about you I don't know. I know you are not what you seem. And I know that you want Alphonso Clay. I may owe you my life, but I also owe it to him, more than twice over. Stay away from him, or I will see that you come to regret it."

For the moment they were alone in the tent. Duval toyed with the idea of killing Bierce on the spot, but swiftly realized there would be a lot to explain. Her explanations just might be accepted by the trusting Fetterman, but not by Clay, not by the owner of those pale blue eyes that seemed to see everything.

"Why, Captain Bierce, I have not the slightest idea of what your talking about," Duval replied in a tone of innocent puzzlement.

"Just remember what I have said." With care, Bierce slowly stood up. He swayed slightly, but retained his footing. The flap to the tent was suddenly thrown back, revealing the pair of sentries who had been posted there since Bierce's poisoning. In strode General Sherman along with Clay and Lot.

"Where is Fetterman?" Sherman asked abruptly.

"The doctor is tending to an outbreak of the bloody flux in

one of the cavalry encampments," Duval replied. "He has already wished the Captain Godspeed, suspecting he would not be back in time for his departure."

"Sure you can make it to the train under your own power, Major?" asked Sherman gruffly.

"I will . . . Major?" Bierce had been brought up short, and stared in confusion at Sherman.

"You are brevetted major in the United States Volunteers, effective today. The paperwork is going north on the same train with you. Sorry I don't have any oak leaves to sew on your straps; but I expect you can get those while you are on leave."

"I hardly know what to say . . ." began Bierce slowly.

"Say anything but thank you," interrupted Sherman. "You are a damn fine officer, and the country owes you more than can ever be repaid. Once you get to Nashville, your orders permit you to go anywhere you like, for as long as you feel the need. Are you going to stay with your family in . . . Indiana is it?"

Bierce swayed and turned paler, and recovered his composure only with visible effort. "I had not intended to, sir. Yet . . . perhaps I will. Perhaps I should. There may yet be time for the youngest. I should at least try." Bierce's eyes assumed a melancholy, even haunted appearance. With a visible effort, Bierce drug his attention from some dread inner landscape and back to his commanding general. "In any event, I appreciate your coming, but I can get to the train on my own—so long as Major Clay and Lieutenant Lot are kind enough to carry my kit."

"I'm going there anyway. General Thomas is taking the same train as you, on his way to Nashville. The army's top brass is going to see him off." Sherman paused, and cast a glance at Clay. "In fact, Major Clay has an interesting idea to trap the traitor who tried to murder you—a plan in which you can be of material assistance."

"What are your orders sir?"

* * *

In the end, it took Bierce half an hour to walk the quarter mile to the switching yard. At one point Clay was on the verge of calling for a halt and ordering a stretcher; but a glance at Bierce's pale, determined features told him it would be an unforgivable injury to the young officer's pride. Twice Bierce had stumbled slightly, and both Clay and Lot made as if to grab an arm and steady him; but before either of the friends could actually do so, Duval would have Bierce by the arm, helping him to regain his fragile balance.

As they came up to the depot, they spotted dozens of aides and horses, waiting at a respectful distance while a smaller group of officers talked by the last car of a waiting train. As they slowly approached the latter group, it resolved itself into an assembly of Sherman's top leaders: Generals Howard Slocum, Logan and Davis as well as Colonel Kitching were gravely making their fare-wells to the majestic-looking George Thomas. Kitching spotted the approach of the newcomers and murmured something to his superiors. The entire group turned as one and saluted formally. Sherman returned the greeting with a sloppy half-wave, and then spoke directly to George Thomas.

"Thomas, hope there are no hard feelings about the assign-ment at Nashville. I need someone there who's good at defense, and there's none better than you. Sorry about the health of a lot of the troops I am sending with you, but they won't need to march so much on the defensive, and I need all the healthy ones for the coming campaign."

The dignified Virginian looked at Sherman for a long moment before replying. "I understand. I am to keep Hood out of Tennessee with whatever you can spare me, while you march with our best men to glory against Georgia militia." The complaint was only implied, but for someone like Thomas it was the equivalent of slamming his hat on the ground and cursing.

"Nothing personal, Thomas, but we're going to be moving Goddamn fast, and speed is not your strong suit." Sherman was seemingly oblivious to the combination of shocked and angry looks the other officers gave him. Thomas was respected by his colleagues more than Sherman would ever be, and the indifference to Thomas' feelings grated.

Surprisingly, it was the murderous Jeff Davis who was first to step forward and take Thomas' hand. Casting a disdainful glance at Sherman, he said "General Thomas, it has been a privilege and an honor to serve under you. Tennessee will be Union so long as you are in command." The other officers hastened forward to add similar farewell compliments. Meanwhile, Clay and Bierce detached themselves from Sherman's party and approached the platform. Clay threw Bierce's carpetbag up to a waiting private, then gave a supporting hand to the still unsteady Bierce as the latter carefully stepped up onto the platform of the passenger car. Bierce turned and leaned down, bringing his head close to Clay's in a conspiratorial posture.

"Last chance," whispered Bierce. "If you're right, you will be making a target of yourself to the assassin."

"It is the only way, Bierce. Now, talk while looking at the group of officers and point."

A grim look on his face, Bierce looked at the group surrounding Thomas, pointed, and raised his voice. "It's him Clay. Can't prove it, but it's him."

Clay turned slowly and stared at the group of high-ranking officers. Their attention had been drawn by Bierce's loud, unpleasant voice, and all were now looking at the two majors. The cold look of implacable hatred on Clay's face was not forced. He was reasonably certain that one of those surrounding Thomas was a traitor and a murderer. He turned back to face Bierce and said in a voice carefully modulated to carry to the puzzled officers "Do not concern yourself. I will obtain the proof, and put an end to him." Then lowering his voice to where only Bierce could hear he added "That should assure he will not have an accomplice try to murder you in the North, and concentrates on me."

In a similarly low voice, Bierce responded. "That is what concerns me. I'll be safe in the North while someone plots your death. You may be overestimating your ability to protect yourself. Perhaps I should stay after all . . ."

"Nonsense!" hissed Clay. "You have already done more than enough. Leave the rest to Lot and myself, and concentrate on restoring your health." Suddenly, Clay fiercely gripped Bierce's hand; the young officer grimaced with pain. "I know you will never entirely escape what was done to you," whispered Clay intently. "Nevertheless, you are a strong man and will survive. You have a life to live, and things to accomplish. Do not sacrifice that to the horrors of the past." Clay then stepped back, and formally saluted.

"Watch you back," Bierce said softly, staring uneasily at this man who could see into his soul. Then he waved to Lot and Duval and said in a louder voice, "Lieutenant, Miss, farewell and good luck." Then with a meaningful last glance at Duval, he turned and shuffled into the passenger car.

Clay turned, and saw George Thomas approaching him with his slow, measured gate, product of an injured back that had never properly healed. Only Clay was close enough to notice how the general grimly set his jaw as he grabbed the car's handrail, or to hear the slight groan as he pulled himself up onto the rear platform. He slowly turned, and fixed his stern gaze on Clay. "You seem embarked on a dangerous course of some sort," he said in his soft Virginia drawl. "Be cautious, the army cannot spare you just yet." He then turned and entered the car, leaving Clay too astonished to salute.

Lot walked up. "What did General Thomas say?"

Clay waited of a long moment before replying. "He knows we

are setting a trap of some sort for some one. I wonder if it is as obvious to the traitor?"

"You can't afford to assume otherwise." Lot looked over to the knot of officers around Sherman. All but Davis saluted and strode off to rejoin their waiting aides and horses. Davis and Sherman remained locked in some serious conversation. Clay and Lot walked over, and then waited at a respectful distance. Suddenly Sherman clapped Davis on the shoulder and said "Then get to it, Jeff." The emaciated general formally saluted his commander, cast a sour look at the two young officers, and strode off to join his own aides. Sherman stared moodily after him for a moment. Then he abruptly turned and addressed Clay and Lot.

"Well, it's done. You're lives may not be worth spit. I hope for your sake one of these men is not a traitor. Hope for the country's sake, as a matter of fact."

"The risk must be taken," replied Clay. "May I ask what you just told General Davis?"

The train gave a shrill whistle, and began its long journey north. "Hell, you can see in just a moment. I told Davis to have some of his boys start to tear up the railroad as soon as that train clears the depot. He'll have a couple of his regiments following the line north until they run into Forrest's boys. Ah, watch."

In the distance Clay and Lot could see Davis on horseback, giving a brisk order to a young officer who stood in front of scores of soldiers, most of whom carried crowbars and axes. The young officer saluted smartly, turned, and gestured to his men. With the train hardly out of sight, they attacked the rail line. Faster than seemed possible the lengths of metal were pried up and the wooden crossties piled into a heap and ignited. In the dry, hot weather it took barely a minute for the pile of wood to become a bonfire. Pairs of sweating soldiers threw lengths of metal rail on the growing fire. In less than five minutes the middles of the rails began to glow dull red. Pairs of soldiers, their hands protected by heavy gauntlets, picked up the rails by their relatively cool ends and carried them hurriedly to a nearby telegraph pole. Placing the glowing middle against the pole, they pulled mightily until the softened metal began to give, and kept pulling until the rail was twisted into a hairpin shape. They repeated the process while some of their comrades moved down the line, tearing up more track and building more bonfires for the gleaming rails. Clay nodded his head approvingly.

"Very efficient," he said, almost as if speaking to himself. "The rails will cool into a shape useless for repairing the line, while the ties are consumed by the act of mutilating the rails."

"Davis is sending parties of his boys up the line, so different sections of the road can be simultaneously destroyed," answered Sherman. "He has parties already working on the branch lines; nothing is going to move by rail in Georgia for the rest of the war."

"Don't the soldiers complain about the hot, hard work in this climate?" asked Lot.

Sherman favored the young officer with one of his grim smiles. "Davis tells me they are enthusiastic. They see the end of the war coming, and don't mind working hard to make it come faster. Matter of fact, he tells me some of his boys have come up with a nickname for the twisted rails. They call them 'Sherman neckties.'" The general chuckled. "I love the boys in this army. There isn't anything they will not do for me."

Suddenly, Sherman sobered. "Including burning the heart of Georgia." He began to walk away from Clay and Lot, as if he had forgotten their presence. "They will help me make Georgia howl," he muttered, leaving the two friends to look uneasily at each other.

Teresa Duval expertly worked the reins of the medical supply wagon, avoiding another one of the seemingly endless potholes in the dusty road. She spared a glance backwards, where a cloud of dark smoke on the horizon marked the spot where Atlanta burned. She smiled, and turned her attention back to the road. '*Served the Limey-loving bastards right*,' she thought.

She glanced to her left and right, and noted with satisfaction the smaller pillars of smoke that dotted the horizon. Sherman had spread his army out in a column sixty miles wide, with orders to remove for the use of the army any food or material of military use from any farm and plantation they encountered, and to burn any that they could not carry away. Officers in charge of the foraging parties had been given strict orders to not burn houses or abuse the civilians themselves. However, Duval knew that order would be more honored in the breach. Every man jack in Sherman's army had lost friends, sometimes relatives, to Rebel fire, and they were anxious to inflict pain with interest on the South. This did not bother Duval, she had seen Ireland during the Famine.

Duval noticed two horsemen weaving through the knots of marching soldiers in front of her, and recognized them as Clay and Lot. Since the very beginning of the march they had made a habit of riding off on their own. Duval knew that Clay was tempting the traitor to make an attempt on his life by ranging far away from the main columns, even though his plan had never been explained to her in so many words. The risks he was running created strange, unfamiliar feelings in her breast. She utterly denied to herself that those feelings were akin to dread or panic, and maintained a surface appearance of doe-eyed placidity.

As he pulled up alongside her wagon, Lot nodded a greeting and said, "Still on the move, Miss Duval? I would have expected you to set up camp by this late in the afternoon, to tend to incoming casualties."

"No need for that, Lieutenant," she responded. "The Lord has blessed us with few casualties so far, which are easily handled by the regimental surgeons. It is best that I stay on the road until dusk, so that the reserve supplies are as close to the head of the army as possible." She hesitated, and then asked "Cannot you persuade the Major to take a larger escort on his . . . scouting? He is more likely to listen to you than to me."

Lot grimaced. "I truly wished I could. It is all I can do to persuade him to take me along."

Clay guided his horse up to join the slowly moving wagon. Although it did not seem possible for him to have been close enough to overhear the exchange between Lot and Duval, he obviously had. "Taking an escort would defeat the purpose, Miss Duval. The traitor is obviously careful, and will attack only when he feels I am vulnerable. The best course is to establish a pattern of riding about, apparently concerned with other matters. In fact, I have just about concluded that the Lieutenant's presence may be deterring him. Jeremiah, I may have to forego the pleasure of your company the next few afternoons."

"I have told you before, I will not permit you to go alone," replied Lot in a voice that for him was unusually harsh. "We are in this together, Alphonso."

Clay looked speculatively at his cousin and friend. "Suppose that I were to order you to stay behind?"

"Then you would simply have to court-martial me for insubordination and disobedience in the face of the enemy. I doubt you would want that kind of disgrace to come upon a Clay, even one who does not actually bear the Clay name." He paused, and then added "Besides, would you truly expect a Clay to behave otherwise?"

A ghost of a smile flickered across the major's face. "No, I expect not."

"May I be so bold as to ask what you intend for tomorrow?" said Duval with apparent indifference, not taking her eyes from the road.

"I understand that General Davis' main body is guarding the left flank of the march," replied Clay reflectively. "Perhaps the lieutenant and I will take a ride over, to inspect his operations on behalf of General Sherman."

"You suspect Davis is the murdering traitor," Duval replied evenly.

"I never so much as implied anything of the sort," said Clay.

Duval suddenly looked directly at Clay. She was no longer doe-eyed; her glance showed anger, impatience—and something else. "I may be many things, Major Clay, but a fool is not among them," she said in a low voice. "Besides, everyone knows how he killed General Nelson up in Kentucky, and did not dance on air for it. Why could he not kill another Union General?" 'Or a major,' she thought but did not say.

Clay barked an unpleasant laugh. "Why indeed not, Miss Duval? I have already had one of Sherman's couriers take a message to the good General Davis, informing him that I will be at his head-quarters tomorrow, but not informing him as to why. If he is the traitor, he may feel compelled to take some hasty action, especially since he knows the lieutenant and I will be riding by ourselves across land where civil order no longer exists, and deserters from both sides roam almost at will. He would be correct in thinking it would be possible for almost any kind of unfortunate incident to occur to two lone riders. Of course, our protection will be that we will be alert for a more specific threat than the occasional looter or bushwhacker."

As the small party had been speaking, they had approached a farmhouse and barn situated close to the road. The foragers had already been there. Although the house was intact, the barn was furiously burning, while a family stood nearby with devastated looks on their faces. In the yard the bodies of several large hogs lay on an improvised bonfire; apparently the foraging party had not been able to carry away all of the livestock, and had killed and set afire what they could not take. The smell of burning pork made Duval's mouth water, although she did not feel particularly hungry.

"Miss Duval, we should camp for the night in the yard of this farmhouse," said Clay abruptly. "There is a well and outhouse available to us, which we are unlikely to find as easily in the light left to us. Besides, no other Union units have taken claim of this site, yet. Crowding will not be an issue."

As Clay's party turned into the yard, the old farmer shot a murderous glance at them, then hustled his family into the farmhouse without saying a word. Duval looked at the house thoughtfully as the door slammed shut, then said to Clay "It would be much more comfortable to rest in clean beds with a roof over our heads. Why don't you evict those traitors, and let us have a bit of luxury tonight?"

Clay looked at the burning barn, then at the mound of slaughtered livestock. He was silent for a moment before replying "There are children in that family; one a girl of no more than eight, I believe. It will be a hard winter for them. Let them keep what comfort they can. You can make do in the wagon, while the lieutenant and I can rest comfortably enough on our blankets."

Duval hid her anger at Clay. Whenever she began to think that he understood how the world worked, that it belonged to those with the strength and belly to take whatever they wanted, Clay would show some contemptible speck of "honor". She almost spat at the mere thought of that hypocritical English notion. She held her rage in check, and sweetly said "Let us then set up under that oak tree at the far side of the yard."

The sleeping Duval shifted uncomfortably in the narrow space she had made in the crowded bed of the wagon. Normally, Duval slept

soundly throughout the night no matter how rough the circumstances, seldom having dreams—at least any that she cared to
remember. But the annoying galloping of the occasional frantic
army courier just fifty yards from where she slept, combined with
her discomfort, gave her a rare restless night. She dreamed, and
dreamed of the past, combining memories with fantasies in a
way she could have disentangled only with difficulty when she
woke—if she had ever remembered more than snatches of her
dreams. She found it strange that she occasionally had dreams
of her past before the age of twelve, a past she seemed curiously
unable to recall when awake.

In one particularly vivid dream sequence, she was a twelve-
year old, listening to a furious argument between her mother
and father; in her dream, she did not think it odd that she could
see neither of their faces. She seemed to recall that the argument
had taken place many times before. Her mother was angry at her
father for "meddlin' in politics and not mindin' where the next
meal will come from," while her father muttered something about
"fey woman, who listens to the sprites and fairies," and that he
should have known no good would come from marrying a witch
such as her. The voices grew louder, the insults viler. In her dream,
the young Duval tired of it and went out into the dark night; her
departure unremarked by her battling parents.

She picked her way across the farmyard and into the fields
beyond, scanning the ground in the dim light of the gibbous moon
for something, anything to put in her stomach. In a loose patch
of earth she spotted a potato and scooped it up eagerly, hoping
that it was something edible that had been missed by her parents.
Disappointedly, the root felt mushy in her hand, and even in the
dim light she could see the black corruption that blighted the
tuber; the foul disease that was starving the Irish while the English
landlords and their minions partied in Dublin and Belfast, or

faraway London. She briefly thought of trying to choke it down; but remembering the nausea that a previous such experiment had generated, she cast the corrupt object aside, wiping her hand clean on her dress of the foulness. She knew she was luckier than many Irish. Her father owned his land, and had some livestock husbanded to feed his family while tens of thousands starved to death in the countryside. But now that the last of the animals were gone, Duval knew that her father would have to dip into his small horde of gold to buy food to keep them all alive.

In her dream, she strolled slowly across her father's fields, trying to think of things other than the gnawing hunger in her belly. Like how she agreed with her mother that Father was foolishly wasting his time in political agitation; time that could be better spent in helping his family to survive. Her father would always angrily rail against the British, saying that all of Ireland's problems came from the absentee English landlords and their cruel land agents who were squeezing the life out of the people, and that Ireland would never be happy and prosperous until it was free of the English yoke. Silently Duval agreed with her mother, who thought it was foolish to be concerned with the rabble, English or Irish; the rabble who had burned her grandmother alive for being a witch were undeserving of her father's concern, reflected Duval in her dream.

She had crossed the field and entered a small copse of trees. Suddenly feeling the weakness of hunger, she decided to sit with her back to one of the trees and rest. Past experience had shown the argument between her parents would continue for some time, unpleasantly loud, and she saw no reason to return home until they had exhausted themselves. In her dream, she felt her eyelids begin to get heavy, when suddenly she became alert at a distant sound.

The sound seemed a combination of a wail and a scream, coming from far off in the distance. Although the uncanny sound seemed to be coming closer and louder, Duval felt no fear, only an avid curiosity; she could not imagine what could emit such an unearthly noise. Then she caught a glimpse of movement in the part of the field she could see between the trees. The moonlight was strong enough to show a figure gliding across the field toward her, a figure seemingly surrounded by fluttering rags of cloth or linen. The eerie wail clearly came from the figure, which was making straight for Duval, who was puzzled as to how it could see her in the deep shadows of the copse. '*This must be the dread being of which her mother had muttered such frightening things,*' thought Duval, '*this must be the herald of death, the banshee.*'

In her dream, she thought in a detached way that she should run, or at least cower in fear at the approach of the dread apparition. In the way of dreams, she felt only curiosity at the sight of the approaching creature. With a sudden leap forward, the figure was before her, howling so loudly it should have deafened Duval, but did not. Duval simply stared curiously up at the banshee's face, observing a pale, unearthly beauty. Somehow, in the dim moonlight, she could see that the creature's eyes were a pale blue. The screaming suddenly diminished to a low moan, almost a whisper; the figure bent forward and took Duval's chin in its long-fingered hand. The young girl and the ageless spirit looked steadily into each other's eyes for what seemed to Duval to be an eternity. Duval still felt no fear, only puzzlement at the look of sad pity on the unearthly countenance. Then in the blink of an eye, the banshee was gone; the faint echo of a wail rapidly fading to nothingness.

As if a spell had been broken, Duval leapt to her feet and began running toward her home. She knew that the banshee was the herald of death; all country folk knew that. If it had not come for her, then it must have come for Mother or Father, she thought in her dream. She feared that the spirit had come as a prophecy of death to one or both of them. In the dream she remembered being frightened for them, which struck her as strange, being that in her waking life she felt no fear for anyone, not even herself.

As she ran she could see her home, now wreathed in flames; a small group of people in the front yard. She could not imagine who had come to help. Most of their neighbors had starved or fled the area in search of food, and the ones who were left hated and feared her mother, believing her to be a witch. It was only when she was almost upon the small knot of figures in front of the burning house that she saw that three wore the red tunics of the militia, and skidded to a halt. In her dream, she felt that she should have turned and run, but she simply could not. She stared at the figure of her father, hanging from a branch of the shade tree in the yard. She could not decide what was more shocking, his head tilting at an impossible angle or the fact that it was his own belt twisted around his neck. She turned to see her mother on the ground with a beefy, grunting soldier on top of her; his hands pinning her arms to the ground while his torso thrust furiously in a parody of the act of love. In her dream she felt she should be doing something, anything, but could not; all she could do was watch, her eyes meeting her mother's agonized gaze.

Duval suddenly felt a rough hand on her shoulder, and was spun around to face a slovenly soldier with the stripes of a corporal on his tunic. "Well, well, Colleen, we were a wonderin' where you be. The Lord Lieutenant of the county said we were to round up all the troublemakers, including their pups. The few of your neighbors hereabouts said your da had a daughter, and grieved we would be to do an incomplete job. And here you be presentin' yourself to us."

Duval tried to ignore the continuing sounds of her mother's rape. "The Lord Lieutenant told you to kill Father and . . . Mother?"

"Not in so many words, Colleen, not in so many words. But I

ask you now, what would be the point of bringing in traitors and their whelp to a nice jail and hot meals, when there ain't enough food for the loyal subjects of the Queen. Might as well sport with the woman as well. I'll tell you something about your ma. Your neighbors've been informing on your folks, mainly because of your ma. Probably didn't care about your da's treason, being Irish and all, but they hated her, and that's a fact. Said she was some sort of witch, in league with old Nick. Said all kinds of bad happened to those who crossed her, or her man. Yes, it was easy as anything to find out that your folks . . ."

The man on top of Duval's mother suddenly howled. "The bitch bit me!" he exclaimed with hurt surprise, holding a hand to his face, blood seeping from between his fingers. The third soldier advanced to help his friend, who was hindered by his loose trousers. However, before he could reach the man, Duval's mother leaped to her feet and snatched the bayonet from the scabbard attached to the rapists' dangling belt. The man yelped with fear, but, to the shock of all, she reversed the blade and rammed it into her belly with such force that the point protruded from her back. She turned her eyes toward her daughter and whispered "Remember." Then her eyes glazed and she fell, dead before she struck the ground.

The corporal sighed with regret, "Ah, that is a shame. And before I had my chance." He turned his eyes toward the young girl, noticing her figure was surprisingly full for a girl of twelve. He grinned wolfishly. "Well, if I can't have the ewe, the lamb will have to do. There's good meat on you, even if you look a wee bit starved. Still Colleen, there is an easy way for a good-looking lass like you to earn a spud."

"I suppose there is, corporal," she replied, and without ado began shrugging off her dress. All three soldiers, even the wounded man who had attacked her mother, gazed with admiration and lust at the firm, supple body that was quickly revealed. They did not look at the eyes, which were coldly darting about, calculating distances and angles. "I want you first," she said to the corporal in an emotionless voice, "but I don't want them watching. I would like a little privacy."

"Certainly," the slovenly excuse for a soldier said cheerfully. He turned his attention to his two companions. "Take a break, boys. I'm taking Colleen around back, where we tied the horses." He took the arm of the now-naked girl and roughly led her around the still-burning house to where three tired nags nickered uneasily. When they neared the horses, the corporal suddenly seized her and kissed her roughly.

In her dream Duval did not resist, but said "Wait. I want to look good for this. Do you have some gear I can use? You know, a mirror, comb—that sort of thing?"

Breathing heavily, the corporal looked confused for a moment, then his face brightened. As Duval had hoped, he said, "Sure, and I've got a mirror in me shaving kit." He went to one of the horses, and removed a small leather satchel from the saddle-bag. He started to open the bag, but Duval interrupted him. "Let me, corporal. You should start undressing yourself. I want this to be a special experience for you."

Smiling from ear to ear, the man replied "Colleen, it is a true pleasure to meet a lass who takes such care in her work." He tossed the small bag to Duval, then clumsily sat down to start removing his boots. He had just succeeded in removing the second one when a small but surprisingly strong hand grabbed him by the hair and jerked his head backwards. He started to yelp with surprise, but before he could shout, a cold piece of steel slashed across his throat, severing his windpipe. He collapsed flat to the ground, eyes bulging with surprise and dawning horror, and made futile attempts to stem the spurting blood with his hands while only a bubbling gurgle escaped his mouth. As he began to lose consciousness, he saw the beautiful young woman step into his field of vision, naked except where spurts of arterial blood had splashed her body, casually holding his own razor in her right hand. His last thought was how strange it was that a girl covered in blood could smile so sweetly.

Duval spent only a moment staring down on the dead man with satisfaction. Then she turned and went to the horse that had belonged to the corporal, where she had already noticed two large horse-pistols in saddle-holsters. She remove the pair of guns, and checked to confirm percussion caps were in place on each; glad that her father had spent so much time teaching his only child about firearms. Then holding a pistol in each hand, she moved her arms behind her, like she was hiding a surprise gift from a child. With no hesitation she walked quickly around the side of the burning house and towards the remaining two soldiers.

One soldier was still clumsily trying to bandage up the wound in the face of her mother's rapist, who was seated on the edge of a water-trough; neither noticed Duval until she was only a dozen paces away. The unwounded soldier caught a glimpse of her and began to straighten up. He frowned and said "Where the hell is . . ." then stopped as he saw how the girl was splattered with blood. Surprise paralyzed him for just a moment, but that moment was enough for Duval to cover the remaining distance, take her left arm from behind her back, and fire the large pistol into the center of his chest. The .54 caliber bullet knocked him backward several feet, killing him instantly. The rapist howled and scrabbled for his musket which lay beside him, but Duval calmly brought the gun in her right hand from behind her back and fired it into the center of his face, turning his head into a horror of broken bone and gore.

Duval dreamt that she stood looking at the bodies of the soldiers for some time, a strange, pleasurable sensation deep in her belly; a sensation she had never felt before, but which was more enjoyable than anything else she had ever experienced. Then, letting both pistols fall to the ground she strode to the well and drew up a bucket of cold, fresh water. As she sluiced the gore from her naked body, she gasped with pleasure, and began to plan her future—a future in which Ireland would play no role. She would need to bury her parents, and that would take several hours; but the soldiers' bodies could be left for the crows. She would take their horses and arms, and sell them in Cork; that should raise enough money to buy her passage to America, a land that loved the English as little as she. As she dried herself and began to slip her dress back on, she reflected that there would be a task to perform before she took the road to Cork. Only one neighbor was left close to her father's farm; only one family who could have peached to the English, a family that was always casting evil eyes at Duval's mother. She decided she would pay a short visit to that family, to settle accounts on behalf of her parents. She was sure there would be no interference; the famine had largely depopulated the country hereabouts.

Then a frown flitted across her face. Food was the problem. What little her parents had perished in the fire, and the traitorous neighbors were likely to have little of their own. How could she survive in the week or more it would take to reach Cork? She briefly considered butchering one of the horses, but quickly discarded the idea; she knew what passage to New York would cost, and would need to sell all the nags to have a chance of meeting that cost. Then she looked down at the bodies of the two soldiers that she had shot. Prime, healthy specimens, she decided. Well developed thighs and upper arms; those would be the best cuts. Cooked and salted, there would be more than enough for a week. She walked over to where she had dropped the corporal's straight razor, picked it up and carefully inspected it, seeing the mark of

Wilkinson, the maker of swords and the most expensive razors. She looked at it carefully, watching how the light from the burning farmhouse gleamed off its high-quality steel. '*A very fine, very expensive blade,*' she thought. She realized this razor would mean a great deal to her in the future. She turned toward the bodies and began to advance . . .

"Miss Duval, Miss Duval," came the cultured voice of Alphonso Clay.

Teresa Duval's eyes flew open, and she saw Clay's head framed by the early-morning sunlight streaming in through the entrance to the wagon.

"My apologies for awakening you, Miss Duval. However, I know how seriously you take your duties, and would not wish you to oversleep." Clay hesitated ever so slightly, then added, "In any event, it appeared that your slumbers were . . . disturbed, and that it might be doing you a favor to awaken you. Lieutenant Lot has obtained some prime bacon, and is frying it for our breakfast. You are welcome to join us, if you like."

She was suddenly aware of the aroma of frying pork. Her mouth began to water. It was not that she was that hungry; it was rather that the smell reminded her something. Something she could not quite remember, but she had the feeling she had enjoyed that something immensely. She tried to remember, perhaps something in her dream. However, the dream was already fading from her consciousness, leaving only the vaguest of impressions.

"Yes, Major, I believe I will accept your offer." A smile of anticipation on her face, Duval allowed Clay to offer her a hand down from the wagon. As she cheerfully advanced toward Lot and the waiting breakfast at the campfire, Clay looked at the expression on her face, and frowned slightly.

* * *

It took until that afternoon for Clay and Lot to catch up with General Davis; the saturnine commander was definitely not a headquarters general, and was constantly on the move about his column. They finally located him on the southern bank of a deep creek, shouting curses from horseback as his men manhandled three-inch cannon across a pontoon bridge. On the far bank of the bridge were a few score soldiers, along with a heart-rending sight: nearly a thousand blacks of both sexes and all ages, some with bundles of pitiful belongings. Slaves who had fled their bondage to follow an uncertain future behind the Federal army. Clay and Lot cantered up to Davis and saluted. The general ignored the salutes, and continued his conversation with a horseman to his right; Clay recognized the rider as Colonel Kitching.

"Colonel, get those God damn guns of yours off that bridge!" growled Davis. "My rear guard still has to come across, and I expect the God damn Reb cavalry to show up at any moment."

Kitching seemed to take no offense at the general's curses. "My boys are moving as fast as they can. You can see for yourself there are only three more cannon to bring across. Then the rear guard can come across, and we can break up the bridge. It may not look like much, but that stream's too deep for cavalry to ford; we'll be secure enough then."

"Pardon my interruption," said Clay smoothly. "However, General Sherman has charged me with inspecting the left flank, and reporting to him on several matters. He is especially interested in your precautions against attack by Confederate cavalry. Normally mounted soldiers are not much of a threat to infantry; but spread out as the troops are, occupied with the destruction of property with military value, he is somewhat uneasy."

Davis turned his dead eyes on Clay; the pallor of his face was interrupted by two bright spots of color on his cheeks. "Don't tell me my business, you arrogant little bastard! You think I don't know the risk? Bad enough with Joe Wheeler out there; I just thank God Hood took Forrest with him to the west. Why do you think I'm so God damn anxious to get those cannon off the bridge, and the rear guard across?" Davis took a deep breath, and turned his attention back to Kitching. "Colonel, I may have spoken harshly to you just now. If so, you have my apology. You are a fine officer, always doing more than required, even handling such sensitive things as prisoner exchanges . . ."

The sound of a flurry of shots from the opposite bank interrupted Davis. The escaped slaves began to scream in fear; all turned to look across the stream and saw several hundred horsemen galloping over a small hill, aiming straight for the bridge. The last of the cannon had just finished crossing, and the lone regiment on the far bank acting as rear guard began to crown onto the shaky pontoon structure. The colonel in charge of the regiment apparently had lost control, as the men were obviously panicked. Only one lone platoon at the very rear even bothered to fire a few wild shots at the approaching horsemen before themselves bolting for the crush at the bridge.

Davis looked about him and spat an obscenity; there were only a couple of under strength regiments within immediate call. Still, the general did not hesitate; he put the spurs to his mount and began galloping among the milling soldiers, ordering their officers to shake their men into skirmish lines and to fire across the river at the horsemen, being careful not to hit their comrades still squeezing across the bridge. A small, thin young man at the front of the horsemen held up his hand, and the galloping cavalry skidded to an almost comical stop; the young commander knew his men's pistols and carbines were no match for the Union muskets being fired from the far bank. The last of Davis' men were now on the bridge, with the black refugees beginning to crowd on it. Davis stared at the far bank, and snarled; the grey horsemen had dismounted and were carefully dodging from piece of cover to piece of cover, denying the Union soldiers easy shots. Clay and Lot saw what Davis saw; the Rebels would soon be so close that there short-range weapons would be effective against the Union Springfields. At that point, their superior numbers would allow them to overwhelm the defenders and capture the short pontoon bridge. Once that happened, Wheeler and his cavalry could cause considerable havoc in the unprepared rear areas of Sherman's left flank. Suddenly, Davis spurred his horse toward the bridge, followed closely by Colonel Kitching. Clay and Lot followed, heading straight for the action, curiosity overcoming discretion.

"Cut the Goddamn bridge loose!" shouted Davis in a voice that seemed far too loud to come from such a sickly frame.

"Sir, you cannot do that!" exclaimed an appalled Kitching.

Davis turned to the artilleryman, murder in his eyes. "Our boys are across! We got to cut it loose before Wheeler can take it!"

Kitching would not give ground. "There are still a thousand contrabands across the river! You know what Reb cavalry will do to runaways!"

"I don't give a Goddamn for the niggers!" Davis turned his attention to an artillery lieutenant who stood to the side of the stream of refugees, only a few more bluecoats left before the stream of terrified blacks would begin to reach the near shore and safety. "Lieutenant! Sever the ropes holding the bridge. Now!

"Disregard that order, Lieutenant!" screamed Kitching. "The General has no right to issue such an inhuman command!"

In a lower, dangerously controlled voice, Davis said "So, you would defy me in the face of the enemy," and began to move his hand toward his holster.

Without preamble Clay vaulted off his horse and became a blur of motion, arrowing straight toward the pontoon bridge. In the seconds it took him to reach the bridge, his custom German saber had appeared in his hand as if by magic. With two swift strokes the ropes securing the right side to wooden pilings were severed. Then, in an acrobatic feat that should not have been possible, he made a running start toward one of the pilings, leapt up and with his right foot launched himself even higher, sailing with apparent grace over the last of the soldiers struggling onto the shore, landing hard just beyond the left side of the bridge. Lot cried out, thinking Clay must have injured himself; but he was wrong. Clay sprang to his feet, sword still in hand; with a blur of motion, the two ropes securing the left side of the bridge to the bank were severed. The swift current began to carry the detached end of the pontoon bridge downstream; the unbalanced strain caused the ropes on the far bank to break loose from their moorings, and the bridge began to accelerate downstream, carrying more than a score of frightened black refugees. Two suddenly cried out, clutching bloody wounds; the Confederate cavalrymen were taking potshots at the unarmed, helpless runaways.

The mass of escaped slaves remaining on the far bank were in a frenzy of panic as Southern horseman dashed at them. Some dropped to their knees and pled for mercy; their pleas were rapidly cut short by flashing sabers. Union soldiers held their fire for fear of hitting the refugees, watching the massacre with impotent rage. Meanwhile, hundreds of panicked blacks plunged into the stream attempting to swim across. Many were poor swimmers, or could not swim at all, and the winter rains had swollen the stream rendering its current fast and treacherous. Many of the stronger made it to the far shore, where willing hands dragged them from the water; but many more disappeared beneath the surface or were swept downstream where a rapids filled with jagged rocks awaited them.

Lot had stood as frozen as a statue, utterly shocked by his friend's actions. Then rage replaced astonishment. He ran to where Clay stood on the bank, watching the appalling chaos with apparent detachment. Lot seized him by the shoulder and spun him so they were face-to-face. "Why, Alphonso, why? Look at them! God damn you, look at them! How could you condemn those Christian souls . . ." Lot's voice choked up; letting go of Clay's shoulder, he waded into the shallow water to help the survivors who had reached the shore, despite the patter of Confederate bullets that kicked up little geysers around them. Suddenly, the roar of several cannons firing at once rang out; Kitching had turned his guns around, and was firing at the Confederate cavalry. Having no effective cover or means of replying to artillery, the horsemen sullenly retired. Suddenly, their was silence, save for the moaning of wounded survivors and the muttered curses of soldiers going to their aid, chief of which was Lieutenant Jeremiah Lot.

Clay stood unmoving, simply observing the chaos and his friend's humanitarian efforts. Then, with an absolutely blank expression on his face he turned and walked away from the riverbank, his departure noticed only by General Davis, who frowned as he looked at Clay's retreating figure.

The column was on the march, now with the black survivors of the river crossing firmly embedded within it instead of trailing behind. General Davis noticed this as he road along the line of march with his staff, looking for stragglers or other signs of indiscipline. On several occasions he considered barking an order to eject the contrabands from the column, so it could march with greater ease. However, on each occasion he saw a number of soldiers glance darkly at him, then avert their eyes sullenly. Davis was a competent general, and knew better than to push his men without a pressing cause.

He also noticed that Clay and Lot no longer rode together. Once Clay trotted his horse up to that of the lieutenant; who then put the spurs to his own mount. Davis mulled several things over in the dark recesses of his mind, then reached an unwilling decision. At the next rest stop, he told his aides that he would not be needing their services for a quarter of an hour, and that they should relax as best they may. He rode over to where Lot had dismounted in order to help some soldiers distribute army crackers and water to a group of exhausted and demoralized refugees. He slid off his horse and wrapped the reigns around the branch of a convenient tree, holding himself erect with some effort. Then he stiffly approached the group; the refugees seemed to collectively cringe, while the soldiers saluted, including Lot, whose expression gave the lie to the respect implied by the salute. Davis touched his hat in return, then said "Lieutenant, I need to talk to you in private. You will come with me." Davis turned and headed toward a nearby meadow; reluctantly, Lot followed. When they were out of earshot of the nearest soldiers he suddenly stopped, placed his arms behind his back, and seemed to stare intently at the far horizon. Lot stopped beside him. Without looking at the lieutenant, Davis began to speak.

"You're related to Clay, aren't you? Don't try and deny it; your both of the same height and build, and are always together. Served a lot of years in the South, and know how it works with the plantation owners and their ... property." He waited for some denial from Lot; hearing none, Davis sighed and began to speak again. "Never talked about such things with a nig ... a black man before; but the good of the service requires me to talk to you now. You think I was wrong to cut the bridge loose, don't you?"

In a strained voice Lot asked "Does the General require an answer?"

Davis chuckled grimly. "No, I guess not. Tell me Lieutenant, what do you think would have happened if I hadn't given that order?" Without waiting for an answer Davis suddenly turned to face Lot directly. "God damn you, I'll tell you! Wheeler and his butchers would have sabered their way across, overwhelmed the small rear guard, and slaughtered every last one of your Goddamn precious contrabands, besides wreaking havoc in the army's rear areas and forcing Sherman to turn around and deal with him. As it is, we saved Sherman from a major problem; and about half of the contrabands got across one way or the other. Half is better than none. Anyway, Clay saw all that, saw it in an instant, while you and Kitching did not. He acted for the greater good, and will carry a burden of guilt for the rest of his life; while you and Kitching would have kept your consciences clear, at the cost of even more lives."

Davis turned to face the horizon again. Without looking at Lot, he continued to speak. "As I said, spent a lot of time down South before the war, got to know you Southerns pretty damn well. Clay is like all the Southern gentlemen I ever ran across, only more so. I think he might die rather than show weakness, even to—maybe especially to—those he feels closest to. I think he feels just as sorrowful for the contrabands who were lost as you do; maybe more so, as his actions condemned them. He has to live with that guilt. I know about that, too. I was quick to anger, but didn't think things through. Didn't matter that there was no trial . . ." Davis trailed off, while Lot looked at him curiously, realizing the general was alluding to the murder of General Nelson.

"Anyway . . . kin is kin, no matter what side of the blanket it's on. You can do as you like; but if I were you, I'd take Clay aside private-like, and let him know he did right in your eyes. Wouldn't mean anything from me; hates my guts. Guess it would mean a lot from you." Davis was silent for a long moment, his eyes fixed on the horizon, and then still not looking at Lot said "Well, that's it . . . Lieutenant. Git."

A thoughtful Lot saluted formally, turned, and headed back to the column. Davis remained staring at the horizon for a very long time.

Lot caught up with Clay as the latter rode silently beside Duval's medical wagon. Lot brought his own mount up beside Clay and matched the plodding pace that was being set. Clay neither looked at nor spoke to Lot; his utterly blank expression remained focused on the road ahead. For some minutes the two friends rode mutely side-by-side, subject to an occasional curious glance from Duval. Finally Lot broke the silence. "Strange man, General Davis. He felt you did right at the bridge, but seems to think I should be the one to tell you so."

Clay said nothing.

Lot took a deep breath. "Alphonso, I owe you the deepest apology. I was carried away by the horror and tragedy of the moment, and did not stop to consider that you had done the best for all concerned."

"Did I?" asked Clay softly, without looking at Lot. "And to whom should I make my apologies? The dead refugees collectively? Perhaps the mother I saw go under for the final time with her child? Maybe the old man who used his last strength to shove a child to the shore before the current carried him away to die? Tell me Jeremiah, which of them would be the appropriate recipient of my regrets?"

"You did what needed to be done, Alphonso," replied Lot gently. "More innocents would have died without your actions; I can see that now. You did not hesitate because you were stronger than me, better than me."

An explosive, ugly laugh erupted from Clay's throat. "You believe that? Let me tell you, I am not a god, and do not enjoy playing the role of one." He turned to look at Lot. "There is nothing for which to apologize, old friend. You were right to be disgusted with me. I am disgusted with myself, no matter how correct the action was when considered in cold blood. It was inhuman of me, unforgivable." He turned away, and murmured "I am not a god . . . no matter what Father would have liked."

Frowning at the enigmatic final comment, Lot said "Alphonso, you are not inhuman, merely strong. Strong enough to do what is necessary, no matter how grim it will be. Despite my initial . . . feelings, what you did at the bridge does not diminish the respect and love I feel for you, and always will."

Clay seemed about to say something when suddenly his head turned forward. "Cannon and musket fire. Heavy. It would appear that the Georgia militia is making a stand."

"I hear nothing," said Lot.

"It is very faint, but it is there."

"How can you be sure it is the Georgia militia?"

"The fire is heavy, too heavy for scouts to be the enemy. Hood is off to the west and north. The militia is the only organized force that it could be. Foolish, very foolish. They have at most four thousand. Even spread out like it is now, Sherman's army will grind them up." Clay glanced at Lot. "There should be a lot of confusion; most of those we suspect are in this wing of the army. Shall we give the traitor a target?"

Lot hesitated slightly before saying "No time like the present." With no further words the two friends put their spurs to their mounts. From her perch on the driver's seat of the medical wagon, Teresa Duval watched them arrow toward the sounds of the battle that only Alphonso Clay could hear. There was a strange constriction in her throat which she could not understand.

The battle was over by the time Clay and Lot reached the scene. Spotting Generals Slocum and Davis conversing under the shade of a tree, their mounted aides at a respectful distance, the friends galloped up, dismounted and saluted formally. Davis touched his hat absently and continued to murmur to his superior, who answered him in short, sharp sentences.

Clay stared speculatively at Major General Henry Slocum, commander of Sherman's left wing and Davis' immediate superior. He suddenly remembered that just two months ago Slocum had been a mere division commander, demoted from the Army of the Potomac in something like disgrace; in the command reshuffle after Hooker's resignation and McPherson's death, he had received two major promotions in rapid succession. Clay decided he could not ignore the fact that Slocum seemed to have benefited most from the acts of treason that had been committed.

Slocum noticed the new arrivals, and acknowledged their salutes. In a voice that held a strong New York accent, he said "Major Clay and Lieutenant . . . Lot, is it? I know you have a special brief from General Grant, but as you can tell, I am somewhat busy at the moment. Whatever you want, it will have to wait."

Clay ignored the dismissal. "With respects, sir, I will not take more than a moment of your valuable time. What has happened here?

Slocum's weary, pinched features showed his irritation. "A little matter of a battle, Major, if you must know. Idiot militia thought to actually hold us back. I don't care if it rains militia, it cannot hold against trained professionals. Once word spread of what my boys found yonder, nothing could hold the men back; they swept right over the Reb line in a matter of minutes."

Slocum had gestured to the large oak near which his aides clustered. Clay had already noticed the four blue-clad bodies hanging from its branches, and had dismissed them as deserters summarily punished. However, he looked closer, and now noticed the cardboard placards hung around their necks, on them the word "Looter" scrawled in black paint.

"Some of Wheeler's cavalry must have done that," said Slocum, answering Clay's unspoken question. "Took my men prisoner, and murdered them."

"Sir, why haven't you taken them down?" asked an appalled Lot.

"Wanted the boys to see what the Rebs have done. Wanted them to know they are not fighting 'gentlemen,' but mad-dog traitors. Put some vinegar in them; they went right over the top of the Rebs. Didn't take many prisoners." Slocum turned his attention to Davis. "Jeff, you and your staff better go appraise the situation on the battlefield, find out if any Reb units were able to withdraw intact, and if so in which direction. I've got to report to Sherman as soon as may be."

Davis saluted silently, mounted his gelding stiffly, and put the spurs to the horse; his aides trailing behind him like the tail of a kite. Clay said "Sir, I believe we will go forward ourselves and make our own appraisal. General Sherman may appreciate more than one point of view."

Slocum gave the two friends a sour look, and replied "Do as you wish, Major." Clay and Lot both saluted, salutes that Slocum deliberately did not return, and galloped off in the direction Davis had taken.

It only took a minute for them to reach the site of the battle. Both quickly drew up their mounts and surveyed the scene, wrinkling their noses at the acrid smell of gunpowder. Lot muttered "Lord have mercy on our souls;" Clay merely looked about dispassionately. There were only a scattering of blue-clad corpses on the field; the Union wounded having apparently already been removed. However, as far as the eye could see the ground was littered with silent forms clad in butternut. "This was a massacre," said Lot, a rising note of horror in his voice. The two friends rode into the middle of the field of death. Suddenly, Lot dismounted and began franticly darting about from body to body, turning some over to see more clearly their features. "God in heaven, Alphonso, these are children. Children!" Tears began to stream down the black lieutenant's cheeks.

Clay glanced about the battlefield, and confirmed Lot's discovery. There were a few adults mixed in with the boys; but those adults had clearly been in their sixties, or even seventies. Without emotion, Clay observed "The Confederate Conscription Act called up all fit men between the ages of sixteen and sixty; the militia now consists of those younger or older than those limiting ages."

Lot looked up at his friend with a stricken face. "Alphonso, we've slaughtered children and grandfathers here."

"It is tragic, but not the fault of the Union. Richmond put muskets in their hands and ordered them to kill our people. Our side could only respond in one way." He looked about the field, where isolated figures in blue walked or rode about the field. "This would have been a good place to make an attempt on my life, with the confusion attendant on the conclusion of a battle acting as cover; but I see no one acting suspiciously in our vicinity. Come, let us catch up with the column, taking our time, and keeping watch while pretending indifference."

Lot did not move, or even appear to hear. His gaze was fastened on the body of a boy of no more than ten lying face to the sky; the top of his head had been removed by a shell fragment, the eyes just below the red horror were filled with innocent amazement. Clay looked at his cousin and friend for a long moment, unaccustomed feelings flowing through his very strange heart. Gently he said, "Jeremiah, he is past the cares of the world, and is now in a better place, a place where evil men will not use his life for their own ends. Come, let us leave here."

Reluctantly, Lot turned and mounted his horse. Eyes straying to the dead child, he asked "Which way, Alphonso?"

Clay gestured to his right. "Down that county road over there. It heads in the general direction we need to go. More importantly, there appear to be a number of trees and buildings along it; good cover for an ambush. Let us go slowly, and hope the traitor takes advantage of the opportunity. Keep alert without being obvious."

As they began trotting down the road Lot said in a low voice "As I said before, this is madness, Alphonso. We may not spot an ambush until the shot that kills you is fired."

"It cannot be helped. The traitor is careful, and would avoid an obvious trap. If he kills me, then it is your duty to avenge me." Clay gestured at the Spencer carbine that was in the scabbard of Lot's saddle. "I know just how good a shot you are, especially with a rifle. Whether or not the traitor's shot kills me, I have little doubt you will put paid to his career of murder. No, my mind is made up; the risk is considerable, but it must be taken. Honor demands it."

"Honor demands that you die?" asked Lot incredulously.

"It did for all those children behind us," responded Clay somberly. "I will do no less."

The friends rode slowly along the road, appearing to be in no particular hurry. Clay seemed totally oblivious to the surroundings, while Lot's eyes darted frantically back and forth, trying to uncover a hint of an attempt on Clay's life. He suddenly noticed a number of figures ahead of them to the left, by a magnificent Grecian mansion set back some hundred yards from the road; transferring his reins to his left hand, he placed his right hand on the butt of the Spencer. The fact the figures were mainly blue-clad gave no comfort; their unknown enemy would be wearing the blue. As they slowly rode up, they could see that the crowd was composed of about twenty soldiers, mixed with a somewhat larger number of blacks. Clay and Lot reached the group, dismounted, and tied their horses to a convenient hitching-post. Clay asked in a loud voice "Who is in command here?"

An officer stepped forward, seemingly too young to shave but with ancient, weary eyes. "Lieutenant Pierce, 37th Indiana," the officer said, saluting.

"Major Clay and Lieutenant Lot, attached to General Sherman's headquarters," responded Clay, returning the salute. "What is transpiring here?"

"This is one of Wade Hampton's plantations," he replied, gesturing vaguely behind him. "My colonel ordered me to take some boys and make sure everything of value was removed."

"One of?" asked a surprised Lot.

The young officer shrugged. "My colonel tells me Hampton has lots of places like this."

"Hampton is the richest man in the South," replied Clay. "He is said to have more than fifty thousand acres among his various plantations, and own more than twentyt thousand slaves. A power unto himself. They say Richmond is afraid of him, and does whatever it can to keep him placated."

Pierce shrugged. "My colonel said something similar. We figured that it would be an easy thing. Seize the livestock, take the valuables, free the slaves, and raise a little hell to give Hampton something to remember us by. Well, it looks like all but one of the overseers skedaddled, taking the portable wealth and house slaves with them. They left only those field hands who were not fit to travel, and . . ." The young lieutenant gestured behind him, where about thirty blacks lay on the ground, being given food and water by hard-bitten soldiers who were acting surprisingly solicitous to the contrabands. Lot took his first good look at them, and gasped; Clay gave no overt sign of shock, a sudden motionlessness of his posture giving the only sign of his feelings.

The slaves, male and female, had all been mutilated and physically abused in various horrible ways. Some lay of necessity on their stomachs, their backs a mass of recent weeping wounds and ancient ugly scars inflicted by the whip. Others had horribly mutilated arms and legs, the wounds apparently inflicted by some kind of animal bites. A few wept uncontrollable as Federal soldiers clumsily tried to offer succor; many more law apathetically, accepting the food and water but otherwise acting as if they were unaware of their surroundings.

"We all heard up north tales of what was done to slaves, and in the campaign so far we had seen some that had been busted up by their owners," said the young officer in a low voice. "But nothing like this. Doesn't make sense. They're valuable property. Doesn't make sense to do something like this to something you own. My boys got the story out of those willing to talk; not all were. Seems Hampton and some of his friends like to really go at those who acted the slightest bit uppity, or who ran. Would sic bloodhounds on them, then flog the meat off their backs while they were still bleeding from the bites."

Clay turned to look at the young lieutenant. "Are these all?"

"All those still alive. Some didn't survive the dogs, or the floggings. Some of the contrabands say some were just taken away and never seen again. Probably were sold south, but these here figure they were killed somehow. Can't blame them, I suppose."

"You say one of the overseers was captured," said Clay in a soft voice. "I would like to see him."

Pierce gestured to the open door of the mansion. "A couple of my boys have him in there. I told them to persuade him to show us anything of value that might have been hidden." He glanced at the mutilated blacks, and a hard look came over his young face. "Told them not to be gentle. If you'll follow me, I'll take you to him."

The three officers mounted the imposing steps, turned right and found themselves in a room that had undoubtedly been the owner's library. The large desk and chairs were of mahogany, and the bookshelves reached the twelve-foot ceilings. However, the books had largely been pulled down from the shelves and thrown into untidy piles. Two soldiers loomed over a disheveled figure slumped in an armchair, a large, powerfully-built man who nonetheless looked badly frightened; the split lip and the beginnings of a black eye showed his fears were not unreasonable. One of the soldiers turned to the new arrivals, and half-saluting said "Lieutenant, we've worked this Johnnie over pretty damn good. He's still saying there are no hidey-places for crops and livestock, or for silver and such."

Clay walked over to the prisoner, and looked down at him mildly. "So, are you responsible for the injuries to those human beings out in the yard?" he said in the softest of voices.

"Not those'uns," he mumbled.

"Really?"

The overseer looked up at Clay with tired, defeated eyes. "I won't lie to you. Out in fields I would lay on if they slacked, or if they talked back. But niggers are property, and you don't break up good property for no reason. Tried talkin' to Mr. Hampton once to ease off on what his friends an' him were doing. But he told me if I kept actin' like a nigger-lovin' Republican he would fire me, and make sure no other plantation in Georgia would hire me."

"So to keep your position you acquiesced in the torture and murder of human beings."

The prisoner looked down, and mumbled "Got a wife and three little ones. This is all I know."

"You apparently did not try to learn anything else," said Clay mildly. Something in one of the piles of books caught Clay's attention. He bent over and picked up two large, ancient-looking volumes. Without looking at the prisoner, appearing absorbed in inspecting the books, he said "How did Wade Hampton and his . . . friends come to cause such injuries?"

Still looking at the floor, the overseer replied "Tried not to see too much. Sometimes he would take them as tried to run away and make a . . . hunt of it. Give them a head start and release them bloodhounds out back. Mr. Hampton and his friends would ride after them on horseback; sort of like a foxhunt, I guess. Sometimes they'd bring the nigger back, bleedin' something awful. Sometimes didn't bring the runaway back at all. Still, that wasn't the worst. Sometimes, not often, they'd git together after dark. They'd take one of the field hands, usually a woman or pickaninny, out to the woods to the north and west. Mr. Hampton would tell me and the other help to stay in the house, and never mind what we heard."

"Did you never become curious about what happened at these . . . events?" asked Clay, who still seemed absorbed in the two volumes he had recovered.

"No, and if you'd have heard the drumming and screaming that came here when the wind was right, you wouldn't have been curious neither."

Lieutenant Pierce looked curiously at Clay. "Sir, what do you have there?

"Two extremely rare books, Lieutenant. One is *The Necrominicom* by the Arab Abdul Alhazard. Although this copy seems to be of the inferior John Dee translation. Even an inferior copy of this work is quite valuable. The other is of some sentimental value to me: *Unausprechliken Kulten* by Friedrich von Juntz, who happens to be my maternal grandfather. It would appear that Wade Hampton and his friends are somewhat eclectic in their intellectual interests. With your permission, I would like to take these books as personal souvenirs."

"Don't see why not, Major. They may be valuable, but my boys will not take to hauling old books all over Georgia."

"My thanks," replied Clay, as he placed the volumes carefully on the corner of the mahogany desk. He then unsnapped his holster and drew his Smith & Wesson revolver. "And now, I regret I must . . ." His words were interrupted by a commotion. With surprising strength the wiry Jeremiah Lot had jerked the large prisoner out of the chair and hustled him out into the hall and through the front door screaming "Run! Run for your life! Get your family and keep running until you are far away from here!" The prisoner caught something in Lot's voice that convinced him of his danger, and despite his injuries took off like the Devil was behind him. As he ran through the yard some of Pierce's men made as if to stop him. However, Lot shouted "By order of Major Clay and Lieutenant Pierce, that man is not to be molested! Let him go!" Lot watched briefly to make certain the overseer was on his way at top speed, then re-entered the library. Pierce and his two men stood with confused looks on their faces; while Clay stood frowning, his pistol pointed in Lot's general direction.

"You should not have done that," said Clay, a chilling, ominous tone in his voice, a strange light seeming to gleam from his pale blue eyes.

"Alphonso, I love you too much to allow another . . . incident like in New Orleans," replied Lot, looking unwaveringly at the pistol in his cousin's hand.

Clay was frozen still as a statue for some seconds, then finally said, "Very well, you may be right." He then turned to Pierce. "Lieutenant, where are the bloodhounds kept?"

A note of unease in his voice, Pierce replied "They are kept in a kennel just to the left of the back porch door. Why?"

"I will be only a moment," replied Clay. Still holding the revolver, Clay stalked out of the library. Pierce turned to Lot and asked

"What the hell is up with your major? He is acting like he is a few cards short of a full deck."

"You don't know the half of it," replied Lot. "A good man, but he responds . . . unpredictably when he sees injustice. We are lucky that he did not . . ." Lot was interrupted by the crack of a pistol shot, followed by the yelp of a dog. Pierce started, while his men looked uneasily at each other. A few seconds later there was a second shot; a few more seconds, a third. A fourth. A fifth. Then uninterrupted silence.

In a few moments they heard footsteps coming down the hall, and Clay entered the library, just finishing sliding shiny metallic cartridges into his revolver. He snapped it closed and reholstered the weapon, then walked over to the desk and tucked the two large volumes under his arm. He looked directly into Pierce's eyes and said "Burn this place and everything in it to the ground." Pierce noticed that the strange light was gone from Clay's eyes. Without waiting for a reply, Clay left the room.

Pierce looked confused. "Uh, Lieutenant, we have orders from Sherman himself not to deliberately burn civilian houses," he said to Lot.

"Sherman is far away, and Clay is right here. If I were you, I would burn it, and praise God nothing worse happened."

Teresa Duval had been rejoined by the wagons under Dr. Fetterman. Together they had set up a temporary hospital in a large barn, and were being kept busy enough by the relatively few casualties the Georgia militia had inflicted before being destroyed. Normally she would have been quite happy dealing with blood and mangled flesh, but Fetterman had destroyed her mood when he had brought in a half-dozen captured Confederates who had volunteered to work as hospital orderlies. She carefully hid her feelings from Fetterman, but every time she heard one of the

English-loving bastards utter something in their drawling accent that aped the British upper classes, she came very close to committing an indiscrete murder. Only her sense of self-preservation gave her the strength to drive the ravening demons back into the dark corners of her mind.

Suddenly a form appeared in the door of the barn, and Duval's heart leapt at the site of Clay's spare frame; she hardly noticed Lot following behind him. "Good afternoon, Miss Duval. I trust you are not overwhelmed by the casualties."

"She does well as always," replied Fetterman on her behalf. "One casualty is one too many; but the battle was short enough that we are able to help all those needing immediate assistance. I thank the Lord Sherman gave me permission to use some of our prisoners from the Confederate regulars to provide assistance."

"No luck, Major Clay?" asked Duval brusquely, not quite meeting his eyes.

"None so far. However, one can always hope. This was always a long-shot plan; but a long-shot is better than a no-shot."

There was a sudden commotion outside the barn; horses neighed, and a wagon creaked. General Sherman's high, fluting voice was heard. "Goddamn it, get someone out here! A good officer is like to die!" Two of the prisoners rushed out with a stretcher and staggered back in carrying a man who alternately sobbed and screamed. His legs both ended in bloody rags just below his knees; a tourniquet on each limb kept him from bleeding to death.

"Goddamn Rebel bastards!" shouted Sherman wildly, glaring at the prisoners acting as orderlies, who carefully did not meet his stare. "Happened right in front of me. Was talking to this captain, as he marched along at the head of his company, when *BAM*. An infernal device blew him near twenty feet in the air, taking off both legs. Don't know how he's survived to reach here."

"Put him on the empty cot over there," commanded Duval

calmly. Along with Fetterman she approached the cot, gazing with outward calm and inward pleasure at the ruin of the young officer's limbs. "We will be able to save his life, if he does not die of shock. We will have to complete the amputations of course; both will be below the knees, which will facilitate the fitting of artificial legs."

"Let me administer the ether while you prepare the instruments," said Fetterman, while the young officer thrashed wildly.

"Sir, what do you mean 'infernal device,'" Lot asked Sherman.

"A keg of gunpowder, buried in the road, with some clever plunger connected to a percussion cap, arranged so that the pressure of some poor bastard placing his foot on it will cause the explosion. Some call these damn things torpedoes. Don't care what they are called; coward's weapons are what they are. We've been running into a few; more as we approach Savannah; making the boys nervous and slowing down the march." Sherman's eyes lit upon one of the Confederate prisoners sponging off a wounded man. "Well, the Goddamn Rebs planted these things, and the Goddamn Rebs can dig them up. You and you and you," said Sherman, pointing in rapid succession to three of the orderlies. "You Johnnies have got a new duty. You're going to be right out in front of my main column, right in front. Anyone gets blown to Hell, it's going to be you!"

"General, you cain't do that," wailed one of the prisoners. "We is prisoners, and the laws of war say prisoners cain't be put in harms way."

"I am the only law in Georgia! You will do as I say, or I will hang you higher than Haman!"

The only officer among the prisoners stepped forward; a lanky man with a haggard expression, whose red collar proclaimed him to be an artilleryman. "General, with your permission, I would like to volunteer on behalf of the men. I am better qualified than they to spot the signs of such a device, and to disarm it without undue risk."

"And I imagine you planted a few of them yourselves. What's your name?"

"Lieutenant Samuel Flournoy, sir. And yes, I did plant a few such devices. I regarded them as against the laws of war, and told my superiors so. However, they ordered me to participate, and I felt honor-bound to do so." The rebel looked steadily at Sherman, neither defiant nor afraid.

Gruffly, Sherman said "You didn't need to reveal that. Why did you?"

Flournoy shrugged. "It is the duty of an officer to protect his men as best he can. Your order is barbarous," and Flournoy paused meaningfully, "but since you are determined to give the order, I really have no choice but to assume responsibility and volunteer for the duty."

"Very well, you have your wish." Sherman paused, then almost angrily added "Lieutenant, I hope to God you survive this war. Now come with me. My aides will take you up front, and get you any tools you need to disarm the infernal devices." Flournoy saluted slowly and correctly, and walked out of the tent with dignity, closely followed by Sherman.

"A brave man," murmured Clay approvingly.

Before she could stop herself, Duval said "I do not want them brave. I want them dead."

Lot looked at Duval with shock, Clay with cool calculation.

"Haven't heard from you in a while, Clay," growled Sherman, not taking the binoculars from his eyes. "Guess your plan of making yourself bait didn't pan out."

"No sir, it would appear not." Standing at the top of a low hill with members of the general's staff, Clay looked at what was occupying Sherman's attention: a fort at the mouth of the Ogeechee River, and beyond that the town itself. There was an intermittent drizzle from the gray December skies; but it did not limit visibility. Sherman would have been surprised to learn that Clay could see as much with his bespectacled eyes as the general could see with his powerful army glasses.

"What is keeping Hazen," Sherman grumbled. "He's got to take Fort McAllister now, today, or this army is going start to starve."

Clay nodded. "It is hard to live off the land when the land has been as picked over as much as around Atlanta. Still, things are going the Union's way in general. The taking of Atlanta changed the whole mood in the North, and was probably the main reason for McClellan's defeat and Lincoln's re-election. The South can no longer count on victory coming from a change in government."

Sherman took the binoculars away from his face and growled "I'm concerned in the here and now. If Fort McAllister falls, Union warships can sail right up to us with everything we need. Only a few days after that, we will take Savannah. Only question is whether General Hardee will stand and be destroyed or slink off to the north. He must know he hasn't a chance against us, in the town or not. Hell, if he has ten thousand able to hold a musket I'd be damned surprised." Sherman sighed. "So Clay, what do you want to do."

Clay's normally placid features were set in a grim frown. "I have failed, plain and simple. As soon as we have established communication with the Union fleet, I request permission for Lieutenant Lot and myself to take ship and rejoin General Grant's staff."

"Guess there's nothing else to do," replied Sherman. "It just seems just so Goddamn hard . . . wait a second." Sherman brought the binoculars back up his face, just as the sound of cannon and musketry reached the soldiers on the hill. "There goes Hazen!" yelled Sherman, something Clay could confirm with his naked eyes. They watched the distant line of blue figures scramble up the steep earthen slope leading to the fort's parapet; some fell, but most went straight over. In less than a minute the stars and bars had disappeared from the flagpole. The crowd on the hilltop cheered and pounded each other on the back; all save Alphonso Clay, who looked on as if only mildly interested.

"Goddamn Hazen and his boys! Goddamn them!" shouted the manic Sherman. "He can take his Goddamn time about things, but when Bill Hazen says he will do a thing, it is done! The campaign is now officially a success; the rest will be mopping up."

At this point a couple of soldiers approached the general, escorting Samuel Flournoy, whose ashen features and stiff expression showed just what he thought of the easy Union victory.

"Beggin' your pardon, General," said one of the soldiers, a grizzled corporal running to fat. "Mickey and me thought this might be a good time to be askin' the General a favor, even if it ain't quite regular, not going through the officers and such."

Sherman looked at the two presumptuous soldiers, appearing amused by them. "So, what favors can I give two fine specimens of my army."

"Well, it's not for us exactly, although we would sure be grateful," said the corporal. He gestured to Flournoy. "You see, Mickey and me have been assigned to watch this Johnnie here dig up torpedoes, makin' sure he don't run away. Well, he's never tried, but he has dug up twelve of those damn infernal machines, takin' his life in his hands each time. Figure he's saved a lot of boyos doing that, but it's like this: those things are tricky, and it's only a matter of time until one blows him to glory. Don't seem right, somehow. Sam Flournoy seems like a good egg, even if he is Reb, and he's risked his life enough, says me and Mickey. So if you don't take strong exception sir, me and Mickey would take it as a personal favor if you let this Johnnie here have a chance of livin' out the war, and send him to the officer's prison stockade. Sir."

Sherman looked first at the corporal, then at "Mickey", and finally at Flournoy with his intelligent, bird-like eyes. Finally he said "Well, never heard of my boys asking a favor for a Reb officer. Don't see how I can deny it. Flournoy, you're off the duty."

"Sir, I will escort the prisoner to the stockade," interjected Clay unexpectedly.

"That's all right then," said Sherman. Just then someone shouted that the Stars and Stripes were being raised over Fort McAllister. Everyone on the hilltop cheered and turned their attention to the spectacle; everyone but Clay and Flournoy. "Lieutenant, please come with me," said Clay. Flournoy assented with a stiff nod, and the two began the short climb down the hill and back to the area where headquarters staff had pitched their tents.

As they walked side by side, Clay suddenly spoke. "You may wonder why I have taken this opportunity to escort you."

"The thought has crossed my mind," said Flournoy dryly.

"You are a brave man, a true gentleman in every sense of the word, and deserve some consideration above that normally accorded prisoners of war. I see that you are a married man." Clay pointed to the wedding band on Flournoy's finger. "Any children?"

Flournoy hesitated a long moment before replying. "My wife was expecting our first child when last I heard from her. She must have had the baby now, or. . ." Flournoy left unsaid the hazards of childbirth. "It is not knowing that is the worst."

"I assumed as much. I would be pleased if you would join me in the tent I share with Lieutenant Lot. It is not much, but it is better than what is accorded prisoners, even officers. You can have a decent meal, and prepare a long letter to your wife, assuring her that you are safe, and will be restored to her soon. You realize the

Confederacy has lost, and that the war will be over in less than six months."

A sad expression on his face, Flournoy replied "I am afraid that is my assessment as well."

"We will not speak of the relative merits of our causes. The important thing is that you will live to see your family again. A few months in a prison stockade will be unpleasant, but endurable, especially when one has some money to buy the little extras that corrupt guards can make available."

"I have no money," replied Flournoy. "It was taken from me when I was captured."

"I will see that you have a modest sum."

"Why are you doing this?" asked Flournoy.

"Call it the courtesy of one gentleman to a better gentleman who has suffered from the fortunes of war. Ah, this is where we cut off. The Lieutenant and I were fortunate enough to find a camp spot off the beaten path. Hardly anyone uses this particular trail, and it is so quiet one can almost forget one is in the middle of a vast army. There, you can see the tent . . ."

Flournoy's arm shot out, seizing Clay by the shoulder, arresting his forward motion. "Do not move," he hissed, and with his other arm pointed to some moist, disturbed soil into which Clay had been about to step. "I have seen the signs before. I could be wrong, but I believe there is a torpedo buried in the path."

Clay frowned. "In the middle of Sherman's headquarters camp? That scarce seems possible."

"It may have been placed there before the army arrived here. In any event, I recognize the subtle signs. Could you get some spades, any digging implement that you can find? I will stay here and make sure no one stumbles into this device."

Clay briefly considered the possibility that Flournoy was

deceiving him, and creating an opportunity for escape; but after a look at the strained, pale features of the Rebel officer, he decided that Flournoy was sincere. Without another word, Clay went in search of the implements.

An hour later, Flournoy had uncovered most of the infernal device. As Clay and Lot watched, he ever so gently removed a percussion cap, ever so gently disarmed a spring backup. Flournoy staggered upright, and then went to a nearby patch of grass, where he collapsed, drenched in sweat despite the cool weather. "It is safe now. At least safe enough. I wouldn't smoke or build a campfire near it."

Clay and Lot approached the hole, where the half-buried device lay. Squatting on his haunches, Clay peered intently at the device. Suddenly he asked "Is this design typical of Southern torpedoes?"

Flournoy had produced a dirty handkerchief and was wiping sweat from his face. "As a matter of fact, no. Usually a small keg of gunpowder is used. Here, an artillery shell was used as the explosive device. Of course, you appreciate with our limited industrial base, the South must improvise a great deal."

"Improvise a great deal," echoed Clay. Suddenly Clay produced his own handkerchief and began to clean the side of the shell from clods of earth still attached to it. Letters began to appear, letters of the Government that had commissioned the shell. However the letters were not those that should have been expected, not "CSA" for the Confederate States of America.

They were "USA": United States of America.

CHAPTER 4

"TREASON FLED BEFORE US FOR RESISTANCE WAS IN VAIN . . ."

A cleaned, shiny three-inch shell sat on a spread of newspapers in the middle of the desk that graced the elegant library. Sherman stood by the window, puffing furiously at a cigar, staring at the sliver of ocean that could be seen from the gracious townhouse he had made his Savannah headquarters. Jeremiah Lot stood uneasily by the closed door, dividing his attention between Sherman and Alphonso Clay. Clay himself was seated in a Queen Anne armchair that had been drawn up to the desk, his gaze locked on the shell, fingers tented just below his chin.

Sherman turned from the window and threw the butt of his cigar at a spittoon; he missed, but did not seem to notice. "Well, Clay, where does this leave us? I've got a Goddamn city to secure, and an army to reprovision and put on the road. And now you tell me a traitor is still active."

Clay spoke as if he had not heard the general. "What do I know that I do not know?" he softly murmured.

"Eh?" responded Sherman, brought up sharply by Clay's comment.

"What do I know that I do not know?" Clay repeated, his eyes still focused on the shell. "I suspect that the traitor is one of four officers, but am unable to narrow it down any further. The traitor is safe so long as he takes no further action; yet he seems desperate to kill me. Therefore, he thinks that I know something that would identify him. Yet I do not!" Clay suddenly slapped the left arm of the chair in frustration, so hard that the noise resembled a pistol shot.

"Have you considered that the torpedo may not have been intended for you?" asked Lot unexpectedly. "Our tent was off the regular path, and for two days we had no visitors—except for General Sherman." The black officer looked meaningfully at the scarecrow-thin commander of the army, who started slightly at the suggestion.

Clay finally removed his gaze from the shell, and looked at his friend. "That is true. Someone could have observed the visits of the General, and thought to take the chance. That way the traitor would be removed from the scene when the assassination took place. Otherwise, it is hard to imagine how he could kill General Sherman—or myself—and survive the attempt. Of course, one motive does not exclude the other; the device could have been intended for me, knowing that on both prior occasions when General Sherman visited our tent I escorted him back to the main encampment. Two for one, as it were, with the death of the highest-ranking Federal officer in the South as a bonus."

Sherman grunted noncommittally. "You imply you have a list of suspects in mind. Why haven't you shared their names with me?"

Clay rose from the armchair, and faced Sherman with something like the formality of parade-rest. "Two reasons, sir. First, although I have a number of suspects, only one is in fact the traitor; and I hesitate to place even a temporary cloud on the honor of an innocent gentleman. Second, I doubt you could conceal your knowledge of his possible guilt from the traitor, and hence prematurely alert him to his danger."

"Damn you Clay, I can keep a secret, and as commander of this army I have a right to know. I order you to tell me who you suspect."

Clay's face became completely expressionless; with a slight shrug of his narrow shoulders he began to speak.

"Very well, sir. Assuming the traitor is not a madman, he must feel he would benefit from the deaths of Major Bierce and General McPherson. I believe that in the attacks on them treason was only incidental, that the murderer was driven by a motive even more heinous and venal than mere politics. It is fairly obvious to an intelligent observer, and has been since late this summer, that the Confederacy is doomed, and that the death of no single leader, no matter how important, can save it. I am driven to the conclusion that the motive is advancement—selfish, personal advancement."

Sherman's bird-like eyes focused intently on the slightly-built officer. "Explain yourself. How can what's been happening advance anyone . . ." Sherman's voice trailed off, and after a moment he softly said "Son of a bitch."

Clay nodded. "You see it now, sir. Very obvious, once you accept the fact that someone you know and trust, someone you see daily, is willing to murder for worldly success."

"The Goddamn bastard set McPherson up, didn't he? And Mac didn't see it, even after it happened."

"I fear that is the case, sir. Someone whom General McPherson trusted implicitly gave him bad intelligence data. Very bad indeed. He was told that Johnston's line was very weak at Kennesaw Mountain. Knowing how you favored McPherson, the murderer could be assured you would take his advice. Undoubtedly aware of your, ah, stormy temperament, he anticipated you blaming the general and relieving him; not knowing the depth of your personal ties to McPherson. Further, it was not out of the question that you yourself would be relieved after such a debacle. Earlier in this war many generals were relieved for less, and this would open up another high rank for advancement. Once again, the criminal misjudged the situation, underestimating your influence with General Grant, and forgetting the great reliance of the President on your brother, Senator Sherman."

"God damn. God damn it to Hell," said Sherman with what was for him unusual solemnity. "There are only a handful of men who could benefit from that. I would trust any of them with my life."

Clay nodded. "You see why I was reluctant to burden you with suspicions until I could narrow the range of suspects to one. However, let us go through them.

"You must consider General Oliver Howard. He is the man who has benefited the most from the events in question. Before Kennesaw Mountain he was a mere division commander, under a cloud from his disastrous performance with the Army of the Potomac. Within three months he has shot right through the rank of corps commander to be placed in charge of your Army of the Tennessee. And if anything . . . untoward were to happen to you, he is one of the two officers who is best placed to succeed you."

"Goddamn it Clay, I just can't believe it of Howard. He is one of the hot-gospel Christians, always praying when he isn't fighting. Besides, whatever happened back East, he has proven himself a damn fine general out here."

"That may be the very point, sir. It would appear his dismissal from the Army of the Potomac may have had more to do with army politics than his performance; performance during which he lost his right arm. He may have brooded upon that, and convinced himself he was justified in taking . . . extreme measures to gain a position he felt he deserved. As for his professions of Christianity, I have known people who were very public in their faith only in order to divert attention from their true characters."

Clay smiled slightly, but did not elaborate before discussing his next suspect.

"Then we must consider General Henry Slocum. Many of the factors that apply to Howard apply to him as well. Like Howard, Slocum lost command of a corps in the Army of the Potomac more due to politics than failure to perform, and arrived in your army a mere division commander. Although recent events have formally raised him back to the command of a corps, he is in fact acting as an army commander alongside Howard. If something were to happen to you, if Howard is not your replacement, then it would undoubtedly be Slocum."

"To someone with no morality, the chance of becoming the top Union general after Grant might justify murder," observed Lot.

"Indeed," responded Clay with a nod. "Men—and women—have murdered for far less. Therefore, we also need to consider those who have benefited at a less exalted level, or who may simply want revenge for having been denied promotion."

Frowning, Sherman asked "Who would that be?"

"For one, consider General John Logan, commander of your 15th Corps. I personally witnessed his rage when you denied him General McPherson's command after the latter's death. It is at least possible that he engineered his superior's death in hopes of receiving his command, and harbors a murderous grudge for not in fact receiving it at that time."

Sherman turned and walked over to the window. He stared at the distant ocean for some moments before speaking. "I meant no reflection on him personally. He is a good corps commander, but not the stuff required for command of more than one corps. Besides, he is a brave and patriotic man; he could not have been responsible for the attacks of Bierce and McPherson."

"Brave and patriotic men have committed murder throughout history," responded Clay. "Bitterness can twist even good men in strange directions. For instance, it may have done so with General Jeff Davis."

"Eh?" grunted Sherman. "How would he benefit from what's going on?

Clay answered a question with a question. "Tell me sir, why did you not consider General Davis for the positions now held by Generals Howard and Slocum? Is he not able to handle an army?"

"Hell yes, Jeff's able. One of the finest Goddamn generals in the army. It's just . . ." Once again, Sherman trailed off without finishing his sentence, looking thoughtful.

"It is because he murdered General Nelson back in Kentucky," supplied Clay. "Somehow he evaded punishment for that. That is a mystery in itself, although I suspect political influence was exercised at the highest levels to preserve an able commander for the Union. However, no matter what influence protects him and no matter how skilled a general he is, he will never advance beyond corps commander. Such appointments need the confirmation of the Senate; and it is simply politically impossible for the killer of General Nelson to obtain that approval. That is why you did not consider him for promotions, is it not, sir?"

Sherman sighed. "Yes, that's about right. I even wrote privately to my brother, asking him if the fuss over the Nelson business had died down in the Senate. John let me know in no uncertain terms the Senate would not stand for Davis' promotion."

Clay continued. "Therefore, we have a man who won his way up through the ranks, earning his commission in the field. A man who believes himself to be better than those who have been promoted over his head, due to their West Point connections. A man prone to hatred and violence. We cannot dismiss him from consideration."

Sherman grimaced as if tasted something foul. "Goddamn it Clay, you have just named my four best commanders! Anyone else you would like to include?"

Clay smiled slightly. "I would have liked to include General Hooker, for several reasons. Unfortunately, although he could have been responsible for the first attempt on Bierce's life, he was far to the north during the other attempt."

A frown on his face, Lot said "One thing bothers me. All of these men are known by sight to everyone in the army. How could they hope to commit these atrocities undetected?"

Clay shrugged. "Remember that two of the assaults took place at the height of battles. Ironically, in such situations you can be surrounded by thousands of people and go undetected, as those people concentrate on simply staying alive. In addition, it is not unknown for a high-ranking individual to have a lackey bound to them by hero worship or the like. Such an individual could perform the actual deeds under the instructions of the murderer."

"So what the hell do I do?" asked Sherman angrily. "Arrest all four? Do nothing until they try again? Just what do you suggest?"

"It would not be feasible to arrest them all," said Lot. "Aside from the injustice done to three innocent patriots, this wounded country could hardly stand knowing of yet more widespread treason in the highest ranks of their leaders."

Clay nodded. "The lieutenant is correct, sir. I fear that I must continue to present myself as a target to the killer; perhaps dropping ambiguous hints to the generals that only a guilty mind would understand."

"So what should I do, Clay?" growled Sherman. "Post bodyguards around you day and night?"

Clay shook his head. "As I have pointed out before, that would defeat the purpose. The criminal is far too clever to expose himself unless he feels assured of success."

"Goddamn it Clay, I can't continue to let you expose yourself like . . . like . . . human bait!"

"With deepest respect, sir, the final decision is mine, not yours. I intend no disrespect to your rank and your honor when I say that I am actually not part of your command, not part of your command structure. I answer directly to General Grant, and through him to Secretary of War Stanton."

Sherman glared at the mild-looking young officer, and only brought his temper under uncertain control with a visible effort. "Do as you like then. I've got enough to do getting this army on the road."

"Already, sir?" blurted Lot. "The men have barely settled into quarters after an epic march, and it looks to be fairly steady rain for the next few weeks."

"No choice," growled Sherman, fumbling for another cigar and lighting it with a friction match. "Got a message from Grant off one of the supply boats. He wants me to leave a small garrison in Savannah, and take the rest of the army overland, through the Carolinas and into Virginia."

Clay, who was rarely surprised, blinked his astonishment. "Now, in this weather?"

"It's an order Clay, and a damn good one. Sam is holding Lee in the trenches around Petersburg, the railway center guarding the approach to Richmond. He can't seem to break through; Bobby Lee is good on the defense, I'll give him that. But Marse Robert can't maneuver. The moment he leaves the trenches, Sam's superior numbers will just chew Lee to pieces. Besides, leaving the trenches means the Rebs give up Richmond, and the war is as good as over. So Sam wants me to march the boys overland; brushing aside what little the Rebs have and tearing up anything that could help Lee, and at the end of the march we join up with Sam and finally finish off the traitors."

Lot gave a low whistle, while Clay slowly nodded and said, "I see. It is the end. After four years, it will finally be the end."

Sherman, who had been puffing furiously on his cigar, suddenly coughed asthmatically and looked sourly at the cylinder of tobacco. Then he said "Grant ended his message by saying 'I think if the thing is pressed Lee will finally surrender.'" Sherman suddenly grinned savagely. "I think I'm going to press this thing."

Jeremiah Lot could not recall feeling quite so uncomfortably in his entire life. The light but steady rain had thoroughly soaked him to the skin long ago, while the cool temperatures of a Southern winter guaranteed that moisture reaching his skin chilled him to the bone. His discomfort was augmented by the unsteady gait of his horse which occasionally lurched wildly in struggling its legs free of the sticky mud churned up by the preceding thousands of soldiers and their vehicles. Still, Lot felt he could not complain: his friend sat on his own horse with ease, apparently insensible to the chill from his wet uniform. Furthermore, most of the soldiers within sight looked cheerful, even boisterous, despite being on foot and having to deal with the sucking mud firsthand. Mostly to take his mind off his own discomfort, he decided to draw this to his friend's attention.

"Alphonso, after what these men have been through, being forced to march through the freezing mud should have placed them near mutiny. But just look at them! They positively act like they're on some picnic, laughing and joking as they trudge along this sorry excuse for a road."

"They see the end, Jeremiah. Most of them had probably given up on seeing victory, or even surviving the war. However, now they see victory clearly in the distance, and a chance to survive to reach it." Clay hesitated, then added "Besides, there is another factor—one that will bode ill for many people."

"What is that?"

"Do you appreciate the true significance of crossing the Savannah River, as we did yesterday?"

"Of course. We are now in South Carolina."

"We are now in South Carolina," echoed Clay. "The first state to attempt to secede from the Union. The first state to call for Civil War. In all other Confederate states, even in Georgia, there are pockets of sincere loyalty to the Union. Not in South Carolina. The men hold this state more responsible for this national tragedy than any other state in the Union. I fear for the people of this state."

Lot was astonished; he had never before heard Clay utter a word of sympathy for the Rebels, civilian or military. "Surely it will not be worse than in Georgia."

Clay did not look over at his friend, but only shook his head slightly. "Mankind is sometimes capable of the most sublime nobility, and sometimes of the most appalling depravity. Sometimes the impulses exist simultaneously in the same breast. One must always keep that in mind. That is why we will pay a brief visit to General Oliver Howard, the Christian General, using as an excuse the order entrusted to me this morning by General Sherman. We will approach this as we have before. I will appear indifferent to any threat, while you will keep unobtrusively alert behind me. I assume that your Spencer is cleaned and loaded?"

"Of course, Alphonso," replied Lot grimly, patting the butt of the Spencer in its scabbard.

"The question was rhetorical, Jeremiah. I had no doubt." Clay became silent, and reflected on the events of the day before yesterday that had reminded him of the need to talk to another ostentatiously Christian person . . .

The town of Savannah was in a state of controlled chaos as wagons were being packed, supplies distributed, and units reorganized for the upcoming march. Clay had paid a visit to the wharves where the Union transports were disgorging supplies and taken on the wounded and sick for transport North, in hopes of finding letters from his estate manager. In this he had been disappointed. However, as he left the warehouse that acted as he army's temporary post office, he spied Teresa Duval on the gangplank of one of the transports, talking to a young naval officer. Although she was nearly one hundred yards away, Clay could clearly see her hand several envelopes to the man, and a small object that glinted yellow. The officer touched his cap, and Duval turned and strode swiftly down the gangplank and into a street, disappearing from view. Clay briefly considered accosting the naval officer and demanding the letters, but uncertain that they would have anything to do with the traitor he sought, and unwilling to start an interservice conflict, he decided to let the matter pass. Thoughtfully, he entered the street leading to Sherman's headquarters, and had almost dismissed the matter from his mind as irrelevant when a voice right behind him called his name.

"Why Major Clay, what a pleasant surprise." The surprise was not pleasant; Clay whirled to find a smiling Teresa Duval looking directly into his eyes, smiling the sort of smile worn by the Mona Lisa.

"Miss Duval, my apologies, you startled me." In truth, Clay was more than startled; he knew his hearing to be unnaturally acute, and simply could not imagine how she had come up behind him without his hearing a sound.

"I need to visit General Sherman's quartermaster and make sure some supplies Dr. Fetterman wants are in fact delivered to the hospital wagons. It would seem you are also going in the same direction. Would you care to escort me? The streets are full of rowdies, some the worse for drink; I was quite worried on my way here. A Christian lady would feel better with your protection."

Clay threw his head back and emitted several barking laughs; he was quite sure that Teresa Duval was one of the most dangerous people currently in Savannah, more than capable of handling anything that came her way, and that she had only the most nodding acquaintanceship with the Bible. Then recovering his composure, he replied "It would be an honor," and offered her his arm. She took it lightly, and the two began strolling down the street.

After a moment, Duval casually commented "Of course you saw me give the letters to the naval officer. I expect you found it strange that I did not use the Army post."

"I assume that you are aware that the military censors examine many letters going north, to prevent the transmission of sensitive military data. I would imagine your letters contained . . . delicate material that you did not wish to be scrutinized by bored army clerks."

Duval gave Clay a doe-eyed glance, smiling sweetly. "Just so. Very perceptive of you, Major."

"Letters to your dear mother?" asked Clay in an ironic tone of voice. His obvious doubts did not disconcert her; she smiled again.

"We all have secrets, Major. Perhaps it is time we exchanged some. As a pledge of good faith, I will go first. I am on the payroll of the Secret Service, and whenever I can do so, submit detailed reports on this army to Allan Pinkerton. In his own way, he entertains the same kinds of suspicions as do you."

As they strolled up the street, Clay favored Duval with a brief glance and an ironic smile. "With respect, Miss Duval, that is obviously not the totality of your secrets. I spotted you hand at least two envelopes to the Navy officer. If all of your 'sensitive' communications were to him, one envelope would have been sufficient."

Duval stiffened slightly with surprise, but then relaxed. After all, she thought, this kind of sharpness was why she found Clay so alluring. Among other reasons. "True enough Major; I have given you one of my secrets, but not all. Now it is your turn."

"I am a private man, Miss Duval. I do not care to share myself with others." They were now approaching Sherman's headquarters.

"Oh come, Major. You must have shared secrets with others in your life. I am certain you have done so with Lieutenant Lot. And besides, you must have a sweetheart back in Kentucky who . . ."

Clay dropped her arm like it was a red-hot poker. He whirled with shocking speed, and staring at her with icy blue eyes said in a quiet voice "I believe this is your destination, Miss Duval. If you will excuse me, I have other calls on my time." With a swift, shallow bow and a click of his heels, he had turned and was striding away. Duval looked after him thoughtfully. *'That settles that,'* she thought. *'He definitely is not a nancy boy. There was a woman in his life. She had not left him, or he her; there would have been a trace of bitterness in his manner. No, he showed only pain; she is dead. That is well enough; once less problem to resolve.'* Smiling to herself, she turned and entered Sherman's headquarters.

"Alphonso, are you all right?"

Clay started, realizing that his attention had wandered while he had mulled over his encounter with Teresa Duval. Straightening his posture, he muttered "Just tired, Jeremiah. Just tired. Ah, I think I see our destination. Whenever you see so many mounted officers, a general cannot be far away." The two friends urged their mounts into a canter, and shortly made their way through the crowd of aides. Their number was explained by the presence of two general officers: the darkly handsome John Logan, and his immediate superior Oliver Howard, the Christian General. However, Howard was not behaving in a very Christian manner. Deftly controlling his mount with his only arm, Howard was berating a fuming Logan.

"Sir, your inability to control your men comes perilously close to dereliction of duty. Look at what they are doing. Just look!"

Lacking a second arm with which to point, Howard indicated the horizon with a furious jerk of his head. Clay and Lot followed the gesture, and saw what had inspired the general's rage: distant pillars of smoke, stretching as far as the eye could see. Not the dozen or so that had been observed at any given time during the march to sea; literally a hundred or more, with no doubt many times their number outside of their immediate sight. Lot gasped, and had to work to retain his composure. Clay merely shook his head slightly, as if disappointed by some minor occurrence.

Logan's normally saturnine features were further darkened by barely controlled anger. "Sir, it is beyond my power to entirely control my men. I am confident they will leave off their mischief if a military situation arises. Their readiness is not an issue."

"Beyond your power, or beyond your desire?" thundered Howard. "I have only to look at the horizon to see evidence that they behave as Vandals or Huns. They would only dare to do so if they knew that their officers, and above all you, did not care!"

Logan's visage darkened further. "Sir, you know what my boys have been through—those as have lived to reach this point. Most of them have been in the army since '61, risking death from the enemy or disease every day, Most have seen their friends, sometimes relations, buried in unnamed graves. And why?" Logan's controlled features suddenly slumped into a mask of hate. "Because of Goddamn South Carolina! Sure, the others states went along, but I would wager a dollar to a turd none of the bastards would've had the balls to secede without South Carolina showing the way! And now my boys are here, on the soil of the state that triggered off this Goddamn tragedy. My boys can do what they Goddamn like in this state, burn what they like, take what they like, hump what they like, and I don't give a Goddamn!"

Glaring, Howard began to open his mouth; but before he could respond to Logan's tirade, Clay cantered up and smoothly saluting, interrupted the impending command catastrophe. "Pardon the interruption, gentlemen, but General Sherman has entrusted an urgent order to me that affects you both." The two generals simultaneously turned amazed and furious glances on Clay, astounded that their confrontation had been interrupted by a mere major. Before either could say anything, Clay spoke again with even greater impertinence as he extended a sealed letter toward Howard.

"Gentlemen, General Sherman made me familiar with the contents of this order. It is vital and urgent, requiring immediate action. The execution of the order would be impeded by any sudden . . . alteration in the command structure of the army."

"Goddamn you Clay, how dare . . ." began Logan.

"Govern your intemperate language," interrupted Howard in a steely voice. "It is unpleasant in the eyes of the Lord, as well as mine." The fuming Logan retained enough control to do as his commander told him, while Howard clumsily clutched the envelope in the hand holding his reins, tearing open it open with his teeth and extracting the paper enclosed with no little difficulty. Frowning, he said "You were correct, Major. This takes precedence over my disagreement with General Logan. I will have to defer his discipline for insubordination to another time." Turning his attention to Logan, he added "General, we are ordered to wheel to the left and advance on Columbia."

"Columbia?" sputtered Logan. "We're barely two days' march from Charleston. Charleston, the place where it all began! The boys are itching to show that Goddamned town the price of treason."

"I am sure that General Sherman knows that," replied Howard. "I imagine he also knows the Rebs know that, and have concentrated what little they have for a last-ditch defense of Charleston. I was not looking forward to taking the town. The Rebs may be on their last legs, but they still have some fight in them." Nodding, Howard continued speaking as if to himself. "Yes, they will have stripped

Columbia bare of almost every soldier. We can walk into the state capital almost unopposed, and in the process cut all supply lines to Charleston, which will then fall of its own weight." He focused his attention once again on Logan. "General, you will immediately get your corps into marching formation, and direct it toward Columbia. We will be the right flank of the advance; Slocum and his boys the left. Anyone found out of column without an officer's orders will be summarily shot, without a court martial. No looting of any kind; speed is essential. Is that clear, General Logan?"

The former Congressman's eyes smoldered with anger; but he slowly nodded, saluted, and rode away without a word. Howard turned his stern, Old Testament prophet features toward Clay and Lot. "Please be so good as to inform General Sherman that his orders have been received and are being obeyed." Then with an appraising look at the pair, he added "Just the two of you have been riding about?"

Clay nodded in agreement.

"The countryside is infested with deserters from both sides and civilian bushwhackers," said Howard. "Let me assign a trusted officer to escort you back to Sherman."

"That will not be necessary," replied Clay. "The lieutenant and I are perfectly capable of defending ourselves."

Howard shrugged slightly. "As you wish." With his only arm he deftly turned his mount's head, and began to gallop toward the east, followed by a string of orderlies who had been waiting respectfully at a distance.

As they disappeared down the road, Lot said "I wonder if General Howard is the one, and had a minion who would try to quietly murder you on the way back to Sherman's headquarters."

Clay shrugged. "If he does, we are still likely to encounter him. Part of me hopes that the murderer is Howard, so the suspense and danger will come to an end. Part of me hopes that it is not, as it would be a blow to you personally to see such a professing Christian unmasked as a traitor and hypocrite."

Lot shook his head sadly. "Do not worry on that account, Alphonso. I am well aware that the Devil can quote scripture; it would have no effect on my faith."

Clay smiled slightly, wistfully. "Very well then. Let us retrace our steps not too quickly, giving an evil-doer time to catch up with us." Careful to keep their mounts at a slow walk, Clay and Lot proceeded along the road toward Sherman.

Teresa Duval drew the medical wagon to the side of the muddy road, out of the stream of trudging soldiers; she knew that the horses needed some rest, and a chance to crop some of the grass that grew on the side of the road. She was impatient with the needs of the animals, but was aware that their usefulness would be impaired if she drove them too hard. She sat on the driver's seat for some minutes, watching the animals eat; becoming increasingly bored. Then an idea struck her: Clay and Lot had left their personal effects in the medical wagon. Included among them were the two books that Clay had liberated from Wade Hampton's mansion. She had been quite curious about them, but something in Clay's manner had indicated he would not appreciate any request to examine his finds. Well, she reflected, Clay is gone for most of the day; she could now satisfy her curiosity with no one the wiser.

With surprising ease she slipped into the bed of the wagon and with no detectible sound extracted the two books from Clay's carpetbag. One she quickly saw was in German, a knowledge of which not being among her many unusual talents. She looked at the heavy Gothic lettering of the title page and slowly sounded out the volume's name and author: "*Unausprechlichen Kulten* Von Friedrich von Juntz". She frowned slightly at that. She remembered hearing Clay once comment that his mother's maiden name was von Juntz. It seems that this could have been written by a relative of Clay's, which would explain his interest. Deciding to inquire further into this at another time, she smoothly tucked the volume back into Clay's carpetbag, and turned her attention to the other, larger volume.

This one was in English, but an archaic English she could barely understand, language that reminded her of the bits and pieces she had read of that damned English scribbler Shakespeare. She turned to the title page, and saw that it was something called *The Necromonicom* by some Turk-sounding person named Al-Hazred, ostensibly translated from the Arabic by John Dee in the year of our Lord 1602. She again frowned slightly at that, for a different reason. Although she could remember only bits of her childhood, she seemed to recall hearing in her youth of John Dee. Some wizard, she seemed to remember, dead for many generations, but still talked of with fear and awe in the Irish countryside as an alchemist who had done magical things for the damned bastard Elizabeth of England. She had a brief flash of memory, of some aging priest whispering to her father while she watched, about how the wizard Dee had summoned up the storms, and the things hidden by the storms, that had destroyed the Spanish Armada before it could liberate Ireland from the yoke of England. Superstition, she thought then and she thought now. Still, it was interesting that here she held a book that had been translated by the long-dead mage.

Idly, she began idly leafing through the pages, wondering why this volume had been important enough to Clay to merit rescue from the burning Hampton mansion. Something caught her eye, and she stopped turning pages, concentrating on the one that had drawn her attention. Although the archaic English was difficult to decipher, she was able to make out what was said. Her first impulse was to laugh; but then she remembered the translator, and the terrible reputation that followed him down through the centuries; it was clear that he believed what the infidel had written in his book. Further, the fact that the intelligent, intellectual Clay considered the volume worth rescuing from Hampton's mansion gave her pause. She turned to another page, and something else caught her eye, then to another, then to another. Soon she was perched on a crate of medical supplies, utterly engrossed by the ancient tome. '*Could it be?*' she wondered. Could what she was reading possibly contain a grain of truth; more pertinently, could it possibly explain Alphonso Clay?

Although engrossed in the book, her sharp hearing detected the approach of a pair of horses. Quickly and smoothly she returned the ancient tome to the exact position it had occupied in the carpetbag, and fastened the latch. Grabbing a large role of bandages at random, she exited the back of the wagon, and feigned surprise at the return of Clay and Lot.

"Major Clay, Lieutenant Lot. I take it your expedition was without success."

"Part of me is thankful that is so," responded Lot.

"There will be other opportunities," responded Clay. "General Sherman has informed me that at dawn this army will begin a force march on the state capital at Columbia."

Duval nodded thoughtfully. "I thought as much. I have already supervised the loading of most of the medical supplies. Once I change the dressings on the more badly wounded, I can start seeing to their transfer to ambulances."

"I pray the more severely wounded can stand the jostling on the road," said Lot solemnly. "Miss Duval, may I be of assistance in your tasks? I have no immediate duties."

Somewhat surprised at the offer, Duval responded. "I have the assistance of a number of prisoners; but if you wish, another pair of hands is always welcome." She turned her attention to Clay. "Major, would you care to help as well?"

The fastidious, aristocratic Clay generally considered himself above such labor, but Lot's offer had shamed him. "I would be honored, Miss Duval," he replied with a slight bow.

Duval smiled slightly. Things were beginning to go as she had planned.

Sherman, Howard, and Slocum stood on a low hill that overlooked the approach to the small, orderly town of Columbia, their respective staffs at a distance. Through field glasses, they carefully examined the fields between them and the beginning of Columbia proper; units of blue-clad figures maneuvered, but did not fire. An occasional, solitary gray-clad figure appeared from time to time at the capital city's outskirts; none of them fired, either. A solitary Clay stood at parade-rest slightly apart from the generals. He had come to confess final defeat, and ask permission to take a supply boat north. He was awaiting a moment when Sherman's conference with his top commanders would conclude. Entranced by the sight before him, Sherman showed no signs of dismissing Howard and Slocum.

Finally, Slocum turned to Sherman. "With respect, this is nonsense," the gaunt New Yorker said. "Hardee is just using this truce to evacuate his men to the north before we encircle the town. Give us the order and we will sweep down and bag the lot; we must outnumber him ten to one. Our caution is getting embarrassing. Even old 'Slow Trot' Thomas is showing us up. He took the dregs and rejects of our army, and has just totally smashed Hood at Nashville."

Sherman took the field glasses from his face and frowned. "The delay is necessary. It was Jeff Davis, your own Goddamn corps commander, who accepted the white flag from Hardee. They've got a lot of our boys, who were moved from Andersonville before we took that hell-hole, in there. You saw what those we did manage to free looked like."

"I did indeed," said Howard quietly. "They were starved in a way I would not have thought possible. Unbelievable that Christian men could behave thus, even toward those they regard as enemies. If there are more such souls down there, their only chance will be to get back into our hands, and immediately receive decent food and medical care."

"Need I remind both of you that Grant has forbidden prisoner exchanges for the duration?" asked Slocum coldly. "The Rebs won't exchange any of our darky soldiers, but send them into slavery, whether they be escaped slaves or Northern-born free men. Until that changes, no prisoner exchanges."

"Hell, I know what Sam said," replied Sherman. "Davis seems to think he can get some of our colored boys back along with those poor bastards from Andersonville. If I can get them, Sam will forgive me."

Frowning, the one-armed Howard asked "Why does Davis think he can persuade the Rebels to exchange our colored troops for some of their own now, when they have steadfastly refused to do so throughout this war?"

"He has placed Colonel Kitching, his artillery chief, in charge of the parley," replied Slocum. "Kitching has shown some skill in dealing with the Rebs when they called truce throughout the last year. He has gotten a reputation as a trusted straight-shooter. In fact, the captain from Wade Hampton's legion who first waived the white flag asked for Kitching by name. And I expect that they will deal in good faith concerning our darker comrades. When that Lieutenant Lot demanded that he be allowed to participate in the negotiations, as a pledge of their faith, they did not object . . ."

Breaching protocol, Clay interrupted. "Lieutenant Lot has been permitted to go into Columbia?" On the word "Columbia" Clay's normally soft, quiet voice seemed to drop an octave, and pick up a disturbing resonance, as if issuing from a deep cave.

Sherman looked quickly at Clay, frowned, and said "I know you and the lieutenant go back aways, Major Clay. However, there is no cause for concern. Say what you may, the Rebs honor truces . . ."

Sherman was interrupted by a distant sound, like the ripping of sheets. He jerked his field glasses to his eyes, and saw what Clay could see aided only by his wire-rimmed spectacles: numerous puffs of smoke emanating from the buildings on the edge of Columbia, and more than a score of blue-clad figures writhing on the ground or ominously still. Sherman spat out a stream of creative obscenities, then took the glasses from his face.

"Goddamn traitorous bastards fired on my boys under cover of a flag of truce! Goddamn it!"

"It might have been an accident," said Howard slowly. "Some trigger-happy private fires, the rest of his company assumes he saw a coming attack and fires, and so on."

"I don't give a rat's ass!" stormed Sherman. "They shot at my boys under cover of a flag of truce, and for that they will pay. Howard, Slocum, form your boys up. I want them charging that town within half an hour!

Without pretense of deference, Clay interjected himself into Sherman's tirade. "Sir, there must be time for the recall of . . . of Kitching and Lot. He . . . they could be killed in the assault, by treacherous Rebels by design or our own people by mistake."

Sherman shook his head vigorously. "Too late for that. Whether or not treachery was involved or only a nervous private triggering a chain of events, a black man in a Union officer's uniform is in mortal danger." Suddenly Sherman advanced on Clay with jerky steps, and seizing him by the shoulders said fiercely "I know what Lot must mean to you. However, the best thing we can do is get into that town damn fast, before it occurs to someone to . . . well, before something bad happens. Go to your tent. We will be in

Columbia in an hour, and I will have the provost on the lookout for your friend." Sherman released Clay as roughly as he had seized him, turned to his general and aides, and began barking a series of orders.

Clay turned and began trudging down the hill toward his tent with mechanical steps, his face an unreadable mask, completely ignoring the gathering noise, excitement, and back-and-forth movement that was seizing the Federal encampment . He came to a stop before his tent's entrance, eyes staring at nothing, arms hanging loosely at his side. He kept wondering over and over why Lot had placed himself in such unnecessary danger, and above all why he had not mentioned his intentions before disappearing into the Confederate capital.

"Major Clay. Major Clay?"

Slowly Clay returned to an awareness of his surroundings. Before him stood Teresa Duval, frowning slightly at his abstraction, holding an envelope in her hand.

"Major, are you all right?"

"Yes," he answered hoarsely. "What may I do for you?"

"Lieutenant Lot left an envelope with me, before he went off somewhere. He did not seem to want to say where, but asked me to give this to you if he had not returned within the hour. Very mysterious." She extended her hand toward Clay.

With the reluctance Socrates must have shown when he took the final cup of hemlock, Clay took the envelope. However, he made no move to open it. Instead, the outside world seemed to go very far away, the confused sounds of the army camp seemed to fade to nothingness, and he was alone with his whirling thoughts. In the space of several heartbeats, a number of thoughts and voices raced through his head, all leading his mind in a single direction.

'Jeremiah would only have left such an envelope if he feared he

would not return, If he feared that, why did he not ask for me to go with him? Because he feared I would be in mortal danger if I went with him; no other reason is possible. Why would there be danger during a prison exchange negotiation? Southerns are capable of deceit and treachery, but not where there are credible witnesses. With the whole army knowing of the truce, and with Colonel Kitching there . . .'

Duval looked with concern at Clay. His normally pale complexion had lost whatever color it possessed; his mouth opened and worked, but no sound emerged. The pale blue eyes behind the spectacles glowed with horror-filled realization. After a few moments Clay finally found his voice. "I now know what I did not know. Kitching. It is Kitching." His voice was barely above a whisper.

Her concern mounting over Clay's seemingly bizarre behavior, Duval asked "Major Clay, are you ill?"

Now he looked directly at her, and spoke in a stronger voice. "I am a cretin, a fool, an arrogant ass. I was so used to looking for treason in high places I overshot the mark."

"What do you mean?"

"Kitching. Kitching is the traitor. So obvious! If I had not been blinded by my assumption it was someone wearing the stars of a general. A mere colonel was not a glorious enough trophy for me; my prior success had fed my pride. Who would have had easy access to Union artillery shells to arrange the trap that would have killed me save for the sharp eyes of Lieutenant Flournoy? Who else could have entered the tent to poison Bierce without exciting your notice, but the commander of the wounded artilleryman who shared the tent with Bierce? Who commanded the artillery battery beside which General McPherson met his death, the noise and confusion of a desperate battle keeping anyone from noticing that an officer had briefly turned his pistol from the front and fired it at a general? Who else was well-known for being eager to undertake any discussion with the enemy occurring under a flag of truce? And when General Davis' men were under attack, during the river-crossing before Atlanta, it was Kitching who argued against cutting loose the pontoon bridge, even though it was obvious that unless fired upon by artillery, Wheeler's cavalry would be over it and wreaking havoc among our troops. Come to think of it, it was Kitching who said he could not fire his guns at Wheeler's men without slaughtering the contrabands, yet when the bridge was gone proceeded to do precisely that. And going back to the very beginning, Kitching's artillery was right beside Bierce when he received his wound. Kitching thought that Bierce would eventually reason it out, or if not I would eventually reason it out. But it was neither Bierce nor myself; it was Jeremiah."

"Why didn't he tell you of this?" asked Duval.

"Because he knew there was still a lack of proof that would stand up in a court martial. When he learned that Kitching was going to again make contact with the Confederates under cover of a flag of truce, he seized the opportunity to force himself on Kitching, hoping to learn something or surprise something that would be enough to send Kitching to the gallows. He knew it would be dangerous, he knew I would insist upon going myself—so he did not tell me." Clay violently ripped the envelope open, scanned the contents of the letter it contained, and letting the paper slip from his hands, turned his devastated eyes toward the sky. "It is as I feared," he said, not looking at Duval. "Jeremiah states his suspicion of Kitching, briefly told his plan—and apologized for any grief that he may have caused me."

Suddenly, both were aware of the sound of volley firing and distant huzzahs; the assault on Columbia was underway. The sound seemed to awaken Clay from his near-trance. With speed that astonished Duval he ran to the tree where his and Lot's horses has been tethered; the Lieutenant had apparently accompanied

Kitching on foot. Clay unwrapped the reins with lightning speed and leapt into the saddle. By that time, Duval had dashed over and grabbed the bridle, restraining the animal.

"I know what you intend," she said fiercely. "It will do no good. There is chaos in the streets of Columbia right now, and you could die from an aimed or random bullet in the blink of an eye. Wait until the town is secured."

Clay stared down at her, his blue eyes glowing with a strange light. She suddenly realized that his eyes were exactly the same color as those of the banshee that occasionally haunted her dreams. He loosed the flap to his holster, and said in a low, quiet voice "Release my animal or I will kill you."

More astonished than frightened, she let go of the bridle and took a step backwards. Clay jerked viciously at the head of his mount until it was pointed in the direction of Columbia, then cruelly dug his heels into the horse's side, spurring it to an immediate gallop. As the dust from the horse's departure enveloped her, Dr. Fetterman rushed up, agitation on his face.

"Was that Clay? Where's he going? I've got to tell him the prisoner Flournoy has escaped from the hospital. When some passing messenger said Columbia was being immediately attacked, he knocked down a soldier and took off like a scalded cat. Don't know what got into him; he knew . . ."

Fetterman found him talking to the air. With speed only marginally less impressive than Clay's, Duval had untied Lot's horse, sprung into the saddle in a most unladylike manner, and was galloping Hell-bent after Clay's dwindling form.

Utter chaos ruled in Columbia. The Confederate defenders had erected street barricades of bales of cotton, bales kept from Europe by the Union blockade and hence only good for stopping bullets. However, there were far, far too few soldiers behind the bales.

As the Union charged the defenders fired one ineffective volley that harmed very few, then fled for their lives, the blue soldiers chasing them through the streets with whoops of triumph. A winter wind was sweeping down from the mountains to the west, swirling dust and bits of cotton from the abandoned barricades through the streets.

Duval sharply reined up her horse as she approached the center of the small town, shielding her eyes from the dust and scraps of cotton being blown about by the strengthening wind as she furiously looked all about for a sign of Clay's horse. Duval had lost sight of Clay in the frantic approach to Columbia, and was desperate to locate him for reasons she would have found hard to put into words. She did not see Clay or his animal; but she did see cheering soldiers pulling down a Confederate flag from a large domed building that must be the state capitol. She galloped over to the marble steps, smoothly slid from the mount, and wrapped the reins around a convenient post, ignoring the occasional curious glance from blue-clad soldiers, most of whom recognized her from her work in the hospitals. She ran effortlessly up the marble steps and into the building's main hall.

There she found what she had expected: the remains of the Rebel headquarters, as represented by a jumble of desks and mounds of paper, and blue-clad soldiers making a number of surly gray-clad officers prisoner. She glanced around until she located the highest-ranking Union officer, a colonel with florid muttonchops whiskers contemplating a moaning Confederate officer lying on the floor; surprisingly sympathetic Union soldiers were trying to comfort the injured man. She suddenly remembered meeting the colonel once; his name was Amos Crenshaw, commander of the 23rd Indiana Infantry. She rushed up to him.

"Colonel Crenshaw, I require your assistance," Duval said with a breathlessness she did not in fact feel.

The colonel turned to her, blinked with recognition, and then said "Why Miss Duval. Looking for hospital facilities? Fortunately casualties have been quite low, Reb resistance crumbling immediately . . ."

"I have only a moment to spare. I must speak with Major Alphonso Clay. Has he been here yet?"

"Been and gone," replied Crenshaw with a frown. "Strode in like the King of Siam and demanded to talk to the highest Reb headquarters officer we got. We told him that captain there was the highest who hadn't already high-tailed it." Crenshaw gestured at the groaning Rebel on the floor, who Duval could see was trying to speak through a mouthful of broken teeth. "After I had pointed out that Johnny, Clay went up to him and asked civil-like where the truce negotiators had been taken. When the Reb seemed to hesitate, out of nowhere Clay hit him the mouth, knocking him to the ground; then he commenced to kick the poor bastar . . . excused me ma'am, poor soul, until he screamed through his bleeding mouth that they had been taken to Wade Hampton's townhouse. Guess Clay knew where that was, because he turned and left without a word to any of us."

"Where might Mr. Hampton's townhouse be located?" asked Duval.

"Go out the front door and turn right. Go two blocks, and then turn right again. You cannot miss it. It is by far the grandest house on that street." The colonel turned and interjected "If you are going there let me get you an escort; the streets are still dangerous. Corporal Wright, can you help this lady . . ." Crenshaw's voice had trailed off; Duval was nowhere to be seen.

Clay had considered kicking open the door to the grand brick structure; but on reflection he decided a stealthy approach might be wisest. He vaulted the railings and dropped silently into the area below street level. Then removing his Bowie knife from beneath his tunic, he made short work of the kitchen window latch. Slithering silently in through the window, he closed it but left it unlatched. Listening very carefully, he detected no obvious commotion within the house; the reveling Union soldiers had not yet begun their joyful task of looting the homes of the high and mighty. However, he did detect the distant sound of murmuring voices; most ears would not have picked up the sounds. Drawing and cocking his Smith & Wesson, he moved stealthily into the main hall.

There the voices were somewhat louder; it took him only a moment to realize they came from a door that appeared to lead to a basement. Softly approaching the door, he tried the handle ever so carefully; the door slid open silently on well-oiled hinges, and the voices increased in volume. He was about to carefully attempt the stairs leading downward to the basement when he detected a motion behind him.

Whirling with frightening speed, to his genuine surprise he found his pistol pointing into the face of Teresa Duval. He was somewhat less surprised to see a Sharp's pepperbox pointed straight at his heart. With a disturbing smile on her face, in the softest of whispers she murmured "Well Major Clay, shall we shoot each other, or form an alliance to see if we can retrieve Lieutenant Lot?"

Clay paused only a moment to consider. To argue with the woman could alert whoever was down below; and in truth he knew she could be a very valuable ally—if she could be trusted. Nodding silently, he turned back to the stairs and led Duval in a slow, quiet descent.

Gradually a segment of the stone floor came into view; it was lit by a flickering light source that was still beyond the field of vision. The sharp click of several pairs of booted feet could be heard, along with rustling noises. Meanwhile, two voices could be heard in intense conversation; Clay and Duval froze on the stairway, intent on catching every word.

"I'm finished. After what you did to the lieutenant, it is only a matter of time—not much time—until Clay figures the whole thing out." The voice of that was Kitching, high pitched with nervousness. "And why in the Hell did you do that anyway? There was no especial need. It would only draw more attention down on me."

An unpleasant laugh was heard in a different voice. "You are a rare piece of work, Kitching," said the voice in an aristocratic Southern drawl. "Not only do you make a hero of that ass Hooker, you are willing to slaughter as many of your own people as need be to restore him to command. And now that you have failed, you want our help in getting to Europe."

"Our goals overlapped!" responded Kitching indignantly. "I know something about your organization, and how it cares more about its own power than the success of the Confederacy, which has lost this war beyond repair. When I first contacted your people, I made it clear that once Hooker was restored to his rightful place— once the pygmies who were jealous of his greatness were swept aside—he would need money for the final step, the ascent to the White House. If Starry Wisdom provided that money, I would make sure that Hooker supported your aims."

Another laugh from the other voice, this one rueful. "You make a hero of that strutting whoremonger Hooker. Personally, I cannot understand it. Be that as it may, General Hampton sent word that your plan had possibilities, and that Starry Wisdom was to support you."

"Some support! You would attempt nothing against Clay, leaving me to try to eliminate him on my own."

"Be grateful you were unsuccessful," said the other in a threatening voice. "Hampton has made it clear he wishes Clay to be left alive, if possible. Clay is more important to us than you can possibly imagine. If you had deliberately killed him, the General's displeasure would have been expressed to you in very . . . disquieting ways."

"Just why is that runtish Kentuckian so important to your people?"

"That is none of your affair. In any event, we must be off before your victorious colleagues take it into their heads to have a look in this building. With you as an escort, and with the passes you have signed by Sherman, we should be able to move through your lines easily enough. From that point, it is up to Wilmington, onto a blockade runner, and off to Bermuda. From there we can regroup, and see what use we can make of you in our plans. What was done to the nigger was done to assure assistance from . . . certain parties in our escape. The Confederacy may be dying, but that is of little import in the grand scale of things. Starry Wisdom lives."

"I didn't know much about your group or your ceremonies, and now I don't want to know more. My God, why did you have to treat that nigger officer that way? Wouldn't a bullet in the head . . ."

At those words Clay leapt from the stairs and made a rolling landing on the flagstone floor, his momentum carrying him to where the stairwell blocked Duval's view. A moment later there was a deep, howling sound—the sound of a wolf being skinned alive. Holding her small pistol before her, Duval glided quickly down the stairs, coming to a shocked halt at the very bottom. Teresa Duval had seen many terrible sights in her life, had in fact been responsible for many of the sights, and had been relatively unmoved by them. The rape of her mother, the hanged body of her father, human flesh roasting on a fire, the objects inside a cabin near Knoxville—all had left her emotions relatively unmoved. However, the sight before her came closest to unnerving her cold, terrible nature.

A motionless tableau was before her. An astonished Kitching gaped at Clay, as did a fleshy, bespectacled man of about forty near him. Near a large table four other men stood frozen in various stages of undress, articles of Federal uniforms heaped on the table they surrounded, along with a glittering pile of coins. Clay looked at none of the men; he stared past Kitching and the bespectacled man. Behind them was a kind of alter supporting large ceremonial candles which gave a flickering, ghostly light to the dim basement. Against the wall was an inverted cross, to which was nailed Jeremiah Lot, the gaping hole in his chest testifying to the fact he was no longer among the living. Another impossibly deep, terrifying howl came from Clay, a howl that seemed to contain all the grief and pain of the universe.

Then, in less than twenty seconds, a number of things happened. One of the men at the table started to draw a huge LeMat revolver; almost casually Clay shot in him the chest, and when the screaming man did not instantly fall, shot him again, silencing the cries for good. Clay then advanced on the stunned Kitching and his bespectacled colleague, cocking his Smith & Wesson. However, the surviving three men at the table rushed Clay without drawing weapons, aiming to overpower him instead. Two shots rang out and two of them fell; one dead from a bullet in the brain, the other screaming as he clutched his bleeding stomach. However, the third man had knocked Clay's gun out of his hand, and was now punching furiously at Clay, who easily dodge the man's clumsy roundhouse blows.

The bleeding, crying man on the floor saw Clay's pistol skid to within a foot of him; painfully he began to crawl toward the weapon. Seeing this, Duval transferred her small pistol to her left hand and produced in her right hand the razor from the cunningingly-concealed pocket of her frock. Flipping the blade open with a flick of her wrist, she took two quick steps toward the wounded man, bent over, and slit his throat from ear to ear, deftly dodging the crimson fountain of blood while muttering "Die, English-loving bastard!"

Suddenly, Clay slipped by his opponent's guard, seized him in a headlock, and snapped the man's neck with a single twist. Duval was genuinely impressed; she had no idea the slightly-built Clay had such strength, and felt rising warmth deep in her belly as Clay threw the body away as if it were a rag doll. However, she noticed that the large bespectacled man had seized an officer's scabbard from the table, drawn the sword it contained, and was lumbering toward Clay with the blade raised high above his head. Duval began to scream a warning to Clay; but with a speed the eye could barely follow, Clay had drawn his own saber and leapt at his opponent, burying his sword to the hilt in the large man's belly before he could bring down his own weapon. An astonished look on his face, the man gagged and died, drawing himself off Clay's sword as he slowly fell to the ground.

Duval then noticed that a desperate-looking Kitching had picked up the LeMat pistol dropped by the first man killed; with horror she saw Kitching was fumbling with the hammer, undoubtedly to allow the trigger to fire the huge buckshot load from the revolver's central barrel. Shooting left-handed, she fired all four barrels of her Sharps .32 as fast as she could cock the hammer. Three of her four shots hit home, and Kitching fell; but as he fell the dying man touched the trigger, and with a deafening boom the pistol went off. Clay staggered, and Duval surprised herself by screaming. Clay quickly regained his balance, and looked with detachment at a rent in his right trouser-leg just above the knee, from which blood oozed rather than spurted. Taking a scrap of clothing from the table, he fussily cleaned his saber before returning it to its scabbard. Then, with the slightest of limps, he walked to where his pistol had fallen; picking it up, he turned toward Duval, gun held loosely in his hand. He looked at the dead Kitching, and back at Duval.

"You took him from me," he said quietly. "He was mine. You took him from me. I had the right . . . I had the right . . ." Clay turned, and looked up at the mutilated body of his cousin and best friend, defaced in an obscene parody of Christ's passion. The gun now pointed at the floor; Duval could now see that a single tear flowed down Clay's expressionless face. Quietly, Duval came up beside Clay and looked at the remains of Jeremiah Lot. Duval had not considered the black officer her equal, but this was not a matter of racial prejudice; she considered no man her equal. She cared only slightly that the man was dead, considering him a religious fool with little knowledge of the real ways of the world; but she cared very much how his passing would affect the man at her side.

Suddenly they heard a pounding from upstairs, shortly followed by the cracking sounds of a wooden door being splintered. The clatter of boots on the upper floor were then audible, along with laughing, cheerful voices, many with Midwestern accents. Very shortly there were breaking and rustling sounds that indicated Wade Hampton's elegant townhouse was being looted with no light hand. Clay made no move nor said any word, continuing to look at his friend's remains as if nothing was happening above them. Finally, three Federal soldiers came down the stairs, a short, lean corporal in the lead. They reached the bottom, of the stairs and came to a skidding halt, clutching their Spencer carbines tightly; eyes wide at the abattoir before them. Finally the corporal spoke.

"Jesus, Mary and Joseph!" he exclaimed in a soft Irish brogue. He looked at Clay, recognized him, and asked "Major Clay, sir?

"Corporal Walker," Clay acknowledged, not taking his eyes off Lot as he reholstered his revolver. Clay had only met the corporal once, at Sherman's headquarters; but Clay never forgot a face, a name, or a voice.

"Begging the Major's pardon, what has happened here? Why is Nurse Duval here with you, and who are these . . ." The corporal's eyes suddenly lit upon Kitching's body. "Sweet Jesus! Colonel Kitching! General Davis' artilleryman! What in the name of all that is holy . . ." His eyes had lit on the mutilated Lot. Religious imagery failing him, he spat out an obscenity.

Clay turned to face Walker, his placid face a picture of self-possession. "Corporal, the men in this room violated the truce that had been called, and took Colonel Kitching and Lieutenant Lot prisoner. They mutilated and murdered the lieutenant, as you see; undoubtedly expressing their innate racial hatred. Miss Duval and I were able to trace the criminals to this lair, and broke in just as Colonel Kitching loosened his bonds and attacked the murderers. Miss Duval bravely assisted me in joining the fight; a fight in which . . . unfortunately the Colonel lost his life. Corporal Walker, I believe you and your men are engaged in unauthorized looting, in contravention of the regulations of the Provost General." The corporal and his men paled as one; the penalties for looting were well known. However, Clay proceeded to put them at rest.

"I care not what you do with or to the property of such . . . animals. Personally, I would say burn this place to the ground, except that the brick and stone construction of this structure would make that extremely difficult. Instead, take everything your men can carry, keeping in mind to watch out for the Provost. In return for turning a blind eye, I would only ask of you two favors."

Relief in his voice, Walker replied "Anything."

"With care, remove Lieutenant Lot from where he was . . . placed, and transport him to the camp. Then, find an embalmer among the sutlers, and prepare a coffin adequate for his transport to Savannah, and from there by boat and train to Kentucky. The soil of South Carolina is unfit to receive his remains; he is going home to Dignitas." Clay strode over to the huge pile of coins, examined them briefly, and then grabbed a handful, which he gave to Walker. "This should defray any expenses. As you can see, these are old coins of Spanish minting; but each should contain the same value of gold as a twenty dollar piece."

Walker looked avariciously at the pile of remaining gold. "What about the rest of that, sir?"

"Call down the rest of your men and decide how to divide it; it is of no interest to me. Do with it as you see fit." Clay began to ascend the stairs; as she moved to follow, Duval's left hand deftly scooped up a handful of coins and deposited them in a pocket of her frock so smoothly that no one seemed to notice.

"Major Clay!" called Walker. "What should we do with Colonel Kitching's body?"

With only a slight pause on the stairs, Clay said "Give . . . it a hero's burial."

Clay was standing on a street corner a block from Hampton's mansion, oblivious to the laughing looters passing up and down the streets, many very much the worse for drink. The shoulder-length blond hair that emerged from the back of his kepi whipped about in the strong cold wind coming down from the mountains to the west. Duval had followed him to this place, curious at his detached state. Finally, she hazarded a question.

"Major Clay, why tell those boyos to give that English-loving bastard a hero's funeral?" For once, she did not hide her Irish accent.

Clay was silent for so long that she began to think he had not heard her. Then he answered Duvall. "I could see no alternative. The evidence is circumstantial, and there are no surviving witnesses from whom to force a confession. It would be only my word, spreading a rumor of treason within the very center of

Sherman's army at the very time this country is emerging from treason's shadow. It would embarrass Sherman and Grant, to no good purpose; yet the lack of evidence would cause many to accuse me of slandering a hero. If Kitching had lived, it would be one thing; as he is dead and beyond causing further harm, let his betrayal die with him."

With a certain admiration in her voice, Duval replied "You are certainly of a forgiving nature."

"Forgiving?" he said, turning his glowing blue eyes directly upon her. Once again, she was reminded of the banshee's eyes that haunted her dreams. "I can never forgive a wrong; a Clay cannot do so. I cannot forgive Kitching, or the abominable, power-crazed Starry Wisdom, for what they did to my cousin and friend, the truest Clay who ever lived." Duval started; although she had suspected a connection between Clay and Lot, she never expected to hear it so openly proclaimed.

Turning away from Duval to look about him at the buildings of Columbia, he continued to speak. "I will never forgive the traitors who ripped this country apart, not to resist oppression, but so they could be free to oppress others, many of whom were far, far better human beings than they. I will never forgive the leaders of the South who tried to destroy what my family had helped build, and end the great American dream so that they could be free to ape the corrupt aristocracy of Europe. I will never forgive the state of South Carolina for leading the succession movement, for being the first to joyfully proclaim treason and lead the rest of the South into the abyss. I will never forgive the city of Columbia for being the place where the first ordinance of secession was passed, and for being the place where our nation's four-year nightmare began."

Clay fell silent, obviously looking at something in the nearby intersection. Duval followed his gaze, but all she could see was a disorderly pile of cotton bales, remnants of a pitiful barricade, the strong winds sending occasional scraps of the fiber whirling through the air. Without a word, Clay began walking toward that barricade; Duval followed closely at his heels, curious as to what was going through his mind. He looked down at the ground near the scattered bales, and saw a Colt percussion revolver lying next to a reddish smudge, apparently abandoned by a wounded soldier. He picked it up, and spun the cylinder, noting that only two of the chambers were discharged. With his free hand he drew his Bowie knife from under his tunic, and with a rapid succession of powerful strokes slashed open several of the cotton bales. As the winds tugged at the ragged scraps of cotton, whirling several high into the air with every gust, Clay thrust the Colt into one of the bales and fired four times in rapid succession. The burning grains of powder shot from the barrel immediately ignited the cotton; fanned by the winds, the flames spread rapidly through the ruined bales, every strong gust sending flaming firebrands of burning cotton high over the city. Clay dropped the empty gun and stepped back several paces, contemplating the conflagration.

Duval had come up beside him. "Fire is such a pretty thing," she said. Clay glanced at her, and frowned slightly at the broad grin on her face. "That mansion and the capitol may be of brick and stone, but most of the buildings seem to be of wood," she continued. "The wind is going to carry bits of flaming cotton all over Columbia; this place will burn like an Englishman's soul in Hell."

Already the roofs of several buildings were alight; Clay and Duval could watch the fire visibly leap from building to building. As the minutes passed they began to hear the hoarse voices of Union officers shouting orders, and began to see lines of soldiers forming bucket brigades from town pumps to nearby houses that had begun to burn. A fire engine pulled by two panicked horses raced by, black smoke belching from the engine. Finally Clay spoke to Duval.

"The streets are becoming increasingly congested. I suggest

we find a quiet spot to watch Columbia enjoy the fruits of its treason. During a trip I made here before the war, I visited the college. There is an attractive park with benches aside from the main building; I suggest we avail ourselves of that vantage point."

A stroll of two blocks along a street frantic with soldiers and civilians brought them to the park Clay had remembered. He stopped and looked at the college building facing the park, its windows already alive with flame. Suddenly, the sound of a woman's screams drew his attention to a small frame house to the left of the large building; the modest home's roof was already ablaze. Clay frowned slightly at what he saw; a woman surrounded by several men in Confederate uniforms was wailing hysterically. Without conscious thought he drew his saber and launched himself at the group, Duval following at a slower pace. However, he skidded to a halt as he reached the group, and after a moment returned his weapon to its scabbard.

The woman was not being attacked at all. He could now see that three of the four standing men were obviously wounded, and just as obviously trying to comfort the pair they surrounded. Three Rebels with what appeared to be more serious wounds lay in the street, fussed over by a black woman in servant's garb. The screaming woman was being tightly hugged by a man in a Confederate officer's uniform; with a shock he saw it was Lieutenant Flournoy.

The woman's screams now became articulate. "My baby, my baby!" she wailed. "Thought I had time to move all the wounded we'd taken in; left her for last upstairs. Then the fire flared. God, I've killed our daughter!"

Hugging his wife fiercely, Flournoy looked over her shoulder and saw Clay. With naked hatred in his eyes, he said "My dearest, you have done nothing wrong; the assassins in blue have done this." He thrust her aside,. "It may not be as bad in the back, I will make the attempt . . ."

"Professor Flournoy, I begs you," said the black maid. "Look at that." She pointed to the open front door, through which a flight of stairs wreathed in flame could be seen. "Poor child is gone; won't help your missus if you be gone too."

Dawning horror on his normally expressionless face, Clay murmured "Again. I have murdered a child again."

Staring avidly at the burning house, Duval said casually. "Do not concern yourself. The runt is a Reb baby; nits make lice."

Clay looked briefly at Duval, then without a word he launched himself at the front door of the house. The Flournoys and the rest gaped as Clay flew through the front door and was swallowed by the flaming stairs. Duval heard a woman screaming, and looked at Mrs. Flournoy; only when she saw the woman silently watching where Clay had gone did Duval realize the screams were her own.

Suddenly a form shot out of the second story window. As if everything was moving in slow motion, she saw it was Clay, kepi missing, patches of his uniform smoldering, tunic loosened, with a small round head peeping over the top of the tunic. He sailed through the air like an acrobat, slowly turning so that he would land on his back; she realized he intended to take the full force of a twenty-foot fall onto the cobblestone street in such a way as to cushion the child. With a sickening thud Clay landed on the street; screaming "*Alphonso!*" she ran to his side.

Clay lay motionless, his eyes closed. Under his tunic a tiny bundle squirmed and cried. Duval wanted to take the child and snap its neck, and would have done so had not Clay's eyes suddenly flown open. The Flournoys rushed to Clay; with fire-blistered hands Clay loosened his tunic, allowing the parents to gently take their daughter from him. "I believe she has sustained no serious injuries," he said.

The mother covered the tiny, squirming face with kisses, while Lieutenant Flournoy looked on in wonder. Turning to Clay, he said "I had never seen my daughter; for a moment I feared I never would." With a pause, he began to speak formally. "It would appear that I am under an obligation to you."

Duval had knelt beside Clay and frantically felt his skull, trying not to look too hard at the red burns developing on his handsome features; she detected abrasions but no obvious fractures, although a more subtle one might be killing him at that very moment. Fearing the answer, she asked "Major Clay, can you move your arms and legs?"

Slight motions of all his limbs followed. "Yes, Miss Duval," he said in raspy voice. "However, I believe I have broken at least two ribs, and have a bullet wound in my leg. Also, there may be internal injuries. It would be unwise of me to rise."

"Don't dare think of it, you stupid bastard," snarled Duval, having briefly returned to her Irish brogue. "As soon as some soldier boys arrive, I will have you carried on a stretcher to where Dr. Fetterman is setting up the hospital tents."

Looking exhausted, Clay nodded slightly. Then, turning his attention to Lieutenant Flournoy. "Lieutenant, I believe you escaped from custody."

"I felt I had no choice. When I heard your troops were taking Columbia, having seen what you had done in Georgia, I felt no compunction in breaking my word to seek out my family and do whatever I could to protect them from harm."

Clay looked at him for a long moment. "The servant called you 'professor.'"

"Yes. Before the war I taught mathematics here." He glanced at the fully engulfed college building, the expression on his face pure bitterness.

Clay nodded slightly. "Miss Duval, I believe you carry a notepad and pencil. Please be so good to remove them and write what I say."

Puzzled, Duval did as she was asked. When he saw she was ready, he began to speak. "Dated the 17th of February, 1865. The bearer, Samuel Flournoy, former artillery lieutenant in the forces of the Confederacy, has been taken prisoner. He and those wounded Rebel soldiers under his protection are as of this date and by my order regularly exchanged and paroled, and not to be molested by the United States of America so long as they respect the peace and obey the laws of the United States." With a flick of his wrist Clay motioned Duval to bring the paper and pencil to him. Duval holding the notebook, slowly and painfully Clay signed "Major Alphonso Brutus Clay, United States Volunteers." Closing his eyes with exhaustion, Clay said "Miss Duval, tear out that sheet and give it to Professor Flournoy." After she had done so he then added "Oh, and give him the gold coins you were carrying for me. He and his family will be facing hard times, and the money could not be better spent."

For a second, Duval froze. She had no idea Clay had seen her pocket the gold in Hampton's basement, and was less than thrilled with having to give up such a sum. However, under the circumstances there was nothing for it but to give Flournoy the money. She briefly considered holding back a few coins; surely Clay did not know the exact amount she had scooped up. She then considered Clay's astuteness, and in the end produced every last one for the astonished Flournoys.

Eyes still closed, Clay said "Lieutenant, the war is over for you; you and your family have survived. Cherish them and rebuild your life and your community. Above all, do not let the horrors of this war embitter you. No good can come of brooding on past wrongs. Believe me; this I know." Clay stopped speaking, and within moments soft snoring indicated he had lapsed into sleep. Duval sat down, and gently nestled Clay's head in her lap; surprising herself, she began to gently stroke his forehead.

The Flournoys and those with them watched the touching yet oddly disturbing scene, while around them Columbia burned.

CHAPTER 5

"SING IT WITH A SPIRIT THAT WILL START THE WORLD ALONG . . ."

"Major Bierce with orders for General Sherman, sir," said Colonel Orlando Poe.

Sherman had been hunched over the papers on the ancient desk placed directly under the capitol dome. At the words his head jerked up. Next to the saturnine Poe stood Ambrose Bierce in a newly-minted major's uniform, carrying a large carpet bag, looking the picture of health; looking, thought Sherman, much like Willie would have looked, had the child lived another twenty years. Sherman wanted to leap to his feet and hug Bierce; instead, he merely nodded at Bierce's jaunty salute, and began to speak in a gruff voice. "Good to see you Bierce. How the Hell did you get back here?"

"Best way possible sir; by boat. Charleston has fallen. Evacuated, really. Once Hardee heard you had taken Columbia, he had no choice but to pull out and head for North Carolina as fast as his legs could take him. The Navy has taken over the harbor, and organized supply convoys. I came in with the first one." Bierce looked around the controlled chaos in the capitol rotunda. "Ah, if Richmond could only see you now, the terrible Sherman setting up his headquarters in the seat of government of the first state to secede. They would surrender in an instant."

"Had no choice but to set up in here," replied Sherman. "Everything burned that wasn't built of stone or brick. This is one of the few places large enough to handle headquarters that's out of the rain. Didn't mean any symbolism by using it."

"Nevertheless sir, very symbolic. As symbolic as the ruins I saw. Who torched this seat of treason? I ask merely out of idle curiosity, not from any disapproval."

"No one gave the order. Already I hear the Rebs are saying I am the new Attila, and deliberately destroyed Columbia. If I had done so, I would have been within my rights, and proudly claimed credit. However, the fact is that some bales of cotton the idiot Rebs used in barricades caught fire, and the wind spread burning material throughout the city."

Bierce nodded thoughtfully. "Colonel Poe tells me that Major Clay was gravely injured in the fire. I would like to see him, once I have delivered my verbal message."

Sherman jackknifed out of his chair. "Hell, I'll take you to Clay myself. You can give me the 'verbal message' on the way. Poe, hold down the fort; won't be long."

The two lean, long-legged officers moved quickly out of the largely undamaged capitol building and out into the devastation that was Columbia. The streets were largely free of debris, and busy with Federal wagons and soldiers. The blocks outlined by the streets were pictures of charred desolation, relieved only by the occasional stout brick building, with morose civilians picking through the remains, looking to salvage anything of use.

"So, what message have you got for me?" Sherman asked as they walked.

"Your coded letter got through. Grant, Halleck and Stanton

are of one mind. Since Kitching is dead, let him stay a dead hero. No point in depressing morale with the war's end so close. They even decided not to tell Lincoln; Abe's a good man, but he simply cannot keep secrets."

Sherman scowled. "Mac died, Lot died, so did a whole passel of my boys. You nearly died, and so did Clay. And Kitching will be remembered as a hero?"

Bierce shrugged. "I see Grant's point of view. Kitching is dead, and beyond the ability to do further harm. The truth would only hurt the Union now."

Sherman glanced at Bierce as they briskly walked. "So why did Grant send you, instead of a coded message? Don't get me wrong; glad to see you up and about. But why the special trip?"

Bierce got a far-away look in his eyes, and took his time before finally speaking. "There is a bit of . . . trouble, relating to my last visit to my parents. My last visit in every sense of the words. I had certain matters to discuss with my father. After he was . . . able to send a telegram, he wired Grant, demanding I be court-martialed on, well . . . a personal matter. Grant called me in for a private chat, and demanded to know why certain things had occurred. I informed the General-in-Chief that I must respect-fully decline to discuss the origins of the dispute between my father and myself."

Sherman laughed harshly. "I don't expect Sam liked that."

"No sir, he did not. Still, Grant is a strange, deep man. He looked at me for near a minute, then finally said he would send me with messages to you, to get me out of Washington until certain things were, I believe he said, 'squared.' Told me that by the time I came back he could guarantee there would be no charges from anyone, army or civilian courts. That surprised me; I was fully prepared to take the consequences of my actions."

Sherman almost asked just what those actions had been.

However, he glanced at the hard, set look of the young officer beside him, he decided to let the matter go. If Grant had decided Bierce could keep the matter private, then that was enough for Sherman. Instead, Sherman pointed to a cluster of tents. "Our hospital tents; Clay is in the second from the right."

Solemnly, Bierce asked "How is he taking Lot's death."

"Not well. Miss Duval says his burns are healing with astonishing speed, and appear to not even be leaving any scars. However, he refuses to talk except to say 'yes' or 'no.' Miss Duval says she fears he may . . . do himself an injury." They had reached the entrance to the large tent, and Sherman paused, took a deep breath, and said "Listen here, Bierce. You were closer to Lot and Clay than anyone else. Maybe you can snap him out of this Goddamn funk he's in. I'd be in your debt if you could." Sherman threw back the flap to the tent, and the two officers entered.

Inside were four cots, but only one was occupied; Teresa Duval hovered over that cot, which contained Alphonso Clay, stripped to the waste and with his left trouser leg slit, showing a glimpse of bandage just above his knee. Duval was applying a salve to red splotches on his hands and face. Clay's bright blue eyes stared blankly through the lenses of his spectacles; he showed absolutely no reaction to Duval's ministrations. The woman heard the officers enter the tent and turned. She nodded familiarly to Sherman, and then paused slightly at the sight of Bierce before saying "General, Major Bierce. I wish we met under better circumstances."

"How is the patient?" asked Sherman gruffly.

"Physically, amazingly well. The healing of the bullet wound in his leg is without complication; while his severe burns are fading with no sign of scarring. Frankly, if I had not witnessed myself, I would not have thought it possible."

"Clay was always a fast healer," said Bierce, as he set down the carpetbag he carried. "I remember when he took a shotgun slug straight through the upper right arm, just before Vicksburg fell; hardly slowed him up half a day."

Duval's nostrils flared slightly, and she stole a quick glance at her patient to see if her memory played her false. It did not. The flesh of Clay's arm was absolutely unblemished, entirely free of the slightest sign of a wound.

Suddenly Clay began to move. Slowly he stood, and saluted Sherman. "My apologies, General, for my state of undress. I have not been in perfect health of late."

"Hell, Clay, you're lucky to be alive. Have a seat and rest yourself."

"I would prefer to stand, general. I am all too aware of how . . . inadequate my performance on this assignment has been. I bear enough of a burden, without having to bear your condescension." Naked down to the waist, one leg of his trousers in tatters, Clay carried himself with the dignity of a Roman senator. Duval looked at the perfection of Clay's torso, and felt arousal—and something else.

"Enough of that horse shit, Clay!" responded Sherman angrily. "You put an end to Kitching when no one else could; no telling how much more harm that Goddamn traitor could have done if you hadn't stopped him."

Clay shook his head. "I should have seen it much, much sooner. Jeremiah saw it sooner than I. Because I did not see it as soon as he, my . . . he died. My failure is something I can never forgive myself. Furthermore, in my . . . disappointment with myself, I undertook ill-considered actions which . . ."

"No more of that crap!" interrupted Sherman loudly, who had his suspicions of how the fire that consumed Columbia had started, and frankly did not care. "You are ordered to leave any actions . . . arising from your discovery of Kitching and Lieutenant Lot in the past."

Frowning, Bierce said "One thing puzzles me, Clay. Kitching must have seen the South was losing the war, even before Atlanta fell. Why did he persist in his treason and murders?"

Clay shook his head sadly, a far-off look in his eyes. "His goal was never to give ultimate victory to the Confederacy. He had a twisted, unhealthy hero-worship for General Hooker, who he must have been convinced had been denied his rightful place by army politics. Kitching was willing to murder, to even give temporary successes to the Confederacy, in order to embarrass and disgrace those who had supplanted his hero. Probably he expected Hooker to be returned to command, and his rise would end only in the White House. Of course, he expected that he would rise with Hooker."

Sherman shook his head with wonder. "Must've been a Goddamn madman."

"With respect sir, I doubt it. Simply evil; believe me, evil explains more wrongs in this world than does madness."

Bierce nodded, then changed the subject. "Clay, Grant entrusted me to deliver two documents to you." He removed a paper from inside his tunic and extended it toward Clay. "This is the promotion of Jeremiah Lot to full captain, United States Volunteers, backdated to the date of the fall of Savannah." When Clay made no move to take the paper, Bierce continued. "Grant charged me to say that of course this will not salve the pain of the loss you must feel. He means it as an acknowledgement from the country to a courageous patriot, who gave his life not only for his country, but for his friend."

Clay closed his eyes briefly; when he reopened them they were watery, although no tears flowed. "I will accept it on his behalf," Clay said in a soft voice as he took the document. "His remains have been sent temporarily to a receiving vault at my estate, awaiting the time when I can prepare a suitable memorial.

His new rank will be reflected on that memorial. You said you had a second document."

With visible reluctance, Bierce produced a second paper from within his tunic. "This is your commission as Lieutenant Colonel of Volunteers, backdated to the date of the fall of Columbia." He extended it toward Clay, who made no move to accept it.

"With respect to General Grant, I cannot accept. It is underserved. Further, I do little honor to my current rank, much less a higher one."

"Whatever you think of your performance, I assure you Grant thinks you did better than anyone had a right to expect" said Bierce. "Furthermore, he has an important new assignment of great delicacy for you. I am not at liberty to describe that assignment. In respect of your talents, Grant feels that a higher rank could ease your path in it."

Clay shook his head slowly. "The General is showing poor judgment. I am of no further use to the cause, or to anyone."

"God damn you to hell, Alphonso Clay!" Bierce suddenly exclaimed. "Jeremiah Lot was the finest man, black or white, I ever had the privilege to meet. He knowingly put himself in the path of danger to save you; to preserve you for the greater good. Will you insult his memory by making his sacrifice a vain one? Do you think he was a fool, an idiot? How dare you imply Jeremiah Lot did not know what was best, for you and for the Union?"

Clay's fists balled, and he stepped forward until only inches separated him from Bierce. "I have killed men for less," replied Clay in a conversational voice.

"Kill me and be damned! It will make what I say no less true. So, Clay, which will it be? Will you honor the memory of Jeremiah Lot, or prove him to have been a sentimental fool who wasted his life?" Bierce looked directly into Clay's glowing blue eyes, and tried not to show fright at the inhuman aspect they displayed. Sherman and Duval remained silent, not daring to interfere.

Finally, Clay's eyes seemed to dim, and assumed a more human aspect. He extended his hand and took the paper that Bierce still held. "I will accept the commission, on one condition," Clay said in his soft voice. "There is a private matter that I must attend to in Washington, a matter requiring less than a day. If at the end of that day I am still physically able to accept General Grant's assignment, I will do so." He looked at Duval, "Please see what you can do to obtain some presentable clothes. I am well enough to proceed immediately to Charleston and from there to Washington."

"Some commissary wagons and their escorts are starting off for Charleston within the hour," said Sherman. "If you feel well enough, he can depart with them."

Dubiously, Clay said "I hardly have the apparel for a journey . . ."

"Not to worry," replied Bierce breezily. "I took the liberty of bringing a new uniform for you." He opened the carpetbag at his feet, and extracted a wrinkled tunic, pair of trousers, and a boiled shirt; on the shoulders of the tunic gleamed the golden oak leaves of a lieutenant colonel. "Fit is probably not that good, but you will undoubtedly do better when you get to one of your fancy-dan tailors in Washington."

Clay looked at the clothes, then at Bierce. "Your thoughtfulness shames me. I apologize for my . . . ungracious remarks. You are a true gentleman, and should be treated as such."

Duval felt a stab of panic at the realization Clay was leaving. Forcing herself to display calm, she addressed the commander. "General Sherman, I would like to request permission to accompany Colonel Clay on his trip north. I am not fully satisfied as to the completeness of his recovery; besides, it has been very long since I have seen my mother."

Sherman looked strangely at her, but finally said "Of course. You have been of more service than I expected a woman to ever be. Thankfully our casualties have been light of late. Dr. Fetterman and the rest of his staff should be able to handle everything." Clay glanced at her, the faintest of smiles on his lips, but said nothing.

"Then let me through a few things into a bag. I will be ready by the time Colonel Clay is dressed." Duval went to where her own carpetbag was stashed and quickly filled it with a few essentials and medical supplies. While she did this, Sherman scribbled a pass granting them access to Army and Navy transportation on a pad he found on an examination table; meanwhile, Clay irritably shrugged off Bierce's attempts to help him dress, and with slow, stiff movements put on his new clothes.

As Clay smoothed the creases in his new tunic, he asked Sherman "Who else knows the truth of Kitching?"

"You mean aside from those of us here? Grant, Halleck and Stanton in Washington, and Generals Slocum, Howard, Logan and Davis. Had to tell the last four, if only to make sure they knew enough to stop inconvenient rumors among their boys. Anyway, I have never liked long goodbyes." Sherman thrust the pass into Clay's hand, then gruffly muttered "Take care of yourself and Miss Duval." Sherman turned and strode out of the tent, pausing only to say "You too, Bierce," as he exited.

Bierce laughed sardonically. "Well, I guess we are not supposed to let the door hit us in our rumps. Still, Grant was anxious. Is everyone ready?"

Duval nodded her assent. Clay walked to the cot he had occupied, where his own carpetbag for his own personal possessions stood open, two books barely visible among its contents. He fastened it shut, hefted it tentatively, then turned to Bierce and replied, "No time like the present."

"Colonel, Madam, our carriage awaits," said Bierce with an exaggerated bow, holding the flap of the tent open for them. The three exited the tent, only to be brought up short by the sight of the cadaverous General Davis riding up on horseback, trailed by several aides. Bringing his mount up sharply, he looked at the oak leaves on Clay's shoulders, and nodded slightly. "Already leaving us Clay?"

Clay saluted. "Duty requires it, General."

"I see you made lieutenant colonel. Made it the hard way." No allusion was made to Kitching, or the humiliation Davis must feel at having harbored a traitor on his staff.

"Harder than you can imagine, sir."

"I expect I can imagine, Colonel. Listen, I know you don't care for me; truth is, I didn't care much for you, neither. Maybe it could be we're too much alike; sometimes we act before thinking, and then have to bear the consequences. Be that as it may, you did a good job for the country . . . and I'm sorry for . . . what happened to Lot. Such things are hard to bear; believe me, I know." Suddenly, the corpse-like Davis thrust out one of his hands; after a moment's hesitation Clay reached up and accepted the offered hand, shaking it firmly. Then, with no further words, Davis released Clay, jerked the head of his mount around, and spurred the animal into a gallop, trailed by his obedient staff. Clay stared after Davis, saying nothing.

"Well, that was damn strange," said Bierce. "What was that all about?

Clay continued to stare after Davis, and said nothing.

Ambrose Bierce lurched to the rear of the side-wheeler steamer, grabbed the railing, and heaved mightily. Nothing actually came out of his mouth; he had lost his stomach's contents a long time ago. However the motion of the tired boat as it pushed its way through the rolling Atlantic left his stomach unconvinced. Finally, the wave of nausea passed and Bierce stood erect, trying to focus on the horizon; he had read somewhere that helped sufferers from seasickness, and Bierce was willing to try anything.

Out of a passageway stepped Teresa Duval, appearing to be the picture of health and contentment. Bierce looked at her and sourly thought that the sea appeared to agree with her entirely. Duval joined him at the railing, and with a sadistic gleam in her eye said "We missed you at dinner, Major Bierce. Is anything amiss?"

Returning his eyes to the horizon, Bierce replied "A minor indisposition. How goes Colonel Clay's recovery?"

Duval lost her sadistic look. "He is not eating, and stays in his cabin, which concerns me. Physically, however, his recovery is astonishing. The burns have almost disappeared, leaving absolutely no scars; I would not have thought that possible, given their extent. His leg wound is not only healing, it seems it will leave almost no mark." She paused, and said with a touch of awe in her voice asked "Are you certain he was shot in his left upper arm?"

"I am. I witnessed the wound being dressed."

Duval hesitated for a long moment, then said with reluctance "There is absolutely no sign of such an injury. None. That is not possible."

"With Alphonso Clay, I would hesitate to say that anything is not possible." Bierce looked around to confirm they were alone at the stern; those passengers who were out of their cabins were apparently on the forward upper deck, from which snatches of banjo music and singing drifted down to the stern. Having confirmed they were for the moment alone, Bierce steeled himself for a conversation he had long dreaded.

"Miss Duval, this is an opportunity for us to discuss certain matters undisturbed. Rather, I should say, 'Miss Doyle—Miss Brigid Doyle.'"

Duval froze with shock; she had not heard that name since she had begun working for Jay Gould, back in '61. "Who is this Brigid Doyle?" she asked with apparent indifference, while her hand slowly crept to the pocket where she concealed her razor—the razor with which she had killed the English corporal, so many years before.

Bierce turned and leaned against the railing, facing the ocean. "Come, Miss Doyle, let there be no pretence among old acquaintances. You have been both clever and skilled in your activities, but not quite as clever and skilled as you believe yourself to have been. During my leave, I spent some time in New York City among the newspapermen. I have been giving some thought to taking that up as a profession, after the war. In any event, I asked some questions, made some inquiries—even talked to some police officers. It seems that you have acquired something of a reputation among crime reporters, and certain officers of the law. Oh, you never leave enough evidence to support an indictment or prosecution, especially since a jury might find it unbelievable that a woman did some of the things they believe you to have done. Still, to certain people you are known, in New York; if it gives you any pride, you are spoken of with some fear."

Her hand had closed on the razor in her pocket. To her own surprise, she responded lightly. "And just what is this Doyle, who has nothing to do with me, alleged to have done?"

Bierce smiled grimly at her. "Oh, Miss Doyle has had much to do with you, ever since she entered New York without the formality of an interview with the immigration authorities. I have paid a visit to Madame LeFevre's in the Bowery, you see, and described you. You were younger then, of course, but they recognized you from my description. Oh, Madame remembers you well. She remembers what you did to that customer who had paid for what she described as 'rough trade,' and what it cost her in bribes to keep her establishment open after the unpleasantness of that nature."

Duval's mouth set in a grim line. '*LeFevre had talked, damn her eyes! I must pay her a visit when I am next in New York.*'

Bierce continued speaking in a quite conversational manner. "A brace of police officers introduced me to a former member of a Bowery gang, recently out of Sing-Sing after serving six years for robbery. He is just a shade of the young man he used to be; Sing-Sing will do that to you. However, he perked right up when I described you to him. He had some choice things to say about his doxie Brigid, who had planned the robbery, then turned he and his gang in for the reward, neglecting to tell the authorities she had spirited away most of the proceeds.

"There are only glimpses of you through the years, until something happens in 1861 and you form some sort of association with Jay Gould. You must have been quite a find for him. Gould is even less governed by morality than the typical Wall Street capitalist, and someone like Brigid Doyle could be useful to him, if she were not such a Mick guttersnipe. It seems a remarkable thing happened about that time. The guttersnipe Doyle disappears, never to be seen again; in her place appears society lady Duval, bearing a remarkable resemblance to Doyle. Duval's manners and poise give her entrance to the homes of the most prominent New Yorkers, including those whom Gould might regard as rivals. Synchronistic ally, the innermost plans of those rivals seem known to Gould; in a few cases, the most troublesome seem to meet unfortunate accidents."

Duval flicked her eyes left and right; no one could see the two of them at this moment. From the upper deck a man with an indifferent tenor was beginning to sing, to the accompaniment of banjo music, "Marching to the Sea," a song celebrating Sherman's victories that was sweeping the North.

Sing the good old bugle boys, we'll sing another song
Sing it with the spirit that will start the world along
Sing it as we used to sing it, fifty thousand strong
While we were marching through Georgia

"You puzzle me, Major Bierce." Duval smiled thinly as she removed the razor from her pocket and flicked the blade open. "Knowing what you know, you choose to reveal your knowledge to me here, on the rear deck, with no witnesses, yourself unarmed and weakened with sea-sickness. Strange, I had not placed you for a fool." Suddenly the smile disappeared to be replaced by a frown, and she made no move toward Bierce. "And you are not a fool, are you?"

From the upper deck the amateur tenor reached the first chorus.

Hurrah, hurrah, we bring the jubilee,
Hurrah, hurrah, the flag that makes you free!
So we sang the chorus from Atlanta to the sea
While we were marching through Georgia!

"No, I am not. All I have learned has been recorded and notarized; three copies have gone to the most unlikely places, with instructions to forward the contents to the United States Attorney should any accident or failure of health result in my demise. You might be able to track down one copy and neutralize it, perhaps even two; but not all three.

A new verse had started.

Yes, and there were Union men who wept with joyful tears
When they saw the honored flag they had not seen in years
Hardly could they be restrained from breaking out in tears
While we were marching through Georgia!

With a note of doubt in her voice, Duval said "Why should I fear such disclosures? You yourself said there is insufficient evidence to prosecute."

"True enough. However, the publicity would end your usefulness to Jay Gould. In fact, it would draw unwanted attention to him. I have never actually met the man. How do you think he would respond to such a situation?"

Duval smiled ruefully. "Not well."

"Besides, there is the matter of Alphonso Clay."

Hurrah, hurrah, we bring the jubilee,
Hurrah, hurrah, the flag that makes you free!
So we sang the chorus from Atlanta to the sea
While we were marching through Georgia!

A lump formed in Duval's throat. "What do you mean by that?"

Bierce smiled lewdly. "If there is one thing I understand, it's women. You want Clay—want him bad. You already know he has the pride of Satan. Do you think he would have anything to do with you, once your actions and origins became public? Besides, I owe Clay, and do not want to see him injured in any way."

Anger welling in her breast, she asked "So what do you want? My promise to leave Clay alone?"

Bierce smiled sadly. "Far from it. I can tell he is drawn to you, even though he may not entirely realize it himself. Against my better judgment, I will tell you one thing, which you must never under any circumstances repeat to him. He once loved Jeremiah Lot's sister. She was taken away from him, sold South, and killed herself after being abused by slavers. It has already twisted him; now that he has lost her brother, I fear his descent into madness."

So we made a thoroughfare for freedom and her train
Sixty miles in latitude, three hundred to the main,
Treason fled before us, for resistance was in vain,
While we were marching through Georgia

"Clay is a dangerous, violent man," continued Bierce. "It is just possible that what he needs is a dangerous, violent woman. Normally, I would worry about you arranging an 'accident' for Clay and coming into his substantial estate, one way or another." Bierce again smiled sadly. "Without a doubt, I suspect that although you would like the money, it is the man who interests you more, God help him. So, set your cap for him, if you like, but be warned: if I ever suspect that my judgment was misplaced, and Clay comes to harm, I will see to it that you are utterly destroyed. If you do not end on a gallows, you will spend the rest of your life hiding under false names in places such as Madame LeFevre's."

> Hurrah, hurrah, we bring the jubilee,
> Hurrah, hurrah, the flag that makes you free!
> So we sang the chorus from Atlanta to the sea
> While we were marching through Georgia!

Duval looked steadily at Bierce for a long moment; then without any obvious motion the razor disappeared from her hand. "Very well, Major Bierce, we have an arrangement."

An unusually large wave slapped the side-wheeler. Suddenly Bierce's stomach spasmed and he bent over, clutching the railing until his knuckles were white. Duval looked at him with contemptuous amusement.

"Well, Major, it sounds like the singing on the upper deck has ended. I was going there, but since there is a lull in the entertainment, I believe I will go to the galley and see if they have some of that excellent pea soup left. I still feel peckish."

At the mention of pea soup, Bierce uttered a strangled cry and recommenced the dry heaves. Smiling, Duval turned and went back inside the main deck.

* * *

Alphonso Clay stood before a full-length mirror in his suite at Willard's, carefully inspecting himself. An amused Ambrose Bierce was an onlooker. Clay minutely inspected the tailored lieutenant colonel's uniform with which he had replaced the ill-fitting one donated by Bierce. Sky-blue trousers were tucked neatly into boots polished to a mirror gleam. Long blond hair carefully pomaded to his satisfaction, he placed his kepi precisely level on his head. He slightly adjusted the holster that contained his Smith & Wesson No. 2; then he carefully evened his spectacles on his face. Finally, Clay nodded in satisfaction and said "I am ready."

"About damn time, you peacock," said Bierce. "Most officers put on the dog before seeing the Secretary of War and Chief of Staff Halleck, but you have carried things a tad too far."

Clay turned to Bierce, his face even more expressionless than usual. "You are mistaken. I am preparing for an important meeting, but not with Stanton and Halleck. As fate would have it, General Hooker has a suite here at Willard's, as well. Apparently he is in town to lobby his friends in Congress, even at this late date attempting to regain high command. You should proceed to the War Department and inform our superiors that I am detained, and will join them . . . when I can. If they ask, tell them my business with General Hooker will not consume above a quarter of an hour."

Dubiously Bierce replied "Well, keep it short, Clay. If you keep those bigwigs waiting too long, there will be hell to pay." With a jaunty wave, Bierce exited the suite. After a moment, Clay quietly said, "Hell to pay, indeed."

As Bierce exited Willard's, he spotted Teresa Duval about to enter the famous hotel. With an exaggerated bow, he declaimed "Ah, the angel of mercy. Arranging more supplies to ship to Sherman's army; or were you paying a visit to the Secret Service in the Treasury Building?"

Duval replied coldly. "None of your affair, Major Bierce."

"Wherever you have been, I hope that you were able to come up with some more cash. Willard's is shockingly expensive, so expensive I was surprised to see you lodging here. Certainly I couldn't afford it, if Clay hadn't insisted I stay in his suite."

"I have no financial worries, as well you know. Where are you off to now?"

Bierce smiled. "State secret, Miss Duval. I can tell you that Clay and I will be shortly meeting with Stanton and Halleck at the War Department."

"Where is Colonel Clay? Shouldn't he be with you?"

"He had some business with General Hooker, who is also staying here, and told me to go on ahead. Well, I bid you adieu. The war waits on no one." Bierce facetiously clicked his heel, and strolled off in the direction of the War Department, whistling "The Yellow Rose of Texas."

Duval stood partly blocking the entrance to Willard's, looking thoughtfully after Bierce. Suddenly, a half-formed notion leaped into her brain. She strode quickly across the lobby to the front desk, and repeatedly struck the bell until she had the clerk's attention.

"I have an important message for General Hooker, to be delivered in person. Which is his suite?"

The clerk, a narrow-chested specimen with a manner as oily as his hair, looked Duval up and down before saying "Ah, another one of Hooker's Auxiliaries," using a popular slang term for prostitute. "They all have important messages for the General. Well, feel free to try your luck. He is on the fourth floor, Suite 417.

"Thank you," Duval said coldly. Hurriedly she strode to the stairs, and ascended four flights two steps at a time; it was a testament to her physical fitness that she was not winded by the time she reached the fourth floor. Quickly determining which way the numbers ran, she hurried to the door of 417, which was partly ajar. Stealthily she maneuvered until she could see through the opening the room's two occupants, both of whom were standing.

The floridly handsome Hooker looked angry. As he fiddled with a pair of green-lensed spectacles, he spoke. "Damn you Clay, I haven't time for this. I'm supposed to meet with Senators Sumner and Wade this afternoon. They think that there is a chance they can force Abe to get rid of Grant, and give me back the Army of the Potomac. What's Grant done with it, anyway? Sat on his ass outside Richmond for six months, that's what. I know Grant is among my enemies, and he is trying to bring me down again; like Halleck and Meade did, like Sherman did. Well, you can go tell you lick-spittle master . . ."

"I am not here to discuss your current plans, as . . . interesting as they may be," interrupted Clay. "I am here to discuss Colonel Kitching."

Hooker now stood very still. "Heard Kitching died a hero at Columbia. Always felt he was a good man. Very devoted to me."

"Yes, very devoted. Very few people will ever know how devoted. So devoted he sabotaged Sherman's attack at Kennesaw Mountain, hoping Sherman would be dismissed and you would assume command. Of course, he had worked his treason through whispering in the ear of the trusting McPherson, so he murdered McPherson to eliminate any trace of his crime. Ambrose Bierce saw enough that he might piece together what happened, so he tried to murder Bierce, twice. In attempting to escape, he was responsible for the death of the finest man I had ever known. Kitching's demise was deserved, and timely."

A muscle in Hooker's left jaw began to twitch. With hands that trembled slightly, he placed the green-lensed spectacles on a table.

"I am shocked to hear such a thing. Are you certain of your facts?"

"I am certain of most things, sir. There is, however, something of which I cannot be certain. I hope that you will be able to help me arrive at certainty."

"And what is that, Colonel Clay?"

"I strongly suspect that Colonel Kitching did not arrive at his scheme on his own. I believe he was responding to the direction of another."

"Who do you suspect, Clay?"

"I believe that you know the answer."

Hooker's florid features visibly reddened. "Just what the Hell are you driving at, Clay?"

"I believe you planted the cancer of treason in Kitching's brain. The fool was so filled with admiration for you he may not have entirely realized you were manipulating him. Whether he realized the origin of his schemes, I suspect you were quite aware of what he intended—and did nothing."

"You're mad, Clay!"

"Perhaps. That does not detract from the validity of my suspicion. You have always had a very high opinion of yourself. I remember the talk earlier in the war about how you would tell anyone who would listen that Lincoln was a fool, and that what the country needed was a dictator. You left little doubt who you thought that dictator should be. You are a man who must have believed yourself a new Napoleon; yet you found yourself serving a man everyone said was half-mad, and finally dismissed in favor of a youngster less than ten years out of the Academy. How the injustice of it must have burned. If an admirer could make your enemies look to be incompetent fools, better yet kill them, you could only rejoice. And your dictatorship could still yet come about, you must have thought. Never mind

McPherson, Bierce . . . Lot . . . the countless brave soldiers who fell at Kennesaw."

Hooker's blue eyes had acquired a glassy, half-crazed look. "You haven't a shred of proof. Not a shred!" His voice became louder, his words slightly slurred. "You are just like the other fools and charlatans . . . envious blacklegs who . . . who were keeping me from my destiny! Well, I'll tell you something Colonel Baby-Killer Clay! Yes, I know all about New Orleans! Think anyone would believe what someone who did what you did might say, especially with no proof? I still have friends in politics, friends who want to ride my coattails. I'll let them take that ride. I can be generous to those who help me gain what is deservedly mine!" A series of tremors shot across the left side of Hooker's face.

Clay sighed. "You are probably right, sir. All the suffering caused by your incompetence, and by the malice of your minion Kitching, may not be enough to keep you from recovering on your march to power. The law may not be able to stop you. However, there is a still a remedy. Do you know my middle name?"

"Eh?" The furious Hooker was brought up short.

"There tends to be significance in how the Clays name their children. They are expected to live up to those names. For instance, my cousin Cassius was named by his abolitionist father after the Roman Cassius, the fanatic defender of personal freedom. My middle name is Brutus—the man who assassinated a tyrant." Casually, Clay unsnapped the flap of his holster and drew his revolver.

"You would not dare! You cannot stop . . . Ahhhhhhhhhhhh . . ." Hooker suddenly clasped his head with both hands, and began staggering to the chair by the table. He threw himself into the chair, still clutching his head, and moaned "Damn you Clay! First the light makes my eyes ache, and then you come in and dare . . . and dare. . ." Suddenly Hooker's hands dropped limply to his sides, the left arm noticeably trembling. Trying to focus his now-glassy eyes on Clay, Hooker said "I was saying . . . I was saying . . . something . . . what the Hell was I saying. . ." Hooker lapsed into silence, and now stared into the distance with unfocused eyes, Clay apparently forgotten.

With a puzzled frown on his face, Clay advanced on Hooker until he stood directly in front of the general. An odd reluctance in his actions, he cocked the revolver in his hand. At this point Duval glided swiftly into the room, and lightly placed her hand on his gun-arm. Clay started, and looked at her with surprise.

"There is no need for you to kill him. Do you recognize the symptoms?"

Clay looked back to the oblivious Hooker, and slowly said "I believe he may be suffering from a, ah, chronic infection."

Duval laughed heartily, heartlessly. "Come, Colonel, there is no need to spare my delicate feelings. The bastard has the pox! Syphilis, to well-educated toffs such as yourself. I saw the symptoms often enough when . . . well, I saw them. When the disease really has a boyo in its grip, their eyes become so sensitive to light they need to start wearing tinted spectacles. They get tremors in one or both arms. They get to feel they are gods, and capable of doing anything or accomplishing anything. And then, they will get sudden, blinding headaches, lose their train of thought, and even seem to go idiot for awhile. Does that not sound like the pig you have there?"

"It does indeed. Perhaps it would be just as well to shoot him; he will undoubtedly recover from this attack and survive for years to come, his life becoming more and more hellish until he becomes a raving lunatic and dies of the rot inside of him. It would be a mercy to end his life."

Duval tightened her grip on Clay's gun arm. "And that is why you should not do it. Killing this bastard would be a favor to him, a favor for which you will swing. Let him live; he has years of agony and terror ahead of him, years of suffering which he richly deserves, and it looks like he will never be well enough for long enough to ever get a high position again. His friends in Congress will learn soon enough what ails him; they will not push the cause of a poxed-out madman."

Clay stood absolutely still for nearly a minute; then he carefully uncocked and reholstered his revolver. Without a word, Clay turned and left the room. Duval followed him, pausing only to quietly shut the door; as she did so, she heard Hooker begin to mutter "Goddamn Clay cannot stop me . . . no one can stop me . . . not the best commander the world had ever seen . . ."

Duval had to walk swiftly to keep up with Clay, who headed straight for his suite without acknowledging her existence. He unlocked the door to his room, entered and nearly closed it in Duval's face. Unaffected by the absentminded rudeness, she slid deftly into the room and finished closing the door herself. Clay looked dully at her, and asked, "What do you want?"

Surprising herself, Duval said "I thought you might appreciate some company right now."

Clay smiled sadly. "I appreciate your concern. However, I am not fit company right now. Besides, after I have composed myself I must attend to some business at the War Department."

"Yes, Major Bierce mentioned something of that. It can wait. You are blaming yourself for Jeremiah's death, are you not?"

"That is none of your business," replied Clay coldly.

"Well, I'm making it my business, you arrogant bastard," said Duval, her anger also surprising her. "Just who do you think you are, God? You and Jeremiah did a brilliant job in smoking out that Southern-loving traitor Kitching; and you even figured out that paralytic bastard Hooker was behind him. Jeremiah took his chances in war, as did you; you were luckier than he, that's all.

If you are looking for someone to blame, blame Hooker, blame Kitching . . . don't blame yourself."

"Who else could I blame?" replied Clay morosely. "Jeremiah Lot was my last connection to . . . her. He was her brother. I not only failed him, I failed . . . her." Clay's face was impassive, but unshed tears glistened in his eyes.

"So that's what this is really about," snarled Duval with sudden viciousness. "Some gentleman you are, mooning after your dead nigger whore . . ."

Although they were nearly of equal height, Clay was able to grab Duval by the throat with only his right hand and slam her against the wall. In a voice that seemed to have dropped two octaves, Clay boomed "No one, not even a woman, may speak that way about . . ."

Duval gave a powerful kick to Clay's groin. Gasping with pain, he released his hold on Duval's throat and staggered back two steps. The razor appearing in her hand as if by magic, Duval slashed at Clay's face. He dodged mostly out of the way, but a thin red line appeared on his cheek. With a guttural cry he leapt at Duval, seizing the arm holding the weapon and slamming it against the wall, causing her to drop it with a grunt. However, she instantly snaked her left leg behind Clay and shoved, causing him to lose his balance and fall backwards, striking his head on the bedstead. Grabbing an unlit lamp as a weapon, she threw herself at Clay, who at the last instant raised a booted foot and kicked her in the stomach, the force of the kick along with her own momentum carried her over Clay and onto the bed. Instantly, Clay leapt to his feet and sprung upon her, pinning her arms.

Panting heavily, faces glistening with sweat, the two strange individuals looked into each others eyes for a long moment. Duval saw something that had the form of a man, but could tell that within he was something more or less than a man. There was something overwhelmingly attractive about the danger he posed. Clay saw a woman who was less than human, a woman who was the antithesis of everything he had adored about his long dead Arabella, a coarse, uncivilized hellion. Despite all that, there was something overwhelmingly attractive about the danger she posed.

Suddenly Duval broke one of her arms free, roughly seized the back of Clay's head, and forced his mouth onto her own, kissing him repeatedly and with wanton abandon. Clay knew he could resist, that he should resist, but the part of him that was not human howled for release. Soon the two were entangled on the bed, their union resembling more a mutual rape than an act of love.

Ambrose Bierce was embarrassed and angry. After Halleck and Stanton had waited for nearly an hour, they had demanded Bierce take the short walk to Willard's and find out just what was detaining Clay. In a foul mood, blaming Clay for being humiliated before the Secretary of War and the Army's Chief of Staff, Bierce strode quickly through the lobby and ascended the stairs rapidly. He reached Clay's door and was about to knock impatiently when he paused. From inside he heard sounds. His amatory experiences left him in no doubt as to what the sounds signified. Surprisingly, it seemed that the people on the other side of the door were going about matters with more than the usual enthusiasm.

Quietly, Ambrose Bierce retreated from the door. '*Well,*' he thought, '*I better go back and tell Halleck and Stanton that Clay is unavoidably detained for another hour.*' As he descended the stairs he thought some more about the sounds. A smile tinged with melancholy crossed his face. '*Better tell them two hours.*'

AFTERWORD

This is a work of fiction. For entertainment purposes massive liberties have been taken with the historical record. For instance, the events surrounding the fall of Atlanta were compressed and simplified, although the death of General McPherson occurred as represented. Another example is Ambrose Bierce's wound; he really did miraculously survive being shot through the head at Kennesaw Mountain, but his astonishing recovery was not as unique as depicted. Be that as it may, where historical characters have appeared I have tried to give a flavor of the real individual, even when they are placed in fictional situations. What follows are brief descriptions of those characters who appear in *Marching Through Georgia*, and indications where some liberties have been taken, for which I plead the informed reader's forgiveness.

CAPTAIN AMBROSE G. BIERCE
SCOUT AND CARTOGRAPHER
ARMY OF THE CUMBERLAND

Ambrose G. Bierce (1842–1914?) Bierce was indeed a scout with Sherman's army who performed numerous acts of lunatic bravery; his commanders thought so highly of him that although he enlisted as a private, he ended the war as a major of volunteers by brevet. He miraculously survived being shot through the head during the Atlanta campaign; within two months he had returned to combat, despite being plagued by blinding headaches and vertigo That would be with him on and off for the rest of his life. Some people attribute his black view of life to damage from this head wound; but the evidence was abundant that he was a strange and difficult personality long before a Confederate bullet injured his brain. After the war he earned his living as a journalist, working much of the time for the young William Randolph Hearst; on the side, he wrote fiction on the supernatural and the all-too natural horrors of the Civil War. His greatest moment of glory, aside from the Civil War, was when he directed for Hearst the public relations campaign against the Southern Pacific Railway's attempt to sneak through Congress a bill forgiving some $70 million in back taxes owed to the Federal Government. The then-head of Southern Pacific, the old robber baron Huntington, was nothing if not direct; he personally accosted Bierce on a street, informing him that every man had his price, and bluntly asked what Bierce's price would be. Bierce's reply is reputed to have been: "A check for $70 million, made payable to my good friend, the Treasurer of the United States;" eventually, that check was written. From this point, his life slid downhill, due as much to his own flawed character as anything else. By 1913 he was seventy-one years old and in constant pain; divorced by a wife he had genuinely loved, who could no longer tolerate his repeated infidelities. One beloved son had murdered a friend in a sordid fight over a girl, before turning the weapon on himself; another had quietly drank himself into an early grave; his daughter wanted nothing to do with him. Telling some people he intended to go to Mexico to join a revolution, and others that he intended to throw himself into the Grand Canyon, he disappeared; no trace of his fate has ever been found. He would have undoubtedly been amused by the mystery he left behind.

BRIG. GEN. JEFF. C. DAVIS
COMMANDER, XIVTH CORPS

Jefferson C. Davis (1828-1879) Davis was an enlisted man in the Mexican American war, granted a commission on the basis of his lunatic bravery. He was a lieutenant at Fort Sumter at the time of the Confederate attack, and can literally be said to have seen combat from the first to the last day of the war. His courage and ability led to his rapid promotion to brigadier general. However, in September of 1862 he had an argument with his immediate superior, Major General William Nelson, and shot the unarmed

Nelson to death. Mysterious political influence kept formal charges from ever being brought against Davis; but further promotion was out of the question. He commanded the XIVth Corps during Sherman's March; in a cold-blooded but necessary decision, he did indeed cut loose a pontoon bridge before numerous escaped slaves could flee Confederate cavalry, as described in this novel. He was in perpetual bad health, probably from liver disease; but it was noted that whenever combat loomed Davis was out of his sickbed and at the front. After the war he reverted to his permanent rank of Colonel. When the last major Indian revolt in California broke out, he was placed in charge of subduing the rebellious Modocs. He did so with such brutality that there were no further Indian disturbances in California.

MAJ. GEN. JOSEPH HOOKER
COMMANDER, XXTH CORPS

Joseph Hooker (1814–1874) Hooker was an extremely brave officer with considerable military ability, but he had two flaws: he seemed incapable of not backstabbing his superiors at every opportunity, and he thought he was a better general than he actually was. Although promoted no less than three times for bravery during the Mexican War, when it ended he resigned his commission and went to California to pursue various business interests, uniformly unsuccessful. When the Civil War broke out, his bravery and ability caused him to be rapidly promoted, despite the fact he was disliked by many in the higher ranks of the Union Army. When Ambrose Burnside was awarded command of the Army of the Potomac, Hooker was furious, feeling the job was rightly his. He began a whispering campaign against Burnside that tainted the morale of the army and ruined whatever effectiveness Burnside had; and after a series of heartbreaking defeats command of the army was taken from Burnside and handed to Hooker. Hooker proceeded to suffer a defeat at Chancellorsville every bit as bad as one of Burnside's defeats; Hooker was relieved of his command and sent west with two army corps to help Grant at Chattanooga. There Hooker did surprisingly well, as he did during the early stages of Sherman's March. However, Hooker's pride and arrogance caused his final downfall at the very moment he was beginning to recover some of his military reputation. After McPherson's death, Hooker felt he should get the vacant command; instead, Sherman gave it to Oliver Howard. Enraged, Hooker threatened to resign, expected the threat would make Sherman give him the command. It did not; Sherman accepted his resignation, and Hooker played no further part in the war. By 1866 Hooker had developed some mental impairment, either from a stroke or disease; he was retired from the army, and spent the remainder of his life an invalid. There is no indication that Hooker was ever disloyal to the Union; however, his relentless backstabbing and scheming causes me no guilt in making him my fictional villain.

MAJ. GEN. JOHN LOGAN
COMMANNDER, XVTH CORPS

John D. Logan (1826–1886) Logan was a Pro-War Democratic congressman when hostilities opened; that was such a rare bird that Lincoln rewarded the untrained Logan with a general's commission. Unlike most of Lincoln's political generals, Logan showed not only bravery but considerable leadership ability and tactical flair. He commanded the XVth Corps throughout Sherman's March. After the war, he converted to the Republican Party, serving as United States Senator from Illinois from 1871 until his death, running unsuccessfully for the Vice-Presidency in 1884.

MAJ. GEN. JAMES B. McPHERSON
COMMANDER, ARMY OF THE TENNESSEE

James B. McPherson (1828–1864) McPherson was a brilliant officer who graduated first in his class from West Point. His sunny disposition kept most from being jealous of his rapid promotion by Grant. Expressing doubts over the horrors of war inflicted on civilians, he nonetheless provided brilliant service until he was killed leading his men in a counterattack during the siege of Atlanta. Grant burst into tears upon learning of his death.

MAJ. GEN. OLIVER OTIS HOWARD
REPLACED HOOKER AS COMMANDER, XXTH CORPS

Oliver Otis Howard (1830–1909) Howard was a mathematics instructor at West Point when the war broke out; he rapidly attained the rank of colonel. In 1862 at the Battle of Fair Oakes he lost his arm while leading his brigade in a desperate charge; for his bravery he was not only promoted to general, but awarded the Congressional Medal of Honor. He was given command of the XIth Corps in the Army of the Potomac. His Corps did not perform well at Chancellorsville or Gettysburg, due more to the inexperience of his troops and plain bad luck than any inadequacy in his military abilities. Transferred to Sherman's army he did much better, and upon McPherson's death was given command of the Army of the Tennessee; he and his army performed superbly for the remained of the war. After the war he was placed in charge of the Freedmen's Bureau, an organization devoted to trying to help recently freed slaves to self-sufficiency; he also helped organize the first university dedicated to African Americans, later renamed Howard University in his honor. A devout Christian and a sincere believer in the equality of all races, he worked hard at the Freedmen's Bureau, but ultimately without success; the stubborn resistance of white Southerners and the post-war Democratic Party doomed his efforts. Later he would be commandant of West Point, and retire at the rank of major general.

MAJ. GEN. HENRY SLOCUM
REPLACED AS COMMANDER, XXTH CORPS

Henry Slocum (1827-1894) Slocum was a West Point graduate who left the prewar army to practice law. When hostilities broke out he joined the volunteers and was rapidly promoted; by the time of Gettysberg he was with the Army of the Potomac, commanding its XII Corps. After the Battle of Gettysberg he was attacked for lack of leadership, although his performance was no worse than many of the Union generals there, and better than some; it would seem that his transfer from the Army of the Potomac was due as much to army politics as to any perceived deficiencies as a general. Slocum certain proved himself to be a very able commander while he was in charge of Sherman's XXth Corps. After the war he spent the remainder of his life in various business and political enterprises in his native New York.

MAJ. GEN. WILLIAM T. SHERMAN
COMMANDER, MILITARY DIVISION OF THE MISSISSIPPI

William T. Sherman (1820–1891) Sherman probably suffered from what we call bipolar disorder or manic depression; his wild mood swings were legendary. There was no effective treatment for that disease in the nineteenth century, which makes his career all the more remarkable. For good or for ill, he was the first modern proponent of "total war", regarding the civilian population and the economy of the enemy as legitimate targets. He had no illusions about war; when in later life an admirer said how glorious and romantic it all must have been in the Civil War, he snarled "War is hell! It is organized murder; you cannot define it in terms harsher than I!" Yet at the end of the war, he was completely opposed to punishing the South in any way; if they would simply swear allegiance to the Union, bygones were truly bygones, as far as the terrible Sherman was concerned. After the war, he was repeatedly mentioned as a possibility for the Presidency; despite the fact that his beloved brother was a senator, or perhaps because of that, he had complete contempt for politics, and repeatedly stated he had no interest in the White House. His sincere denials were often taken for coyness, and his name kept cropping up as a draft possibility. Therefore, swallowing for once his burning hatred of reporters, he convened what we would call a press conference, and uttered the phrase "If nominated I will not run; if elected I will not serve!" There was no further talk of drafting Sherman to run for the Presidency. Even by the standards of the Civil War,

Sherman's bigoted feelings against blacks were embarrassing in their intensity and crudity. However, during the war and later as General-in-Chief of the army, he witnessed how black soldiers were every bit as good as white, and was too intelligent to discount the evidence of his eyes. By the time of his retirement from the army in 1884, he was calling for racial integration of the armed forces; Congressional opposition made that impossible for another 65 years. Perhaps a man should be judged more by where he ends than where he begins.

George H. Thomas (1816–1870) Thomas was often described as having the appearance and dignity of a Roman proconsul. His devotion to duty was absolute; he did not give himself a single day of leave in the entire four years of the Civil War. He had been a child living in the area of Nat Turner's slave rebellion when it occurred. His father died mysteriously about the time of that rebellion. Despite his many ties to Virginia, Thomas did not hesitate in affirming his loyalty to the Union. He gained the first significant Union victory of the war at Mill Springs in January 1862, a victory that essentially ended Confederate hopes for taking Kentucky. He was a corps commander under Rosecrans at Chickamauga; his determined, resolute leadership of his men saved the army from complete destruction after Rosie fled the field. When General Sherman set forth on his march through Georgia, he sent Thomas back (along with frankly second-rate units) to defend Tennessee from counterattacks by the elusive army of John Hood. Hood then placed Thomas under siege at Nashville. Grant ordered Thomas to counterattack; but Thomas refused to do so until he had collected enough men and cavalry to make such a counterattack decisive. An impatient Grant set out for Nashville to personally relieve Thomas of command. However, before he got there Thomas finally moved, utterly smashing Hood's army and destroying it for good as an organized force. As a reward, Thomas was promoted to major general in the regular army. After the war he was assigned to command several districts, ending up in San Francisco where among many things he directed the landscaping of the sand dunes of the Presidio which makes it such a beautiful place to this day. Although he and his only brother were reconciled after the war, his two sisters (whom he had essentially raised) refused to have any contact with him, except for an insulting request that he change his name. His feelings can perhaps be guessed from the fact that before his death he destroyed all of his personal papers, and refused to utter a word about family matters. He never wrote his memoirs, saying only "All that I did for my government is matters of history, but my private life is my own and I will not have it hawked about for the curious."

ABOUT THE AUTHOR

Tracing his Californian ancestry all the way back to the 1830s, Jack Martin developed a passion for American history and the mystery genre. With encouragement and support from his beloved wife Sonia, he began writing the Alphonso Clay Mysteries. Sonia passed away on Christmas Eve 2009. He promised her he would finish the books and become a published author. The series includes: *John Brown's Body, Battle Cry of Freedom, Marching Through Georgia, Battle Hymn of the Republic, and Hail, Columbia!* Martin is also the author of the Harry Bierce Mysteries.

ALPHONSO CLAY MYSTERIES OF THE CIVIL WAR

FROM OPEN ROAD MEDIA

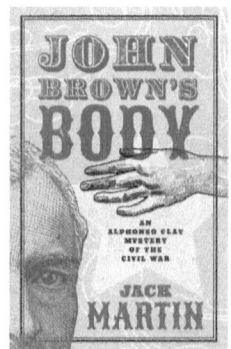

OPEN ROAD

INTEGRATED MEDIA

Find a full list of our authors and
titles at www.openroadmedia.com

FOLLOW US
@OpenRoadMedia

www.ingramcontent.com/pod-product-compliance
Lightning Source LLC
Chambersburg PA
CBHW030412020726
47493CB00003B/1046